BY MATTHEW NORMAN

Last Couple Standing

We're All Damaged

Domestic Violets

LAST COUPLE STANDING

LAST COUPLE STANDING

MATTHEW NORMAN

a novel

BALLANTINE BOOKS

NEW YORK

Published in the United States by Ballantine Books, an imprint of Random House, a division of Penguin Random House LLC, New York.

BALLANTINE and the HOUSE colophon are registered trademarks of Penguin Random House LLC.

LIBRARY OF CONGRESS CATALOGING-IN-PUBLICATION DATA
Names: Norman, Matthew, author.
Title: Last couple standing: a novel / Matthew Norman.
Description: First Edition. | New York : Ballantine Books, [2020] |
Identifiers: LCCN 2019038078 (print) | LCCN 2019038079 (ebook) |
ISBN 9781984821065 (hardcover) | ISBN 9781984821072 (ebook)
Subjects: LCSH: Man-woman relationships—Fiction.
Classification: LCC PS3614.O7626 L37 2020 (print) |
LCC PS3614.O7626 (ebook) | DDC 813/.6—dc23
LC record available at https://lccn.loc.gov/2019038078
LC ebook record available at https://lccn.loc.gov/2019038079

Printed in Canada on acid-free paper

randomhousebooks.com

2 4 6 8 9 7 5 3 1

First Edition

Book design by Debbie Glasserman

FOR MY BALTIMORE FRIENDS

PART ONE

THE DIVORCES

1

E verything that went so thoroughly wrong that spring can be traced back to The Divorces.

Capital *T,* capital *D,* for emphasis. The Divorces.

They came in a set of three, like celebrity deaths and plane crashes, and ruined everything, leaving the once invincible Core Four broken and tattered.

That's what they called themselves: the Core Four. They were a group of friends who'd been together for more than two decades. Their origin story was both convoluted and utterly mundane, because, well, that's how it is with friends.

They met in college at Johns Hopkins. Mitch and Alan had a chem lab together and became fast friends, mostly because they were the two worst students in the class. Megan was the bridge that linked the genders. She lived in Alan's dorm and was way, way smarter than Alan and Mitch, so she helped them through their dreaded science requirements in exchange for occasional access to Alan's Honda Accord. Sarah worked with Megan at the campus bookstore, where they bonded over Margaret Atwood while selling Hopkins hoodies. They scored a couple of fake IDs sophomore year and hit the Greene Turtle one night after work, where they ran into Alan, who'd just smuggled Mitch in through the back door.

Mitch had a minor crush on Megan—a three on a scale of ten—but he never acted on it because Megan called him "buddy" whenever possible and clearly thought he was a bit of a doofus. Sarah could've been persuaded to like Alan if the stars had aligned, but they never did, even in the face of so much casual drunkenness, which was a sign that it was simply never meant to be. Consequently, Mitch, Alan, Megan, and Sarah became one of those flirty but platonic little cohorts that are the foundation of any decent college experience.

And then Alan met Doug while playing intramural basketball. Doug was lights out from three-point range—a natural-born athlete— but he couldn't dribble to save his life. He joined the group from time to time at trivia night in the rec center, and became a permanent fixture one Thursday when they all went to a Counting Crows concert at the last minute in D.C. and had a blast. Sarah and Doug made out during the song "Mr. Jones" and became the group's first couple.

Terry, who had a part-time job at Doug's favorite used-music store, started showing up, too. Terry lived in a house off campus and had a seemingly endless supply of vintage concert T-shirts, which was cool, and he had the best sideburns that any of them had ever seen, straight out of *Beverly Hills 90210*. Sideburns, like Counting Crows, were a thing people talked about a lot in the nineties. Terry was an indie alternative to the typical preppy Hopkins guy, and Megan was into it right away. They started dating almost immediately.

Amber and Jessica were late additions to the group, recruited during blurry nights out in the city. Mitch saw Jessica at a bar in Canton and was instantaneously dazzled by her, despite her enormous flannel and her complete indifference toward him. Mitch famously told Alan later that night that he was "gonna make that girl love me if it's the last thing I ever do." A few months later they were all at a house party in a sketchy neighborhood near Camden Yards when in walked Amber. "Wow, look at her!" Alan yelled over the music—as smooth as ever.

They paired off over the sixteen months leading up to the end of their senior year: Megan with Terry and Amber with Alan in 1998, and then Jessica with Mitch and Sarah with Doug in 1999. Henceforth they were officially the Core Four. And, like any group legit enough to have its own name, they did everything together. This eventually included graduating, becoming gainfully employed, and getting married.

Megan and Terry and Sarah and Doug had their weddings a few months apart in the summer. Both ceremonies were lovely, featuring epic toasts, discarded bow ties, and, in Megan and Terry's case, a break-dancing ring bearer.

Alan and Amber had an ill-advised winter ceremony: always a dicey proposition in the Northeast. An ice storm a few hours before the rehearsal dinner tested everyone's resolve, particularly that of the caterer, who everyone later agreed had to have been on some kind of mood stabilizer.

Jessica and Mitch's wedding was last, in the spring, on Fenwick Island in Delaware, and it was perfect. Well, almost perfect. Two seagulls destroyed the wedding cake during the reception, but the guests were all drunk by then, so everyone would remember it as hilarious.

The Core Four drank together in an endless loop of Fourth of Julys and New Year's Eves and Halloweens and charity bar crawls in the city.

They waited a while to have kids, the Core Four, because what was the rush? And when they finally did, all the Wives but Amber got pregnant in unison. The little ones learned to walk together, wrestled in rented bouncy houses at sweaty birthday parties, and started pre-K at the same time.

Then, when it was time—when parking hassles and crime rates got to be too much—they all moved to the suburbs the same year. Their houses formed an odd square that covered 5.4 miles in the wooded suburbs of Baltimore, Maryland.

They celebrated holidays as a group. They watched the Oscars together. They all got dressed up and went to the Preakness. Their lives were intertwined, their experiences collective and referenced in first person plural—the royal "we." They had keys to one another's houses. They knew one another's garage codes and secrets. They were a big, sprawling, man-made modern American family.

And now that family was broken. By every reasonable standard of measurement, they were adults. Yet, one by one, they failed at the most basic adult institution of all.

Marriage.

MEGAN AND TERRY

Megan and Terry were the first to go down.

Their breakup was a surprise but, looking back, not a *surprise* surprise, because, quite honestly, they seemed to love each other the least. Still, everyone was pretty shaken up by it. The group's reaction, collectively, was: *Holy shit. Megan and Terry? Are you serious?*

Typically in divorce situations, everyone immediately blames the guy. Well, in this case, everyone was right. There was a woman on the side—younger, of course. There was a secret credit card, a secret email address, even a secret Skype account, which, technologically speaking, was pretty old-school. After the divorce, Terry moved to an elaborate apartment downtown and bought the most enormous flat-screen TV he could find. It arrived in a cardboard box the size of a Ping-Pong table.

The other woman—the younger one—was out of the picture by then. She liked Terry and all, and she'd had a lot of fun, but not enough, it turned out, to leave her husband and family in Roland Park.

Everything changed after that. Things snowballed. Dominoes fell. Floodgates burst wide open. Shit hit the fan.

SARAH AND DOUG

Sarah and Doug were next.

This one actually *was* a shocker. Of all of them, Sarah and Doug seemed most likely to make it. For starters, they were the best-looking of the group—the perfect aesthetic match. Sarah was naturally blond and dabbled in Pilates and yoga. Doug had wavy, effortlessly good hair and great arms. They were the kind of attractive that if you didn't know them, you'd assume they had to be monsters. They weren't, though. They were just normal people who happened to look like they belonged in a commercial for home exercise equipment.

The real kicker, beyond their mutual hotness, was that they genuinely seemed to love each other. They kissed in public. They still held hands at movies. He sent her flowers sometimes, just for the hell of it, and she said adorable things about him on Facebook, which was sweet, even though it grossed a lot of people out.

The infidelity thing in their case was more complicated than in Megan and Terry's situation. It was a whole "marriage in the age of the Internet" kind of thing. Sarah started communicating with a long-lost ex-boyfriend on Instagram, which devolved into sexy Twitter DMs. While this was happening, Doug was in the throes of a full-scale email romance with his work wife from the accounting department. The phrase "emotional affair" was introduced and debated extensively in the group. Quiet betrayals were made. Cracks in the foundation were formed. Then the whole thing came toppling down.

When Sarah and Doug announced via group text that they were splitting, too, it felt like when a great restaurant boards its windows in the middle of the night and suddenly no longer exists.

The group's reaction this time was something just shy of full-blown panic. Jesus H. Christ. You guys. What's happening to us?

AMBER AND ALAN

Four months later, it was Amber and Alan's turn.

In terms of perceived marital health, they fit squarely between Megan and Terry and Doug and Sarah. They were solid. They were dependable. Stable. Safe. They were the Subaru Outback of married people.

Sure, Alan drank a little too much sometimes, especially at parties, but who doesn't drink a little too much sometimes at parties? Amber always seemed vaguely discontent—a little depressed—but, again, how could you *not* be a little depressed in present-day America, what with its being an uncontainable dumpster fire and all?

Infidelity wasn't the problem for Amber and Alan—real or virtual. Their issue was that they were never actually in love. Never. Not even in the beginning.

They discovered this six sessions deep into wildly expensive couples counseling. Their friends splitting in such rapid succession gave them permission, finally, to admit it. And, once they did . . . it was such a relief.

I don't think I ever loved you either.

You didn't? Oh, thank God.

Did we get married because we both liked the Cure so much?

I think maybe we did.

They didn't have kids, Amber and Alan, so there was far less drama. Everyone else agreed, for lack of more elegant words, that their breakup didn't count as much as the others, because when childless couples divorce, really, they might as well be two high school kids calling it quits at their lockers.

Here're the CDs I borrowed.

Here's your sweatshirt back.

It's not you; it's me. Well, it's kind of you . . . but mostly me.

Can we stay friends?

That left Jessica and Mitch. The Butlers.

The last of the Core Four.

2

It was a lot to think about, the swift, systematic dismantling of their friend group—of their entire social structure. And on that early spring evening, that was exactly what Jessica was doing. Thinking about it—all of it—as she stood outside Bar Vasquez, watching Mitch through the restaurant's front window.

He was waiting for her inside, wearing his English-teacher blazer, trying to look like he belonged there in the dim, trendy place, which, of course, he didn't. He was forty years old, and it was a Wednesday night, of all unholy things, and it was clear to her just by looking at him that he'd rather be home in his fleece sweatpants watching *Sports-Center*.

She watched him squint at his cocktail menu.

It felt weird spying on him like this, but it was fascinating, too, like doing fieldwork again. When Mitch finally gave up and used the candle at the center of the table as a do-it-yourself flashlight, a familiar match-strike of love flared up in her chest.

Who was she to judge his sweatpants, anyway? She looked down at the tan slingback monstrosities clamped to her feet. How satisfying would it be to kick them off onto the gray Baltimore pavement?

Through the window, she watched Mitch pick up his phone and type. A moment later, her purse vibrated gently.

Woman! Where are you? I'm utterly alone in here.

Still, though, she watched him.

A twentysomething girl in a short yellow dress walked by his table. She was hot, in that obvious way that so many girls in their twenties are hot. Mitch's antenna activated, and Jessica watched her husband discreetly check out the girl's ass.

"You dork," said Jessica, shaking her head.

Lately, she found herself wondering how often Mitch thought about sex.

Some pretty compelling neurological studies suggested that average, healthy American men think about it every seven seconds, but, good God, could that possibly be true? As an experiment, she counted to seven in her head and discovered that it's actually a lot longer than you think.

"Can . . . umm. Can we help you, ma'am?"

It was one of the valet kids. There was a troop of three of them, bored looking, in matching windbreakers. She only noticed them just then, and she realized that she must seem crazy.

"No thanks, guys," she said. "I'm just stalking my husband."

Fifteen years.

Fif . . . *teen.*

That was how long they'd been married.

Sometimes it felt like forever. She'd have to exhale before saying the number aloud, the way you might talk about an eight-hundred-mile car trip. Sometimes, though, it was like they were just getting started. A couple of newlyweds, with all the time in the world.

Either way, it was plenty long enough for Jessica to know exactly what was about to come out of Mitch's mouth at any given moment. So when she slid into the chair across from him and he asked, "What's the name of that drink I like here?" she had an answer locked and loaded.

"The negroni, you dummy," she said.

"That's not the really sweet one, is it?"

"No. Not really. It's gin mostly. Some other stuff."

He tilted his menu toward the candle. "Ah, right. How do you remember this stuff? We haven't been here in months."

"You could just get a beer," she said. "You know, simplify."

He made his good-natured face. "It's date night. I order expensive drinks on date night, and you find me charming. I texted you."

"I know. I just got it. I love when you call me 'woman,' by the way."

They kissed quickly over the middle of the table—corner of his mouth to opposite corner of her mouth—the matrimonial equivalent of a knuckle bump. She picked up her water glass. "To the last couple standing," she said.

They clinked and sipped.

"Are you supposed to toast with water?" he asked. "Isn't that bad luck?"

"At this point, I think we can toast with whatever we want."

"True that, girlfriend," he said, and then he lowered his voice—serious, like a funeral. "It's official, then? *Officially* official? Alan and Amber?"

There was a long, empty table across from them where a big group would sit. She imagined the Core Four gathered around it, laughing, sharing apps, which was something that would now never happen again. "Yep," she said. "They signed the papers this morning."

"Well, shit," he said. "That's that, then."

She drained her water. "Amber emailed Megan, Sarah, and me from the lawyer's office. She wants to get drinks on Friday. Girls' night."

"That's so *Sex and the City*," he said.

He was right. It was a total *Sex and the City* move. But they'd reached a point in their marriage where you don't have to acknowledge each other's rightness all the time. Instead, she surveyed the people around them. "Young crowd tonight."

"I know," he said. "We're like the chaperones. I've been eavesdropping. Believe it or not, most of them are complete morons."

"Don't be cynical. They're young. We were morons once, too."

"You're all morons!" Mitch said, just loud enough, but no one noticed or cared.

A Black Keys song came on, and Mitch tapped the table. "So, your day. Good? Bad? Somewhere in between?"

She thought about the day's patients: an overeater, a college kid with bipolar disorder, and a woman who admitted to recently googling the phrase *How to secretly poison someone.* "It came and went," she said. "Mostly good."

"Same. Teenagers still don't care about great works of literature. Other than that, nothing to report."

This was how they talked about their days, a sort of shorthand. Since The Divorces, though, Jessica wondered if they should be saying more to each other, like with details and complete sentences.

"Oh," Mitch said. "I wanted to ask you something."

"Yeah?"

"Okay, be cool," he said. "Don't look right away. But you see that girl over there in the yellow?"

She glanced, faux casual. It was the hot girl she'd caught him checking out five minutes earlier. She was a few tables over now, her long legs crossed. "Got it."

"All right. Is that a really short dress, or is it a slightly long shirt and she forgot to wear pants?"

Jessica looked again. "Well, aside from basically being able to see her crotch," she said, "I think it's rather elegant."

He pushed his menu to the center of the table and rested his chin on his palm. "Emily's never gonna dress like that, right?" he asked.

"She probably will. The other day she asked me what thigh gap is."

"Wonderful," he said. "How is that even in a seven-year-old girl's brain?"

"Well, she's highly verbal for seven," said Jessica. "And she watches all those Ariana Grande videos on YouTube."

Mitch took a sip of his water. "Thanks a lot, Internet."

She smiled, and so did he, because this part of marriage had always been easy for them. The breezy part. The part that didn't involve their friends' marriages imploding and them being left to quietly wonder, *Are we next?*

"Where the hell'd our waiter go?" said Mitch.

She scanned the place, and her eyes fell on the restroom doors next to the kitchen. She remembered a night years ago, back when this place was called Pazo instead of Bar Vasquez, when they tried to have sex in the men's room. They'd failed, of course, because the sheer logistics of having sex in a public restroom are simply insurmountable. But there was joy in that failure.

"Oh, good," said Mitch. "Here he comes."

Jessica barely heard this, though. She was thinking about how she'd giggled all those years ago, when the Pazo manager knocked on the bathroom door while Mitch held one of her breasts. "Maybe if we stay really quiet, he'll think we died," Mitch had whispered.

"Hey, guys. Sorry about the wait. Can I start you off with some drinks?"

"Absolutely," said Mitch.

"For the lady?"

Jessica meant to say *shiraz*, which was a word she'd said many times before without difficulty. But when she looked up, the waiter was so startlingly good-looking that the word got caught in her throat.

"Sorry?" he said. "Shirrrr . . ."

"Shiraz," she said. "A glass."

"Right. Cool. You, sir?"

"I'll take a . . . *negroni*." Mitch pronounced it slowly, like a determined tourist in an exotic country.

When the waiter was gone, they looked at their menus. The Black Keys song was over, replaced by something clubby that Jessica didn't know. Mitch took a breath, and, of course, she knew exactly what he was going to say.

"What's the name of that thing I like here? Chicken something, right?"

3

The third negroni had been a mistake.

Mitch knew it would be, too, even as he was ordering it, which is how it always goes with fancy drinks: like making a down payment on nausea.

He took a deep breath and rallied as he opened the front door, because you never know exactly what you're in for when you leave a nine-year-old boy and a seven-year-old girl with a sitter. Injuries, emotional breakdowns, night terrors, art-supply disasters, plumbing fiascos. You have to be ready for all of it. But on that night there was only silence.

He hung his keys on the hook. "Hello, hello," he said.

"Hey, guys. In here."

It was Luke, the next-door neighbor kid. He was their go-to sitter, and one of Mitch's students. They found him hunched over his laptop at the kitchen island. Three strong drinks had left Mitch feeling silly, so he went in for a high five. "Luke, my man. Bring it."

They touched palms, and then Mitch improvised some sideways hand slaps and finger grabs.

Jessica gave him a look that asked, *Are you drunk?* And then she told him to leave the kid alone. "Come on, he's studying."

"It's my new thing," Mitch said. "I'm developing personalized handshakes with all my students. We'll work on that one, Luke. It was just a first draft."

Luke laughed. "Okay, Mr. B."

He felt a hit of boozy goodwill. He couldn't help it. He loved it when his students called him Mr. B.

Jessica grabbed two fizzy waters from the fridge and gave Mitch one.

"What're you working on?" he asked Luke. "You look very serious."

"Trig," Luke said.

"Oh God," said Mitch.

"I know. It's a nightmare."

"Well, the good news is, you'll probably never have to use it a day in your life."

"You think?"

"Are you kidding? I'm forty. I don't even know what trig is. Is it the one with shapes?"

"Don't listen to him," said Jessica.

Luke piled some things into his backpack—papers, notebooks, an awful-looking calculator—and Mitch whispered, "Trig is lame, Luke."

"I'll mention that to Mr. Howard tomorrow."

"Damn right. And tell him Mr. Butler told you to."

There was leftover oven pizza sitting on the table. Mitch grabbed some crust and took a bite. It tasted pretty much like you'd expect cold oven-pizza crust to taste.

"How were the kids?" Jessica asked.

"Good," said Luke. "We went all in on Legos."

Next to the microwave, Lego Bart Simpson and Lego Chewbacca sat together in the Lego Batmobile.

"Any trouble getting them down?" she asked.

Mitch caught Luke glancing at Jessica's breasts, and he had to stop himself from ruffling the kid's hair.

"Well, they went to bed with flashlights," Luke said. "Is that normal?"

Mitch avoided looking at Jessica. "It's just a phase," he said. "Now, if you'll excuse me, I'm gonna retire to the bedroom to drink LaCroix in my underwear. Jessica, pay the man."

Jessica rolled her eyes, and Luke laughed again.

"See you fourth period," said Mitch. "And wear your big-boy pants. We're starting *Romeo and Juliet*. Oh, and spoiler alert"—for dramatic effect, Mitch turned and looked back over his shoulder—"it doesn't end well."

Date night had been his idea.

Not just *that* date night—the entire date-night enterprise.

It came to him in a burst of optimism a few months back, after The Divorces started, while he and Jessica tag-teamed the dishes. "We should start going out more," he said. "Like we used to, before the kids sucked the life out of us like little vampires."

In theory, it was a grand gesture of early-middle-age romance. Now, though, pre-hangover on a Wednesday night and looking at his own blotchy face in his wife's full-length mirror, it felt like so many other things in their lives. It felt like one more thing.

He set his khakis on a pile of similar-looking khakis and turned on *SportsCenter*.

Then, at exactly 10:20 P.M., he heard the sound of a car door outside. He went to the window to look. It was James, his next-door neighbor, Luke's dad. For the fifth night in a row, James—not Jim, *James*—was loading his things into his black BMW SUV in the driveway.

Luke's parents, James and Ellen, were splitting, too, because divorce was a virus at that point, and it was closing in on them at zombie-movie speed. Mitch hid behind the blinds and watched.

James wore a Yale sweatshirt and a pair of jeans. He smiled down at his iPhone. The light from the screen caught his teeth, making them glow in the dark. Ellen was out there, too, arms crossed, glaring at him.

A throat cleared. It was Jessica, standing at the bedroom door, there to startle him. "You're creeping again, weirdo," she said.

"I'm not creeping. I'm observing."

"Well, you're observing creepily."

She came into the room and set a laundry basket next to the dresser.

"Do you think that dickhead whitens his teeth?" Mitch asked.

"Of course he whitens his teeth," she said. "He tans, too."

"Really? How do you know?"

"It's April in Baltimore, Mitch. He's a white guy with skin like a Latin R & B singer."

"Man," he said. "That's so nineties."

Out in the driveway, James checked his phone again. Another smile. Mitch wondered who he was texting with.

Jessica stepped out of her heels, one after the other. After all these years, he still had to recalibrate whenever she did this. She was shorter barefoot, obviously, but it was more than that. She was somehow smaller, too, like an actress removing an elaborate costume. She reached back and unzipped her dress, exposing one bare shoulder, and Mitch felt that familiar stir. The topographical map of their sex life featured the typical peaks and valleys, but his body still reacted to hers at nearly every turn, which, he knew, counted for something.

"I like that dress on you, by the way," he said.

She flexed her feet, cracking her toes. "Thanks."

"Luke liked it, too," he said.

She tossed her heels into her closet with a clunk. "Teenage boys are an easy audience," she said.

Outside, James Tetrised more crap into his car. A long reading lamp. A set of golf woods. A duffel bag.

In the bathroom, she let the dress fall to the floor and started brushing her teeth in her bra and underwear, and Mitch fell into bed to watch her. About ten seconds in, she wandered to the window with her electric toothbrush and looked down on James and Ellen.

"You get to creep, but I don't?" he said.

"I'm subtler than you."

"Why do you think Ellen watches him like that?" he asked. "Every night. She just stands out there."

She turned off her brush. There was toothpaste foam at the corners of her mouth. "That woman represents one of the great internal conflicts of my feminist life."

He turned down the TV. "Yeah?"

"On one level, James is a pulsating asshole. Through and through."

"I support that. Particularly in light of the tanning revelation."

"But then there's this mean voice in my head. It keeps saying, 'Maybe the mom jeans and androgynous haircut weren't such a good idea after all, Ellen.'"

"Ouch," he said. "That *is* mean."

"I'm not proud of it."

Back at the sink, she rubbed moisturizer on her face and legs—a nightly ritual. "I watched you tonight, you know," she said.

"You what?"

"I watched you."

"You did? When?"

"At the restaurant. Before I went in. I watched you through the front window for a few minutes."

"How'd I look?" he said. "Do you think my blazer's getting too ratty?"

She met his eyes in the mirror. "I saw you check out that girl."

"What girl?"

"The one who forgot her pants. Remember?"

Obliviousness was a card Mitch played as much as any other husband, but for a moment he legitimately had no idea what she was talking about. And then . . . the girl in yellow. "Ah," he said. "Right."

"Mm-hmm."

He felt his face flush. "In my defense, it was a lot of skin, Jess. Your eyes sort of go right to it."

She climbed into their bed smelling like nighttime. Instead of curling into her spot beside him, she settled somewhere in the middle, legs tucked beneath her. She was in shorts and a tank top now. So much of marriage is spent only half paying attention to each other. Talking while driving. Talking while watching Netflix. Talking while staring at a toddler, or while scanning utility bills or catalogs from the mail or Evites for some distant weekend. But she faced him now, fully engaged, her eyes square on his, and it made their bedroom feel smaller.

"You seemed pretty interested in her," she said.

"It was just a girl in a restaurant. There are millions of them."

"Stop it. Of course you were interested. She was hot."

He sat up and settled against the headboard. "Hardwiring," he said. "Right, doctor?"

She nodded. "If this was ten thousand years ago, you'd've grabbed her by the hair and done whatever you wanted to her."

"Which would've totally ruined date night," he said.

Outside, another car door shut, and Ellen shouted something that sounded very much like "There's no way in hell you're taking the espresso machine, you son of a bitch!"

"Mitch," she said. "I want to continue our conversation. *The* conversation." She put her hand on his leg over the comforter.

But before either of them could say more, there was a noise. Through their closed bedroom door, from the other side of the house, over the sounds of their neighbors' marriage ending, came a shout. That shout was followed by the sound of a little boy running down the hallway.

"Shit," Mitch whispered.

Jessica wrapped herself in a blanket, and three seconds later their son, Jude, stood in the doorway clutching his flashlight.

"Hey, buddy," said Mitch.

"Hey, honey," said Jessica.

"E.T. is in my closet again," said Jude.

"Jude," said Mitch. "Come on."

"I'm serious, Dad."

"Buddy, I promise. He's not."

"I saw him, though."

"You didn't."

"I heard him."

"Jude."

It was a parent-child standoff. Jude clicked his flashlight on and off, on and off. "Can one of you come lay with me?" he said.

Mitch looked at Jessica. She was already reaching for her Kindle.

"Jude. We've been over this. A lot."

"I could hear him breathing. In the closet."

Jessica sighed. It was a weaponized sound, aimed at Mitch.

"Just for a minute?" said Jude. "Till I fall asleep again?"

There was no use in fighting. He'd lost. There are so many losses in parenting, strung together over many years. "Okay," he said. "I'll be there in a second."

When their son was gone, Mitch reminded Jessica that, technically, according to the rotation, it was her turn.

"Mm-hmm," she said.

Outside there was beeping as the rear hatch of James's SUV closed.

"Goddamn E.T.," Mitch said. "I hate that little fucker."

4

B ack to the conversation.
    That conversation. The one Jessica and Mitch were about to
continue having.

It was ongoing: one big conversation in five parts, like a British
detective series.

When frightened Jude showed up in his pajamas with his flashlight,
he interrupted what would've been conversation number four about
how Jessica and Mitch Butler planned to save their marriage.

CONVERSATION NUMBER ONE

The first time they talked about it, they barely even talked about it.
Mitch actually thought Jessica was joking.

They were at the Towson mall.

Luke was watching the kids one Saturday afternoon so they could
do some shopping. They milled around a couple of stores together,
looking at this and that. Jessica asked for, then promptly disregarded,
his advice on a sweater. Mitch let her pick out a new pair of jeans for
him. Eventually, though, as couples in malls do, they drifted apart.

Mitch sat in a massaging recliner at Brookstone, and looked at a
display of Air Jordans at Foot Locker that he was way too old to pull

off. A girl at a kiosk gave him a sample of a new moisturizer for his face. Eventually, he grabbed a drink at Starbucks and just started wandering. A half hour later, when Jessica found him, he was drinking an iced green tea and looking up at an enormous image of a nearly naked Kate Upton in an ad for pajamas.

There are thousands of beautiful, famous women in the world. For Mitch, though, there's just always been something about Kate Upton, which was why she was at the top of a short list that Mitch kept in his head, like an all-star team. This list was no secret. Quite the opposite. Jessica had a list of her own, in fact, of male celebrities, which included Mark Ruffalo, George Clooney from 1998, and, for some reason, Salman Rushdie.

She shouldered up to him and nudged his arm. "Busted," she said.

Mitch sipped his tea and played it off. "We should probably get you a pair of those jammies," he said.

A young mother passed, pushing a stroller with twins in it. A Journey song was coming out of a nearby store. A mall janitor mopped up a spilled soda next to a nearby garbage can. And then Jessica said, "Do you ever think about sleeping with other people?"

Mitch laughed, because what else can you do when your wife asks you something like that?

CONVERSATION NUMBER TWO

The following weekend, they were on their hands and knees picking up strewn Lego pieces in the living room.

Mitch was about to ask her if she thought it was weird that Jude kept putting Darth Vader heads on girl Lego bodies when she said, "That Kate Upton thing. I wasn't *entirely* joking."

"What?"

"I'm genuinely curious."

"What do you mean?"

"Do you?"

"Do I what?" he said. "Do I think about sleeping with Kate Upton? Doesn't everyone think about sleeping with Kate Upton? Isn't that, like, part of the human condition?"

"That's not what I asked."

"It's not?"

She shook some Lego pieces in her hand, like dice. "People," she said. "Do you ever think about sleeping with other *people*?"

Historically, Jessica wasn't a layer of traps, but a series of warning alarms went off in his head anyway. "I don't know," he said.

"Of course you know. Either you do or you don't."

"Well, yeah. I guess. Sometimes."

She nodded.

"Why? Do you?"

"Sometimes."

"Oh."

"It's hardwiring, Mitch. We're human beings."

For Mitch, being married to a therapist had some advantages and some disadvantages. She was unfailingly reasonable. She was incredibly smart. But sometimes it felt like he was talking to a robot that had been programmed to read WebMD pages aloud to him.

"Do you love me?" she asked.

"I do," he said.

"And I love you. You're a human male. Wanting to have sex with one of the hottest women on the planet doesn't make me love you less."

He thought about it. And he thought about Kate Upton. Lego Luke Skywalker looked up at him from the floor. True to form, he was missing one hand. "You're not trying to tell me you had sex with Salman Rushdie, are you?"

CONVERSATION NUMBER THREE

And then there was just last week.

They were writing the kids' weekly activities on a dry-erase board in their kitchen, because that's what marriage is with children: scheduling.

"All of our friends are divorced," she said.

He looked at her. "I know. I've been keeping up."

She jotted down some kid's birthday on the board. "Sex was a big part of all of their downfalls."

"You think?"

"Don't be silly," she said. "Terry had sex with someone else. Sarah and Doug *virtually* had sex with other people, which is a symptom of wanting to *really* have sex with other people. Amber and Alan didn't want to have sex with each other."

"Okay," he said. "But how does that apply to us?"

"How could it *not* apply to us?"

"We're not them, Jessica. You do know that, right?"

"You think we're that different?"

"Of course I do. Just because we *like* them doesn't mean we're all the same people. For starters, they're assholes. We're better than them."

Jessica capped the dry-erase pen.

"Plus, we're happy," he said. "That's the big difference. You and me. All of this." He made a grand, sweeping gesture with his arms, meant to indicate the house and the children and the yard and the kitchen and the activity board and their lives. All of it. "We're happy. Right?"

Emily and Jude were on the back deck messing with the birdfeeder. Just before the kids burst back into the house to tell them about a blue jay that was fighting a cardinal, Jessica replied, "But, Mitchell, are we?"

5

"Okay, bud, first off, it's pretend. E.T.'s a puppet. Or maybe a robot. I can't remember which. Either way, he's one hundred percent not real."

His son looked at him with grave suspicion. They were lying in Jude's room. With the night-light and hallway light on, it was just dark enough for the sticker stars on the ceiling to glow.

"Secondly. And this is more important, narrativewise. Even if he *was* real, why would E.T. want to murder you?"

"He's bad," said Jude. "And his neck is gross. It's like a giant worm."

"Yeah. The neck. CGI wasn't as good in the eighties. But he's not bad. That's the whole point of the movie. *We're* the bad ones, not him. Society. He's a metaphor for . . . I don't know, innocence or something."

Silence followed, and it occurred to Mitch that maybe this wasn't the best time to introduce the concept of metaphor.

"The end was nice, though, right?" he said. "E.T. gives little Drew Barrymore the flowerpot and the ship flies off into the sky? All's well."

Jude shook his head. "I don't like how he sounds when he screams."

Mitch slow-blinked his way into a sigh, and for a while they looked at the sticker stars together.

Jessica had totally called this, of course. The whole thing.

He'd showed her the ad in the *City Paper* a few weeks ago. The Senator, this cool old theater downtown, ran classics on Saturday mornings for families. "Check it out," he said. "Let's take them."

She looked at him like he'd suggested a family outing to test chain saws. "Are you crazy?" she said. "It'll scare the shit out of them."

"What? There used to be *E.T.* lunch boxes. I had an action figure!"

But then there they were, Jude and Emily, scared shitless, watching what Mitch quickly remembered was a terrifying movie. A child alien is left on Earth and then slowly chased for two hours by deep-breathing men in masks. At one point, during the scene in which Elliott's big brother finds E.T. pale and dying in the woods, Mitch looked over at his children, and they appeared not just scared but scarred—for life. They hadn't slept through the night since.

Mitch tugged the blanket up over himself and his son, and told Jude to close his eyes. "Don't worry. I won't leave till you're asleep, okay?"

Jude slid closer. "Promise?"

"Yeah."

One of the big stickers above them—a moon or something—was starting to peel away from the ceiling, and Mitch fixated on it as they lay in silence. A few of the other stickers were starting to peel away, too. After a few minutes, Jude's breathing slowed, and Mitch thought about conversation number three with Jessica.

We're happy.

Long, dramatic pause.

But, Mitchell, are we?

The fact that she questioned this should've stung, but it didn't. Because, he had to admit, it was a perfectly valid thing to ask. For years, the concept of happiness simply hadn't come up in Mitch's head. Nor had the concept of *un*happiness. This was his life. This was *their* life. She was his wife, and he was her husband, and that was the way it'd always be.

Then The *fucking* Divorces.

Everything was open to scrutiny now. Everything needed to be parceled and quantified.

He thought of the last time they'd had sex—a fifteen-minute-or-so operation last week, after *The Daily Show*. He'd picked up an issue of *Cosmo* that morning in his dentist's waiting room and skimmed an article about the many hidden erogenous zones scattered across the female anatomy. As Jessica wiggled beneath him, he stretched her arm out and kissed the humid spot inside her elbow. She laughed and asked him what he was doing.

"Does that feel good?" he asked.

She took her arm back and told him to hurry up and fuck her. "The kids could show up any second."

Jude was passed out now, his eyeballs jittery beneath their lids, and Mitch started to untangle himself from the sheets. But then there was a knock. It was a tap, really. Barely loud enough to hear. His daughter, Emily, stood at the door in comically mismatched pajamas with her hair hanging over one eye.

"'Sup, lady?" he said.

"Daddy?"

"Hmm?"

"Can I tell you something?"

It was a tic, a sign of learning to articulate herself. She'd ask permission to say something before saying it. As perfectly normal as it was for a seven-year-old, it made everything sound very grave, like she was about to report the death toll after an earthquake.

"What is it, babe?"

"I think E.T.'s in my closet."

Good Lord, Mitch was tired.

It was a level of exhaustion you don't experience in your twenties or even your thirties—something exclusive to forty and up, like colonoscopies and pleated khakis. So he held his arms out to his daughter, because it was all he could muster the energy to do. "Okay," he said. "Hop in."

And as she did, as she crawled over him and into bed—as she'd done so, so many times before—she kneed him right in the balls.

6

And that was how Jessica found them.

It was exactly how she knew she'd find them—a sleeping mass of humanity tangled in Transformers sheets. Jude was on his side, back pressed to Mitch. Emily was sprawled out over both of them like a human blanket. *She must've racked Mitch again,* Jessica thought, *because he's holding himself in his sleep.*

Two of her three best friends in the world had recently negotiated for custody of their kids, and Jessica played a ridiculous scene out in her head. A judge—an older lady, African American, kind of an Oprah vibe—asks Jude and Emily who they'd rather live with, their mom or their dad. They pick Mitch, of course. They don't even extend Jessica the courtesy of pretending to think about it.

He lets us put gummy bears on our Froyo!

Yeah!

She touched his shoulder, gave him a shake. "Mitch. Hey. Mitch."

He opened his eyes. "Hi," he said.

"Come downstairs."

"Okay," he said. "Be down in a sec. I'm just gonna shoot Steven Spielberg a quick email first and tell him to go fuck himself."

———

Downstairs, in the kitchen, Jessica ate two Golden Oreos over the sink.

She did it quickly—single-biters—because they were amazing. She ate two more, slowly this time. Outside, through the kitchen window, the backyard was as black as deep space. Five years into suburban living and she still wasn't used to the darkness. When her eyes adjusted, she saw her own reflection in the glass.

She straightened herself and arched her back, assessing things. And then she ate another Oreo, because . . . fuck it.

The hot waiter from earlier must've looked at her breasts no fewer than ten times over the course of their meal. He wasn't egregious about it, like some gawking teenager, like Luke, their babysitter. He just did that quick eyeball dip—the thing men have been doing for millennia and women have learned to live with. She ran through a list of similar looks she'd gotten that day. And then the day before that. And every day since she was twelve and a half. She imagined a relentless wave of male eyeballs, like in a horror movie. Classmates and patients and coaches and teachers and colleagues and neighbor kids and random men she'd never meet or speak to.

As she looked at her reflection in the window, she caught a familiar light out behind the house. It flickered, then held steady. She cupped her eyes with her hands and pressed them to the glass. Luke was sitting on a tree stump in the strip of side yard between their properties, reading a book by the light of his cellphone.

Squeaks and thuds came from above as Mitch made his way down the stairs. "Oh no," he said. "You opened them. You monster."

"Couldn't help it."

He grabbed a handful of Oreos, devouring two in an instant, like a creature from the woods.

"Check it out." She pointed to the window. "He's out there again."

Mitch smiled a sad half smile for his student.

The past few nights, when James was at the house packing, Luke had been there, stationed on his stump. Jessica thought of go-kart rides with her own dad. Go-kart rides and batting cages and mini golf and Saturday matinees and waterslides. Her father was like an every-other-week day camp that concluded with her being dropped off in front of her mom's house. *Till next time, Jessie.*

Mitch ate another Golden Oreo. "Remember when we used to eat regular Oreos, like assholes?" he said. "Then some product-development guy at Nabisco says, 'Let's make vanilla Oreos and call them Golden Oreos,' and our lives are changed forever."

She'd found them at Giant a few weeks ago, under a sign that said NEW FLAVOR. Since then, Golden Oreos had become their mutual obsession. Jessica and Mitch kept them in the highest kitchen cabinet, away from the kids, like cigarettes or porn.

She twisted one in half, licked the frosting. "Maybe they're not really better than the originals," she said. "Maybe they just taste so good because they're different."

CONVERSATION NUMBER FOUR

He leaned against one counter; she leaned against the other.

"Jessica," he said, "did you just turn Golden Oreos into a justification for infidelity?"

She tilted her head. "I may have."

"I knew there was a reason I married you," he said.

"I don't love that word, by the way."

"Infidelity?"

"Yeah. It's judgy. Steeped in negativity and accusation."

"You're right, it is. Open marriage?"

She felt an actual chill. "That's even worse."

"I know, right?" he said. "It's like a key party. Like I should be wearing a bathrobe."

She briefly imagined Mitch having sex with Kate Upton. Since The Divorces, along with directing *Lifetime*-quality courtroom dramas in her head, stalking her husband through restaurant windows, and questioning everything about her own happiness, Jessica got to picture the love of her life screwing a world-famous swimsuit model.

Mitch and Kate Upton in a hot tub.

Mitch and Kate Upton in the back of a limousine.

Mitch and Kate Upton at the Plaza in New York City, the skyline lit up through the window.

He'd be all sensual about it, too, Jessica knew. Gentle and attentive, which was totally his thing when it came to sex. He'd kiss Kate Upton's neck and ears while he moved inside of her, and her big, gorgeous eyes would roll back in her head.

Holy shit, Jessica. He's really good at this.

"Maybe *relaxed* is a better word," she said. "Conceptually speaking."

Mitch nodded. "'The Relaxed Marriage.' It's got a ring to it. Like a Cheever story."

"Only *you* could turn a conversation about sex into something nerdy."

He tipped an Oreo her way. "Touché."

"Love is a feeling," she said. "Monogamy is a rule. One we came up with twelve thousand years ago when we started worrying about property rights."

"That's romantic."

"Nobody ever said reality is romantic," she said. "As a society, we've watched monogamy fail over and over again, but we still put ourselves through it, generation after generation."

Mitch chewed and thought. "How about 'The *Evolved* Marriage'? The world's changing. The environment's different. We're . . . *evolving*."

Jessica had lost interest in finding a label. "You know, in therapy, when someone chea—" She stopped herself. "When someone *evolves* in their marriage. When you ask them why, they almost always say the exact same thing."

"Yeah? What's that?"

"They say they wanted to feel alive again."

Mitch nudged the Oreos her way. "More alive than cookies in your pj's on a Wednesday night in the suburbs, you mean?"

She kicked his knee gently with one bare foot. "I keep thinking about the movie *Love Actually*."

"There's a part of my brain that's always thinking about *Love Actually*," Mitch said. "It's delightful."

"Remember when we watched it last Christmas? That Emma Thompson scene? The Joni Mitchell song? Everyone's so depressed because the bad guy from *Harry Potter* has the affair, right? But think how different the end of that movie would be if Emma Thompson would've cut him some slack. Let him live a little. Maybe it would've saved them."

He took two Oreos and handed her one. "His name was Alan Rickman," he said. "And he was a screen legend."

Outside, a car engine started: a low, expensive-sounding hum. James's BMW. When he pulled away, the headlights lit up the kitchen like an explosion.

"The other day," she said, "when I asked you if we're happy."

"Yeah?"

"I didn't mean that I think we aren't."

"I know," he said.

She sealed the bag and pushed them away. Enough.

Mitch took a piece of her hair and tucked it behind her ear. "But you think we need to be saved anyway, huh?" he asked.

The truth: She didn't know. Maybe. But she was sure that there was a point when Megan, Sarah, and even Amber hadn't known either. In their divorces—maybe in every divorce in the history of divorces—there was a moment when things could've gone either way.

"Maybe this will save us before we need saving," she said.

7

On weeknights, the Butler bedtime routine was ironclad, run with humorless, German-like precision.

Bath. Teeth. Story. Cuddle. Closet check for E.T. Then, between 8:30 and 8:50 P.M., the lights went out.

Like any parenting routine, though, it went straight to shit on weekends, particularly when one of them was flying solo. Which was why at 8:45 P.M. on Friday, while Jessica was out with the Wives, Mitch was only halfway through bath time.

Emily splashed about in a mountain range of bubbles and drew animals on the tile with a green bath pencil. Jude's bath was done, so he was sprawled out on the bathroom floor in pajamas, coloring in an E.T. coloring book. Mitch supervised the operation while sitting on a wooden step stool, drinking a beer from a plastic Orioles stadium cup.

He took a picture of the tile, catching just a glimpse of the back of Emily's head, and posted it to Instagram.

Bath time at the Butler House. #Friyay?

"That's some decent coloring, dude," Mitch told Jude.

"Thanks."

"See? Not scary at all. E.T.'s totes adorbs."

The idea was pretty simple: A kid couldn't be scared of something he colored in a coloring book, right?

But Jude shook his head. "He's not adorbs, Dad."

Emily looked up from her bubbles, her face serious. "Am I gonna turn all white when I die, too, Daddy, like E.T. did?"

"Honey, you're not gonna d—" Mitch pumped the brakes. "E.T. didn't die, guys, remember? We talked about this. He was just sick. Then he got better. Fade to black. Roll credits."

All three of them knew this was total bullshit. E.T. died. He died frightened and tormented, hooked up to fake movie medical equipment, and thanks to Mitch, his kids got to see it firsthand on an enormous screen.

"When are you gonna die, Daddy?" Emily asked.

"Not for a long, long time. Like, an annoyingly long time. My goal is to be a burden on you for many, many years. Someday, Mommy and I will live with whichever one of you has the coolest house."

Amazingly, Emily accepted this without further comment.

"Is Mom gonna be home soon?" asked Jude.

"Not till after you're asleep," he said. "She's having a *Sex and the City* night with her friends."

"What's sex and the city?"

"Nothing. Keep coloring."

When his phone buzzed on the sink, Mitch assumed it was Jessica texting—to remind him of something or to say good night to the kids. But it wasn't. It was his friend Alan of Alan and Amber; of divorce number three.

I'm knocking on your front door. You in there?

Mitch was surprised by how excited this suddenly made him. He hadn't seen any of the Husbands in a month, and he texted back immediately.

Upstairs. Giving kids bath. Come in.

Alan hit him back with a thumbs-up emoji, but a moment later he texted:

Locked. Should I ram the door with my car?

Go around. Back is unlocked, I think. If not, you can go fuck yourself.

He laughed at his own vulgarity—at the sheer childish joy of talking shit to a friend.

"Who are you texting?" asked Jude.

"Uncle Alan's here."

Just as quickly as that surge of excitement appeared, it was replaced by melancholy. The Core Four had always referred to themselves as the uncles and aunts of one another's kids. Could they still do that? Are there rules to pretend-families like theirs?

A single, loud beep came from the security alarm, and then Alan shouted up the stairs. "I'm getting a beer, you filthy animals! And there's nothing any of you can do to stop me!"

"Bring me one, too!" said Mitch.

"Me, too!" shouted Emily, and her laughter reverberated off the bathroom walls like a Mariah Carey song.

Mitch recognized his friend's lanky gait as he came up the stairs. "Where are you guys?" Alan said.

"In here!" said Emily and Jude.

"In the bathroom," said Mitch.

"Oh great. If someone's doing a *numero dos* in here, you're all in big trouble!"

The kids laughed. Tall, youthful, prone to bathroom humor, Alan was their favorite pretend-uncle. He handed Mitch a beer and sat on the edge of the tub. "How's it going, Butlers?"

Mitch punched him in the thigh.

He wore a nice shirt tucked into dark jeans. The top button was open, Mitch noticed, and he smelled like cologne.

Alan touched Jude's wet hair. "Whattya say, Jude the dude?"

"Hey."

"Is that E.T.?"

"Yeah. Dad's trying to make me think he's not scary."

"Well, your dad's delusional. E.T.'s horrifying. Did you let them watch that, man?"

This was great. Even the guy with no kids thought he was a terrible father.

"There's my little lady," said Alan. "How're you, beautiful?"

Emily blushed. "Gooooood."

"I like the bubbles."

"Me too," said Emily.

"We used four capfuls of bubble juice, even though the directions only said two," said Jude.

Mitch took a drink. "That's how we do it on Fridays," he said. "Next we're gonna sniff some of the glue from Emily's art set."

Alan took a drink—at least a third of his bottle.

"You missed one of your buttons," said Mitch.

Alan smiled. "It's intentional. I'm trying something. You like?"

"I don't know. I'm still processing. You look like a suburban coke dealer."

"It's the new me. I'm reinventing myself as a breezy single guy who's so chill that sometimes he forgets to button all his buttons."

"Okay. It's growing on me."

As they watched Jude color, Mitch assessed his friend. He looked different. It was tough to pinpoint how, exactly. It was like when you finally take your car to the car wash after an ugly winter. It doesn't just look clean—it looks somehow new again. That was how Alan looked: new. Or newish, at least.

"Are you divorced now, Uncle Alan?" Emily asked.

"Em," Mitch said.

Alan rolled with it. "That I am, sweetie. Your Uncle Alan's a free bird. Officially. Hide your daughters."

"How was it?" asked Mitch. "Signing the papers. Tense? Weird?"

"Not as bad as you'd think. We hugged. I wanted to do a divorce selfie. That's a thing now on Instagram, divorce selfies. Amber wasn't down, though. Surprise, surprise. She thought it was 'inappropriate.'"

Mitch opened his new beer and poured it into his cup while Alan used shampoo to mold Emily's hair into a full-on Mohawk. "I gotta get some kids," he said. "They're hilarious."

"You talk to Doug and Terry lately?" Mitch asked. "How're they?"

The Husbands texted often throughout the week—sometimes daily. There'd be long chains about the most inconsequential things imaginable. Weeks would sometimes pass without any of them sharing any real, legitimate personal information.

"Oh, you know. Same stuff. Terry's music collection is straight-up bananas now. He's practically got a DJ booth in his apartment. And

Doug's doing CrossFit with twenty-five-year-olds every day after work. He's due for a devastating injury any day now. It's a foregone conclusion."

"Uncle Doug is kinda jacked," said Jude.

"Eh," said Alan. "I could take him."

"Yeah, right," said Jude, turning the page of his coloring book to a picture of E.T. holding out one glowing finger.

"So, what's up?" Mitch asked. "You just popping in? Gracing us with the presence of your exposed chest?"

"I was in the hood. Thought I'd roll by. You're the only one of us who still buys good beer." He was smiling, though, being coy, and Mitch gave him a look, which was all it took. "Okay, fine. Ya got me. Uncle Alan's got a date tonight, kids!"

"A date?"

"With Aunt Amber?" asked Emily.

Alan booped her nose. "Girl, you're killing me. No, with someone else. Someone new. It's complicated."

"Like, a *date* date?" said Mitch.

"Well, I guess that's what you call it. We're meeting at Valley Inn in half an hour. I'm gonna show up a little late, though, just to keep her guessing." He winked. Alan was the only person Mitch knew who could wink in casual conversation without looking like a sex criminal.

"Wow. You've been divorced for like—"

"Forty-eight hours. I know. But, seriously, check it out." He pulled his iPhone out of his back pocket and tapped the screen a few times, revealing the image of a girl.

Mitch took the phone. She was blond. Freckles across the bridge of her nose. Smiling and young. Midtwenties, maybe.

"How'd you meet her? Were you cruising high school parking lots?"

"Shut up," Alan said. "She's not *that* young. She's like twenty-six or something. And we haven't met yet. Not technically."

"What?"

"I know I said I wasn't gonna do the app thing," said Alan. "I was gonna be a purist. But I was at work the other day, and I was like, why not? This is what people do now. This is how people meet people. So I signed up. I'm not kidding, dude. . . . Fifteen minutes later, girls were hitting me up. Pinging me right and left."

"Pinging you? Is that what they call it?"

"I don't know. I'm sure there's a word for it. I felt like Justin Timberlake."

"Justin Timberlake's married, Uncle Alan," said Jude.

Mitch gave his son a high five. "Truth bomb!"

"Good point, Judey," Alan said. "I'm talking pre-Biel here. Vintage Timberlake. Boy-band style."

"But don't these girls know how old and decrepit you are?" Mitch said.

"You'd think, right? But apparently not. In app world *this* is desirable." He showed Mitch his profile picture. He stood outside Camden Yards, smiling, in an Orioles T-shirt.

"Let me see," said Emily. She touched his digital face and smiled, and Mitch imagined the dating future the poor girl would inherit: apps and swipes and robots. Mitch and Jessica met at a bar while drunk, in real life, like God intended.

"Well, you should pace yourself," said Mitch.

Alan snorted. "It's a date, not a half marathon."

"I know," said Mitch. "But you've been an indoor cat a long time now. It's a jungle out there."

Emily licked a drop of water from her nose, and Jude dug into his ziplock bag of crayons. Mitch noticed Alan touching his bare ring finger, feeling for something that wasn't there, a soldier reaching for a limb that's long gone.

"It's actually overwhelming," Alan said. "You have any idea how many women there are out there? Like, *available* women?"

"I don't," he said.

"This is the golden age of being single. They're gonna write books about it someday." He tapped his phone. "I mean, if these things had existed back in the day, when we were young and in the game? My God, none of us would've ever gotten ma—"

He cut himself off, and Mitch felt an emptiness open. Apparently it was the night of mixed emotions. Happiness at the idea of seeing his friend. Sadness at the loss of the lives they'd all once lived. Now emptiness at the implication that he was somehow missing out on something. His face must've shown all this, because Alan segued. "Anyway, I'm babbling. What's up with you guys? How're you and Jess—our lone survivors?"

As Mitch worked through some of the possible responses to this, he was aware that Emily and Jude were watching him, waiting. Half the job of parenting is not saying ominous shit in front of your kids, so he cleared his throat and said, "Well, we miss all you guys."

Which was true. Mitch missed the hell out of those assholes, all of them, the Husbands and the Wives, their kids, their dumb yards and messy houses and crappy beer selections.

"We miss you, too, buddy," said Alan.

There was no joke to be had here. No teasing or sarcasm. Just two old friends in a little bathroom in the suburbs, acknowledging to each other that sometimes things just suck. Fortunately, though, Emily was there to save them.

"Look, Uncle Alan," she said. "I drew a picture of you."

In green bath pencil, next to an elephant on the bathtub tile, stood a smiling stickman with a giant head, huge ears, and a broken triangle nose. It was a perfectly terrible drawing.

Alan aimed his iPhone at the tile. "Sweetie," he said, "I've never looked better."

8

Nine miles away, Bond Street Social was an absolute shit show.
Jessica had known it would be, especially on a Friday night,
but when she'd brought this up to the Wives earlier via text chain,
they'd made her feel old and lame.

It won't be THAT bad, grandma.

Maybe you can DVR Murder She Wrote?

Isn't a shit show kinda the point???

The message was clear. They were three single women, dammit,
and they'd go wherever the hell they pleased. She was the interloper
now, the extra wheel, the other.

Which made it that much more satisfying when Jessica arrived and
saw them huddled together at the back of the bar and clearly miserable.
It was loud, hot, and packed, which were all things they'd once loved
about this place—about all of the places of their youth. She stopped
and took them in before they noticed her: her three attractive, dressed-
up, overeducated friends.

She loved them. God did she love them. But she couldn't help but
hate them a little, too, for allowing their lives to fall so thoroughly
apart.

"Hey, ladies," she said.

"About time!" said Sarah. She tapped her watch, but she was smiling. The Wives were used to Jessica arriving last.

She hugged her friends one by one, and then Amber said, "Okay, so this place kinda sucks."

"Did it always suck like this?" asked Megan.

"I remember it sucking less," said Sarah. "It's like spring break in here."

A shot materialized. Megan held it out to Jessica with a smile that said *This wasn't my idea.*

"Time for you to catch up," said Amber. "We're celebrating!" There was some slurring in her vowels. Amber was a chronic slurrer when she drank.

Jessica took the little shot glass. "How many have you had?"

Amber counted with her fingers. "Not *that* many. I was the first one here, so I got a head start."

The drink was green and murky, like a prop from a movie about teenagers doing dumb things. "What is this, anyway?"

"Remember back in college?" asked Sarah.

"Vaguely," she said.

"Back then, when someone handed you a shot, you just took it, right? No questions asked."

"I also cut my own bangs in college," said Jessica. "Is there a roofie in here?"

"I'm almost positive there's not," said Megan.

"Driiiiink!" shouted Amber. She was teetering in her high heels. She was the tallest of the Wives by a long shot.

As miserable as they looked, they also looked amazing. Lanky Amber in her leggy dress. Sarah in a sleeveless blouse that showed off her amazing arms and sexy collarbones. Megan was lovely, too, in a dress she never would've gone for when she was married to Terry. Tight and short, but classy, too—one of those miracle dresses that accentuates what you want accentuated and leaves everything else alone.

"So, question for the group," said Amber.

Megan, Sarah, and Jessica leaned in to hear over the noise.

"Do you think I could sleep with Mr. Suit Guy over there?"

There was a handsome, well-dressed man nearby with his arm around a woman who was clearly his wife.

"Doubt the missus would be cool with that," said Jessica.

"I don't mean *literally*," said Amber. "Not, like, *reaaaally* sleep with him."

"You mean *figuratively* sleep with him?" said Jessica.

"Yes. Exactly. I'm being hypothetical."

Megan and Jessica laughed.

"Enunciate, hon," said Sarah. "It's too early to be slurring."

"Ha ha," said Amber. "I'm collecting data. This is a fact-finding mission."

"I thought it was a celebration," said Jessica.

"We're celebrating *and* fact finding. I need to establish my sexual range. I haven't had sex with someone who isn't Alan since I was a junior in college. A *fucking* junior in college! I mean, are you kidding me?"

Slurring had become swearing, and Jessica decided it was time to take her shot. Tequila burned her throat, and there was a trace of something sugary. Since The Divorces, she'd struggled to adjust to seeing these women as individual entities. In her mind, they were still parts of couples. Megan still went with Terry. They were moneyed, blunt talkers, distant with each other. Sarah still went with Doug. They bought Vitamin Water in bulk and drove a Volvo. And Amber still went with Alan. They were funny and always arrived in Ubers, because they were usually already half in the bag.

"I bet I could hook up with that guy over there," said Amber. "Maybe him, too." She was just pointing randomly at dudes, like she was leafing through a J.Crew catalog.

"What about that guy?" asked Megan.

"Well, yeah," said Amber. "Probably. If I want to feel like an Amazon woman every time we leave the house together."

"Oh, stop it," said Sarah. "You're gorgeous." As the best looking among them, Sarah was constantly telling the others how beautiful they were.

"Nope," said Amber. "This isn't about looks. This is about *height*. Feet and inches. I've been dealing with it since sixth grade. Guys don't want someone taller than them. It messes with their heads. And I don't want some guy who's shorter than me, quite frankly. You small bitches don't get that. Alan was—well, *is*—six-two. I went all the way up there. So, that's where my range starts. Mayyyybe six-one if I wanna wear flats every day for the rest of my life like an Amish woman. Which, for the record, I do not."

The Wives made skeptical faces, but Jessica knew Amber was right, and she knew that Megan and Sarah knew it, too. There are rules to attraction. Rules to everything.

"Should we get another round?" asked Sarah. "I'm buying. Tito's on me."

No one got a chance to respond, though. A couple of guys with spiky hair shoved through the middle of them like bird dogs, and enough was enough.

"Okay, I'm done with this place," said Amber.

"Amen," said Jessica.

"Where should we go?" asked Sarah.

"Somewhere that doesn't completely suck," said Amber. "That's my one stipulation."

"Agreed," said Megan.

They listed some spots—some new, some old, some Jessica hadn't heard of. Amber suggested Bar Vasquez. "That place is kinda decent, right?"

Sarah and Megan liked this idea.

It was where Jessica had just been with Mitch on date night, but it was too late to protest. The decision was made, and the Wives were already heading for the door.

Her mom hadn't wanted her to marry Mitch.

In Mitch's defense, her mom hadn't really wanted her to marry anyone. At least not then.

He proposed by way of a quote from a Curtis Violet novel, which was just like him. They were sitting on the couch together in the little apartment they shared in Federal Hill—shacked up and poor. It was a Saturday afternoon, and she was studying.

"I'm thinking of assigning this to the kids," Mitch said, holding out a paperback. This was when he was teaching junior high English, before the cushy private high school gig.

"Maybe a little aggressive for seventh graders, don't you think?" she said.

"Nah. It's one of his early ones. Less sex, short chapters, hardly any swearing. Check out this passage. I think the kids'll respond to it. It'll inspire them."

She very nearly told him to leave her alone. She was busy, after all. But when she saw that he'd circled a paragraph with pink highlighter, she knew something was up. Mitchell Butler would sooner key his own car than deface a book.

"Read it out loud. It's better when you actually hear it."

Whatever doubt she had that he was about to propose was erased by the expression on his face. True, unguarded vulnerability. So she read.

"She was better than him in all the measurable ways. Better looking. Anyone could see that, plain and simple. Smarter, for damn sure. A brighter future. The product of better breeding—cleaner, far more ambitious genes. She wore better clothes, too. She had a better all-round disposition, and she looked like an angel when the light hit her just right through their bedroom window. Somehow, though, impossibly, illogically, despite all of this, she was his. Which was why he said what he said. Screamed it, in fact. 'Will you marry me?'"

She left the whole Curtis Violet thing out when she told her mom a few days later. By God, the woman hated Curtis Violet. They were sitting in her old row house in Mount Washington, drinking mint tea.

Her mother didn't immediately respond. The wooden clock on the mantel sounded like a heavy-metal drummer tuning up. The cat, Susan B. Anthony, walked into the room, assessed the situation, and quickly got the hell out of there.

"Well, congratulations then," she finally said.

That might've been the end of it. Jessica might've ignored the tone and accepted the sentiment, but she just couldn't. "How can you *not* like him, Mom? Everyone likes him. That's Mitch's thing—his defining feature. Universal likability. He's like Tom Hanks."

Her mother set her tea down. "I *like* him fine. But to marry you—now? My brilliant daughter? He's such a turkey sandwich of a guy."

"I don't even know what that means," said Jessica.

"You're too young."

"I am not."

"*Dramatically* too young."

"No, I'm not. We're all getting engaged."

Jessica hated how that sounded as soon as it left her mouth. She was referring to the Core Four, but it sounded like she was talking about a cult—a commune with sister-wives and group showers.

The cat came into the room again. She looked around and rubbed her head on the leg of an end table.

"It's okay, Susie B. We're being civil. Jessica's marrying the most likable boy in all of Charm City."

Susie B. turned her back to them and curled up in a sunbeam.

"I will say this for Mitchell. He's the opposite of your father. Kudos there. I'm sure that's why you're attracted to him, by the way. Don't need all those textbooks to tell you that."

"See, then? That's good. You hate Dad."

"True. He was handsome, though. Still is, the son of a bitch."

She felt a burst of defensiveness so sudden and intense that it surprised her. "What the hell do—"

Her mother rolled her eyes. "Oh, would you stop it? Relax. Mitchell is handsome, too. In his way."

"Well, shouldn't you be happy, then? He's handsome. He's got a good job. He's nothing like Dad. Isn't that the goal?"

"The goal? Oh, Jessica. Have I failed you so badly as a mother that you think marriage should be the *goal*? At your age?"

"Not the goal. But the destination, at least." Jessica didn't know exactly what she meant by that, which often happened when arguing with her mother. Her thoughts came out confused and pieced together.

"For women, Jessica, it's a trap. Society set it thousands of years ago, and we keep stumbling into it. It strips us of our power, takes the best years of our lives—our *identities*."

"Our identities? You're being melodramatic."

"You will be defined by someone else henceforth. Mrs. *Mitchell*

Butler. Because it'll always be about him. It's always about the man. Is he happy? Is he still attracted to me? Is he paying enough attention to the kids? Is he fulfilled? Is he losing interest? There's nothing needier on planet Earth than a man. And your needs will come second. Always."

It had seemed so dated, like so much bra-burning, hippie-era bullshit. But now, years and years later, sitting at a four-top table at Bar Vasquez listening to her best friends talk about men, she was forced to consider that maybe her mom had been onto something.

It *was* about them. Megan, Sarah, and Amber wouldn't shut up about guys.

"Maybe I should just focus on finding someone to have fun with," said Amber. "I mean, I can do that, right? I don't need permission."

"Sure," said Sarah.

They'd been there forty-five minutes, and this was how it'd been the whole time. Jessica squeezed her wineglass and tried to change the subject. "Did you guys hear about that thing in Nebraska the other day?" she asked.

They looked up from their drinks and dinners. They'd all ordered heavy, except Amber, who was quite possibly the only woman in Baltimore who'd transition from shots to a kale salad.

"Omaha, I think," said Jessica. "This gay activist group. They went to the top of the tallest building in the city and threw buckets of glitter from the roof. It got caught in the wind and spread for miles. Apparently, it was glorious."

Megan smiled. "Yeah. Saw it on *Morning Joe*, I think."

"God bless the gays," said Amber.

A man about their age passed in a polo shirt and jeans, blatantly checking them out on his way to the restroom.

"Have you ever noticed that if you squint your eyes, all guys basically look the same now?" said Sarah.

Megan laughed.

"We go on cleanse diets and take online spin classes at five-thirty in the morning," said Sarah. "They take a shower and tuck in their shirt and they think they're David Beckham."

"Stop it," said Amber. "He didn't look that bad. And he was tall."

"You know, Amber," said Megan, "as fun as it is discussing dudes for you to hypothetically sleep with, if you want some veteran advice, maybe take your time with the sex stuff."

"I have to agree," said Sarah.

Amber laughed. "What? Why?"

"It's different now," said Megan.

"How's it different?"

Jessica leaned in. "Yeah. How? They still put their *you know* in our *what'sit,* right?"

Megan bit into a shriveled potato. "You can make fun if you want," she said, "but it's true."

"Come on," said Jessica. "Is there really nothing else we can discuss? Books? Movies? Dismantling the patriarchy, maybe?"

"In a minute," said Megan. "Amber needs to hear this. This is her life now, and everything's changed."

"How so?" asked Amber.

"For starters, it's not nice anymore."

"What isn't?"

"It," said Megan.

"And *them*," said Sarah, joining in.

"Sex isn't nice, and neither are men," Megan said.

Jessica imagined Megan and Sarah practicing this, like two midlevel executives clicking through slides on a keynote presentation.

"It's porn's fault," said Sarah. "That's my theory."

"You're damn right it is," said Megan. "I haven't had sex with a guy once since my divorce who hasn't tried to come all over me."

Amber choke-coughed on her drink.

"Same," said Sarah. "Which is such a delight, because God knows that's exactly what we're hoping for."

"Is this the part where I yell 'Check, please'?" said Jessica.

"That's what they think sex is now," said Megan. "Target practice. Oh, please, Troy or Chad or whatever, can you aim for my face? I'm just dying to get it in my eyes."

"Point is," Sarah said, "you should probably check out some porn. At least know what you're getting in to."

"And maybe get some protective eyewear," said Jessica.

Amber shook her head. "Whatever. If I wanted to *not* have sex, I'd have stayed married. Believe me, I'm ready. I'll wear a hazmat suit if I have to. The other day I grazed a guy's hand at Starbucks when I was reaching for the almond milk, and I wanted to put his fingers in my mouth."

"That's actually kinda hot," said Megan.

"I think finger-in-mouth porn is a whole thing now," said Jessica. "Google it." She thought this was funny, but the Wives were dialed in, and a moment of sisterly silence settled over them. Jessica pulled out her phone and tapped out a text to Mitch.

Divorce is awful. We're never getting one.

"It's not just sex, by the way," said Sarah. "That's just part of it. It's them. Guys. *They're* different, too—and these dating apps have made it worse."

"God, the apps," said Megan. "Fuck the apps."

"They're terrible," said Sarah. "Everything is superficial now. Imagine the worst singles bar on earth—fully digitized. Guys are just chasing some physical ideal, some type they think they're supposed to want. And that's not in our favor." She picked up her phone. "You should see the women on this damn thing. Twentysomethings everywhere in bikinis. Girls are hiring professionals to take their profile pictures. Why would some decent guy our age wanna talk to *me*? He can go on his phone and find a hundred versions of me the way I looked fifteen years ago."

Since this was Sarah talking, there was no one there to do her job and tell her how beautiful she was, so Jessica stepped in. "Oh, come on. Look how hot you are. I literally want to bite your arm."

Sarah kissed the air in her direction. "Yeah, but I'm not midtwenties hot. There's no workout class that's gonna make me that."

"Consequently," said Megan, "we get the older guys."

"Older?" said Amber.

"Yep. Forty-year-old guys want twenty-eight-year-old chicks. And now, thanks to the motherfucking Internet, they can have them. Fifty, fifty-five-year-olds? We're right in their wheelhouse. They love us. We're like catnip to them."

Amber groaned.

"Oh, and don't forget about the dick pics," said Sarah.

"Ah yes, dick pics," said Megan. "I remember my first one. A year ago. A rite of passage."

"Me too," said Sarah. "Last year. A lawyer named Chris. I thought he was so sweet, too. He seemed normal. We had drinks. We talked about his daughter's horseback riding lessons for like an hour. Then, I woke up the next morning, checked my phone, and it was wiener city."

Jessica laughed, loudly, and they all looked at her. "Sorry," she said. "It's terrible and all, but you just said *wiener city*."

Their waitress did a flyby, and they ordered another round.

"Yep," said Megan. "In a matter of days, your phone will be awash with high-res male genitalia. Welcome to the club."

Amber, fully defeated, sank in her chair, her kale salad wilting.

Maybe this is part of it, Jessica thought. *Like the dick pics themselves, this is a rite of passage. Your divorced friends show you what it's like behind the curtain, and you're appropriately horrified.*

When their drinks arrived, the Wives ditched all the accoutrements, the swizzle sticks and silly umbrellas, to the center of the table.

"Can I ask you guys something?" said Jessica. She was talking to Megan and Sarah, the veterans of divorce.

"Is it gonna be something sarcastic?" asked Megan. "Collectively, I don't think we're in the mood for that."

"No," said Jessica. "Well . . . yeah, no. I promise."

They sipped and looked at her.

"Do you ever regret leaving them?"

The Wives had discussed The Divorces in exhaustive detail—the causes, the repercussions, the effects. Not this, though. This had never come up.

Jessica pushed on. "I read this thing—a study."

Sarah made a snoring sound.

"Stop it," said Jessica. "This is related. Apparently, an overwhelming number of women regret divorce five years later. Something like sixty or sixty-five percent."

"I don't know," said Megan. "If I could do it over again, maybe I'd just have forgiven Terry and moved on with my life."

"But he cheated on you," said Amber.

"Yeah. And it sucked. I wanted to chop his dick off. But after a while . . . I don't know. Is it that big of a deal?"

The Wives treated this rhetorically.

"Sometimes I do," said Sarah. She sounded pained, like a woman confessing to something. "It's just easier to be married. And Doug used to rub my back every night. It was like this thing—this ritual. Even when we were pissed at each other, or if we'd just had a big fight. Every night."

"Well, this is just great," said Amber. "I should probably switch to wine. I don't wanna puke until I get home."

Bar Vasquez was getting louder. Every table was full now; people were two deep at the bar, waiting.

"I mean, case in point," said Megan. She bit an olive. "If I was still married, and I had the chance to have sex with that waiter over there, are you telling me I wouldn't go for it?"

Jessica, Sarah, and Amber turned to look.

It took Jessica a moment to recognize him. Gorgeous and familiar in a crisp white shirt. It was the waiter from the other night—from date night. Their eyes met across the restaurant.

"Okay, wow," said Sarah.

"Jeez," said Amber.

"Why can't he be *our* waiter?" said Sarah.

"I think I found the top of my range," said Amber.

Megan seemed pleased with herself. "You guys see my point, then? I mean, who could blame a girl for getting with something like that?"

They watched him work for a while, weaving through his tables, delivering bread and drinks.

And then Amber asked, clearly, without a single slur, "Do you think this restaurant has a policy against licking members of the wait-staff?" And despite everything—porn, dating apps, and a city full of creepy older men—the Wives all laughed.

9

The text chime startled Mitch awake.

When she was gone, his senses were always heightened, like a smoke alarm that's too sensitive and freaks out every time you toast a bagel.

He grabbed his phone off the coffee table.

Divorce is awful. We're never getting one.

It was jarring, out of context, but then he remembered that she was with the Wives. He considered his reply for a moment, and settled on understatement.

Deal.

He had been watching a documentary about serial killers on Netflix when he fell asleep, and now his TV was asking if he wanted to watch a different documentary on serial killers. There were some broken Golden Oreo pieces on the coffee table, and two empty beer cans. As far as images went, it was basically the opposite of an inspirational meme. #LivingMyBestLife.

He wondered about Alan's date and how it was going. The beauty of living in the twenty-first century: When you wonder something about someone, you can just text them.

How's the date?

The typing bubble popped up within seconds. He'd noticed this about the Husbands. Since The Divorces, their text replies were virtually instantaneous, as if their phones were permanently affixed to their bodies.

Still on it, Dawg.

Then why are you texting me?

She's in the bathroom. Valley Inn is bumpin.

He included a fire emoji, and then dancing-girl and martini emojis. Alan was big with the emojis.

How is she? You like her?

Even hotter in real life. Check this out. Took 10 mins ago.

An image appeared. A glowing girl and a middle-aged man with his top button undone.

You took a selfie on a first date?

Brave new world, my friend. Gotta go. She's coming back. Oh, BTW, she smells like Starbursts.

Upstairs, Mitch did a quick check on Jude and Emily. They were good for now, sprawled out in that insane way that kids sleep. He lingered at Emily's door, because she was adorable, and he hoped to God that in twenty years she wouldn't be on a date in a bar with some forty-year-old divorced dude with crow's-feet, in the middle of reinventing himself.

He was about to head to bed, but he stopped in the hallway at a framed photo of the Husbands. It was a picture he hadn't noticed in a long time.

Kid pics got top billing downstairs, in the high-traffic zones. Up here, though, along the stretch of light-green wall that connected the three bedrooms, they kept documentation of their pre-kid lives. In this particular photo, the Husbands were smiling on the beach on Fenwick Island. The Core Four hit Fenwick every summer back then. They rented a house as close to the shore as they could afford, and almost never got their security deposits back. Alan set a grill on fire once trying, drunkenly, to make quesadillas, and on two separate occasions, Doug crashed through screen doors.

Mitch could remember the exact moment the picture was taken. Terry flagged down an elderly couple walking a corgi and asked them to take it. Mitch and Alan were flexing, and Doug and Terry were sunburned and laughing. They were all young and happy and thin, and their wives were twenty feet away, in bikinis. He imagined stumbling onto this group now, as a forty-year-old—as the Ghost of Divorces Yet to Come.

Hey, idiots! Enjoy this while it lasts!

"Mr. Butler!"

Mitch squinted at the photo.

"Mr. B. Out here."

Through the hallway window, Mitch saw Luke sitting on his stump. And apparently Luke saw him, too. Mitch pushed the window open and stuck his head out. "Luke. What're you doing out here, you nerd?"

Luke held up his book. "*Romeo and Juliet*. You assigned it, remember?"

"Yeah, but I gave you guys the weekend off. You should be out living it up, enjoying yourself."

Luke looked embarrassed in the low light of his iPhone, and Mitch had about a dozen simultaneous flashbacks to the Friday nights of his own youth. Binge-reading, listening to bootlegged U2 concert CDs, playing *Super Mario Brothers 2* until his thumbs cramped, trying to catch a stray boob on partially scrambled Cinemax.

"Just reading ahead a little," Luke said.

Up in the sky the moon was nearly full, burning big and bright through some passing clouds.

"Well, don't be afraid to take a break. You've currently got a hundred and forty percent in the class, so you're doing okay."

Luke smiled. There was a sound from up toward the front of the house—car doors and packing. James again, still moving out.

"Do you have to go?" Mitch asked. "Are your parents gonna be looking for you?"

"Nah. He's about to leave. When he does, my mom'll go straight to bed. She's taking these pills that knock her out in like three minutes flat. Sometimes she doesn't even make it upstairs."

Teachers have an official log in their brains where they note comments like this—the official ledger of red flags and warning signs. "So, how're you doing?" He nodded in the direction of the driveway. "You know, with all that?"

Luke seemed to think about this on his stump. "She's not even that pretty," he said.

"Who?"

"My dad's new girlfriend."

"Oh."

"I mean, if she was hot, at least maybe I'd get it, you know?"

Mitch was pretty sure that wasn't how it worked. Then again, what did he know? His parents, Bob and Cindy Butler, had been married for forty-two years and spent half the year driving around the country together in an RV the size of a townhouse. They referred to it as the "Butler Cruiser."

"So, exactly how far ahead are you reading?" he asked.

"Just a little."

"How little?"

He looked embarrassed again. Kids like Luke were Mitch's weakness as an educator. For the most part, his job was to guide kids through their English requirements and off into lives of artlessness. The handful of Lukes he got every couple of years made it all seem less hopeless.

"I finished it," Luke said, and Mitch laughed.

"Of course you did."

"Twice, actually."

"That's the thing about books," Mitch said. "No matter what's going on in your life. All the stupid stuff you can't control or fix. They're always there, right?"

"I like that, Mr. B.," he said. "It's deep."

Mitch rested his elbows on the windowsill. "When I was in high school," he said, "I got cut from the freshman baseball team. I was so depressed that I typed out *The Catcher in the Rye* on my parents' computer in a single night."

James's packing sounds echoed into the night.

"Wow, Mr. B. You were an even bigger nerd than me."

10

The Uber driver was being totally unreasonable.

It was something small—a Nissan Something-or-other. Megan, Sarah, and Amber were piled drunkenly into the back seat, laughing. Jessica tried to take shotgun, but the driver put his hand over a duffel bag on the front seat. "I am very sorry, miss, but no." His accent was thick and unidentifiable.

"What?" said Amber, the giantess. She was pretzeled into the middle of the back seat, which made no sense.

"Yeah," said Sarah. "Are you serious?"

Jessica sighed. "Could we just put that stuff on the floor? I won't mess with it."

"Yeah, she's a little person," said Amber. "And she's a doctor, too. Trustworthy."

The driver looked at her through the passenger-side window with pleading eyes. He had a large black mustache. "No," he said. "I must insist. Please."

Sarah and Megan booed from the back seat, and a car honked behind them.

"This is no way to get a five-star rating, dude," said Megan. "One star's really gonna mess up your average."

"But then he'll just give *you* one star," said Sarah. "The whole system is flawed. You give them a shitty review, they give *you* a shitty review."

"It's like nuclear war," said Amber. "Everyone's equally screwed."

"*That* is literally the most intelligent thing any of us have said all night," said Sarah, and the back seat laughed.

They were drunker than she was, Jessica knew, which was a common phenomenon since The Divorces. If there was security footage of the scene, she would look exactly how she felt: like a woman on the outside, looking in.

"Ladies," said the driver, "negative review or no, so be it. I am going to have to ask—"

Megan slapped her thighs. "Well, there's only one thing left to do then," she said. "Come to Mama."

Jessica leaned against the car. "You wanna drive to the suburbs with me in your lap?"

"Why not? It's better than strapping you to the roof like an armoire."

"*Armoire* is an odd word," said Amber. She demonstrated by repeating it three times in a French accent.

"Enough talking!" said Megan. "Hop on in."

"That will not work either, I am afraid," said the driver. More cars were honking. Some pedestrians stopped to watch.

"Dude," said Amber, "we're trying to work with you here."

"The laws of Maryland state that there must be one seatbe—"

"You're not leaving us with a lot of options," said Megan.

"Should we get out, then?" said Sarah. "I'm lodged in here pretty good. Might have to get the Jaws of Life."

Amber tapped at her phone. "How do you call an Uber if you're *in* an Uber? There's no button for that. This app is stupid."

"You guys, wait?" said Jessica.

Inside the Nissan Something, everyone went silent. Megan, Sarah, Amber, and the driver looked at her, waiting. She wasn't sure what she was doing, exactly—at least, she told herself she wasn't. But what she did know was that she didn't want to go home yet.

"Jess?" said Sarah.

"You want us to get out?" asked Megan.

"Should we do more shots?" asked Amber. "I could probably do two more before night-nights."

Jessica looked back at the restaurant. There were people inside. There was laughter and music, the steady thud of bass. Through the blur of the front window, she could see the waiter. He stood over a table, a tray of drinks balanced in one hand. Again: a woman outside looking in.

Jessica didn't want to go home yet.

So she didn't.

11

T he Wives never would've left her there on the street alone under
normal circumstances.

Absolutely not.

"Never leave a ho behind" had been their motto back in college and
the few years after college, when they were young enough to affection-
ately call one another hos. They would've strong-armed the poor
driver until he finally gave in, or they would've piled, drunk and complaining, back onto the street and figured something else out.

But on that Friday night they were tired, and more than that, they
were just plain over it. Consequently, all Jessica had to do was show
them her phone with the Uber app open. "See?" she said. "I'll get my
own damn Uber."

"Okay, that's a lot of cars," said Megan.

She was right. There was a swarm of little black car icons buzzing
around their location dot.

"Just go," said Jessica. "I'll be fine. One of these guys'll be here in
fifteen seconds. I'll probably be home before any of you."

The other Wives collectively shrugged.

"All right!" said Amber. She blew Jessica a kiss from the back seat.
"Roll out! But you're only getting four stars, dude."

For a moment, when they were gone, Jessica stood looking at the front of Bar Vasquez. Laughing people went in and out, handsome guys and pretty girls, and she wondered what she was doing out there, exactly. She looked down at her hands and was surprised to see that they were shaking.

When she opened the door, she nearly chickened out. She would've turned around if the waiter hadn't been standing right there, five feet from the entrance.

"You're back," he said.

Jessica briefly wondered if he was talking to her. They hadn't exchanged a word earlier, while the Wives finished their drinks and dinner and after-dinner drinks, but their eyes had found each other's maybe a dozen times as he buzzed back and forth across the restaurant. And now he was smiling at her, and he was gorgeous. "I am," she said.

"Where's your crew?"

She looked back at the front door as if the Wives might be there, hands on hips. *What the fuck, Jessica?*

"They couldn't hang," she said. "Bunch of lightweights."

His eyes moved to her breasts again, quick as hummingbirds. "That's lame," he said. "Well, let's get you a drink, then. Come on. I just got switched to the bar upstairs."

He led her up some steps to the mezzanine section that overlooked the restaurant. She sat down on a squishy stool at the end of the bar. It was quieter up here than it had been downstairs.

"So, you like this place, huh?"

"What?"

"Well, technically, you've been here twice tonight. And you were here the other night, too. Couple of days ago, right, with . . ."

She almost said "my husband," but instead she let him trail off. Somewhere in her lap, her hand formed a loose fist around her engagement ring. The diamond dug gently into her flesh. "I do like it," she said. "You've got good wine here."

"Gimme a sec, okay?"

He made a few drinks behind the bar—two for a couple at one of the bar tables, two more for the cocktail waitress, who collected them on a tray. And then he poured Jessica a glass of shiraz.

"I'm impressed," she said. "You remember my wine choice. You're a good waiter."

He tilted his head. "A little secret from the pros. We always remember what beautiful women order."

These words had a complex effect on her—a sensation like being in a glass elevator, rocketing upward over an unfamiliar cityscape. Sure, the male gaze is one thing. It's ever-present, laced with ambiguity and aggression. But no one who wasn't Mitch had called her beautiful since she was a college kid, and she could feel an insistent pulse in her neck. "Um . . . *you* know that *I* know that you work for tips, right?"

"Guess I won't charge you for that one, then," he said.

A series of woven veins ran up his forearm and disappeared under the rolled-up cuff of his white sleeve. She imagined tracing their path with the tip of her finger. A couple in their twenties bellied up to the bar and tried to get his attention. He completely ignored them.

"So, ladies' night tonight?" he asked. "Special occasion?"

"We were celebrating."

"Oh yeah? Celebrating what?"

"Divorce." She let the word settle, unexplained, and his attention narrowed. "My friend Amber. She just signed the papers."

"Ahh. Well, that's . . . *nice*? Is that the word? Nice?"

"Believe it or not, you came up in our conversation."

"Me?"

"You caused quite a moral dilemma for us, actually."

"Do tell."

He was blasé at the prospect of a table full of women talking about him. He'd looked like this his entire life, Jessica assumed. No awkward stage, like everyone else. No gawky teen years or braces with rubber bands or acne or baby fat or disastrous haircuts. It was like white privilege, but exclusively for hot people—hot privilege—and it was hard not to resent him for it.

"My other friend, Megan," she said. "Her ex had an affair with a real-estate hussy. You single-handedly caused her to forgive him."

"Oh yeah? How'd I do that?"

The twentysomething couple cleared their throats.

"She said, even if she was still married, she'd have an affair with you in a second. So you've decriminalized cheating. Bravo."

He laughed. "Okay, now *I* need a drink."

"Hey. Do you, like, have a drink menu or something?" It was the twentysomething girl. He slid them a black leather booklet and then poured himself a glass of the same shiraz Jessica was drinking.

She nodded toward the couple. "I take it back. You're not a very good waiter at all."

He swirled his wine. "I have good nights and bad nights. I'm easily distracted."

It wasn't like Jessica hadn't flirted in the last twenty years. She was a human being, after all. But not like this. She wondered if she was doing it right.

"We all dared Amber to flag you down and talk to you," she said. "She's convinced she's gonna die alone. You'd be good for her."

"Like a *How Stella Got Her Groove Back* situation?" he said.

"You know that book?"

"I thought it was a movie," he said, without a trace of self-consciousness, and she tried to imagine him reading but couldn't. Maybe that's the burden of hot privilege. Everyone assumes you don't read much.

"A book *and* a movie," she said. "Either way. Amber was a coward. Said you were too scary to talk to."

He smiled. "Man, women really overthink this stuff, huh?"

"Well, that's a given. It's our defining feature. But what do you mean specifically?"

"Table nineteen, right?" he said. "I was watching you guys earlier, over there in your dresses, all done up. Any one of you could've taken home any guy in here. Snap of the finger."

"Oh? Just like that, huh?"

"Yeah. Just like that. It's like a superpower, and you guys don't even know you've got it. Total waste. With great hotness comes great responsibility."

"This is good to know," said Jessica.

He took a sip, swished it around a little. "Wait," he said. "Which one was Amber again?"

"The tall one. *Really* tall. Like a baby giraffe."

"Oh shit, yeah," he said. "I totally would've hit that."

She laughed, louder than she'd intended. "Well, if you're interested, I can give you her number. She'd be thrilled."

He finally took the twentysomethings' drink order. A beer for the guy, something fizzy with vodka for the girl. When he came back, he told Jessica that he had a confession to make.

"Yeah?" she said.

"I'm lying," he said.

"About what?"

"I can't remember what any of your friends look like."

"Really?"

"Mm-hmm," he said. "I was too busy looking at you."

12

Mitch was dreaming about Alan's date.

Before, she'd been just a picture on an iPhone screen— a smile, shoulders, freckles. In his dream, though, she was fully three-dimensional, and sitting in his classroom.

Even asleep, Mitch acknowledged how cliché this setup was.

He was a teacher, and his subconscious had made her a student. If this were an essay instead of a dream, he'd write something constructive across the top of the first page in red. *Maybe start with a less familiar premise and go from there.*

Dream Mitch was at his desk at the front of the classroom, which looked mostly like his real-life classroom, except there were no windows, and all the desks were empty save for hers, which was right in the middle of the room. She wore one of the school's cross-country uniforms—those little singlet things. He had no idea why. He was lecturing about . . . well, something. He couldn't tell what. Words were coming out of his mouth in a steady, cohesive, academic-sounding stream, and she listened, nodding along, nibbling at a pen cap.

And then she was walking toward him. Her cross-country spikes click-clacked on the hard floor. Then, in a senseless dream jump cut, her shoes were gone, and she was sitting on his desk in those little ankle socks that runners wear. She handed him her iPhone and licked her lips, and he found himself swiping through naked picture after naked picture. On a beach. In a bed. On a yoga mat. Lying on a couch. Sitting in a leather recliner reading a magazine.

Do you like them?

I . . .

Keep going. There are so many. Millions.

And then she was straddling him, and it was so vivid that he could feel the weight of her body pressing down on him. And just as quickly, she was naked, and he was inside of her, and he could feel that, too, as utterly real as sex had ever been.

She was a stranger, this girl. He didn't even know her name. But she was so completely familiar to him. Her skin. Her lips. The flutter of her tongue against his.

Shhhhhh. You don't even have to wake up.

She didn't smell like Starbursts, as Alan had said. She smelled like alcohol, which burned his eyes, and her lips tasted like something he knew. Like vanilla.

"My God, Mitch. You're so hard."

This wasn't dream dialogue—it was actually happening—and when he opened his eyes Jessica was rocking gently on top of him. The room was dark, he could barely see her, but he didn't need to see her, because, of course, it was her.

"Jess?"

"Kiss me," she said. The slightest lisp, the ghost of her childhood speech impediment lingering in the dark.

He kissed her, and she grinded herself harder against him. He put his palms on her hips to slow her down, because it was too fast, but it made no difference. She grabbed the headboard and anchored her legs to the mattress. "Oh fuck," she whispered. "Oh fuck."

"Hold on," he said. "Hon, slow down."

She ignored him, so he closed his eyes and tried to gather himself, which he was able to do for about nine seconds. But then she bit his shoulder. Softly at first—gently, even—then a lightning strike of pain as her teeth sank into his flesh, and it was too much to bear. Jessica and Mitch came together for the first time in as long as he could remember. It was so intense that he didn't even notice their bed breaking until Jessica shouted. The headboard snapped away from the base with a crack and crashed into the wall, and the frame buckled. The box spring hit the floor, and she collapsed on top of him.

For a while, they just breathed. And then Mitch said, "Holy shit."

She rolled off of him and onto her back, and they watched the ceiling fan spin above them. He touched the bite mark on his shoulder, which was tacky with blood, and he said "Holy shit" again.

Jessica sighed, and it turned into a sleepy little laugh. Such a lovely sound.

"You ate Golden Oreos, didn't you?" he said.

"I may have."

He reached over and rested his hand on her bare stomach, tracing his fingertips gently from hipbone to hipbone, and they lay quietly together, wrapped in their sheets, atop the wreckage of their bed.

CONVERSATION NUMBER FIVE

"Okay," he said.

She lolled her head to the side, her breath and heart rate slowing now. "Okay what?"

"Let's do it."

He could've said more, but he didn't. Fifteen years. He didn't have to. She knew what he meant.

PART TWO

THE RULES

13

It took Jessica and Mitch about twenty minutes to come up with the Rules for their relaxed marriage.

You'd think it'd take two middle-aged neurotics longer to work through something like that. But, by the time they sat down on their back deck on that Sunday evening, they were tired and, as it turned out, a little stoned. Jessica would note to herself later that it had taken them longer to decide on the lamp in their entryway than it did to determine the logistics of their infidelity.

It was fully dark, aside from some purple tiger stripes over the horizon, and Jude and Emily were in bed, finally.

Jessica and Mitch could count on one hand the number of times they'd smoked pot since college, but Alan had given each of the Core Four a joint a while back, long before The Divorces, and if any occasion called for casual drug abuse, this was it.

"How old do you think it is?" Jessica asked of the joint.

"Couple years?" he said. "Right?"

"It's gotta be longer than that. Emily wasn't even born yet."

"Time is a very mysterious thing," he said. Which was true. Half an hour ago they were on their honeymoon; now they were forty.

Jessica held the shriveled thing to her nose and handed it back to him.

"It looks like petrified wood," he said.

"Do you think it'll even work?" she asked.

"Maybe," he said. "It's been in my sock drawer."

"Does pot go bad, do you think, or is it like Twinkies?"

"They didn't cover that in season one of *Narcos*," he said.

They were two people asking each other questions that neither could answer. It was a microcosm of marriage. Not just their marriage—*all* marriage. Fidelity. Parenting. Money. Interest rates. Real estate. The stock market. Jumbo mortgages. The differences between LED and plasma. Nobody knows. Everyone's just making it up as they go and hoping to avoid catastrophe.

"There's only one way to find out," he said.

They didn't own a lighter, so Mitch lit the joint with an extra-long grill match from the garage and inhaled deeply, like he remembered doing. After a few coughs that burned straight down to his soul, he felt his brain shake loose, and he smiled. "Damn," he said.

"Really? It works?"

He nodded and gave her the joint. The end had smoldered out, so he fired up another foot-long match. Jessica held the smoke in her lungs for a beat, then blew it out in a long, shaky plume.

"Look at you, Snoop," he said.

A few seconds passed, and she blinked. "You're right," she said. "Damn."

They put their feet up on a big flowerpot and looked out at their yard. The tree stump that Luke had claimed for his sit-in was empty, which was a relief. Unseen wildlife called out in the woods, and they both agreed that their faces felt weird.

"This is fun," she said. "We should do this more."

Was she referring to smoking pot or to just sitting together on the deck? Mitch had no idea which. Maybe both. "Let's move to Fenwick," he said. "Quit our jobs. Sell stuff to tourists."

"We could buy a convertible," she said. "The kids look cute when they're tan. It'd be good for them."

This was a mantra of sorts for Jessica and Mitch, one they returned to from time to time. The first half was always the same—the "Let's move to Fenwick" part. The second half changed every time.

We could paint houses like college kids on summer break.

We could start a vegan bicycling club and wear lots of bracelets, like Johnny Depp.

We could open a bookstore that also sells boxes of wine and gives away rescue puppies.

"So, the Rules," she finally said.

Their faces really did feel weird, like masks made of friendly, slow-moving bees.

"The Rules," said Mitch.

"How should we . . . proceed?"

"Proceed?" He giggled, like a stoner. "That sounds pretty formal. Like there should be an official ledger. Should we find a notary?"

"Shut up," she said. "Rules are important. Guard rails."

"Well, for starters, no lying," he said. "Total honesty."

"Right," she said. "But do we really need to state that? Isn't it assumed?"

Mitch considered this.

"Should we also say no murder?" she said. "Like, hard-and-fast, no killing people."

"Okay," he said. "I get your point."

RULE NUMBER ONE: NO SOCIAL MEDIA FRIENDS

They'd never taken a good look at each other's social follows and friend lists before—they'd never even talked about them, specifically—but Jessica and Mitch knew enough about social media to know that danger lurked there.

There were high school crushes and exes online. There were old hookups, now married and fat, and also old hookups now divorced and hotter than ever. There were co-workers with emotional vulnerabilities and albums full of vacation pics of themselves in swimsuits. There were the ones who got away. The ones who almost were. The ones who maybe could've been if things had all worked out differently.

The past is always present on social media—inescapably so. It helped take Sarah and Doug's marriage down, and they knew it had the power to take theirs down, too.

RULE NUMBER TWO: NO REPEATS

This just made sense.

As a matter of fact, it was the whole point.

What they were agreeing to were dalliances: little breaks from their daily reality. Anything more than once with the same person would be an affair, and affairs were the hideous clichés of middle age. Affairs were ugly and required lies and guilt, and they ruined lives.

"I don't think I could do it anyway," he said. "The carrying-on part. The sneaking around. I'm so terrible at lying."

"You really are," she agreed.

Mitch looked at the joint. He considered lighting it again but didn't. One hit was clearly plenty. Any more and he'd wake up in the middle of the night with his head stuck in a bag of Doritos.

"It'll be like getting a massage on vacation," she said.

"What do you mean?"

"You go once, right?" she said. "You enjoy it. It feels good. It relaxes you. And then you never see the massage therapist again."

Mitch sat up in his chair. "Wait," he said. "What kind of massages are you getting?"

RULE NUMBER THREE:
NOBODY THAT YOU *KNOW* KNOW

This started as "strangers only." It was Mitch's idea, and it was, according to him, the same principle as the social media rule, just re-articulated for real life instead of digital life.

His point was that they had their celebrity hookup lists, of course, like everyone else in the world, chock-full of Uptons and Clooneys. "But there's another list, too, right?" he said. "A list that's more, you know, obtainable."

"What do you mean?" she asked.

"Real people. People we actually know."

"Ah," she said. She understood what he was getting at. Secret crushes. Daily, recurring desires, harmlessly categorized as off-limits under normal circumstances.

"Right?" he said. "We all know people we'd have sex with, all things equal, if there were no consequences."

"True," she said.

"Those seem like land mines to me," he said. "Probably even worse than our Facebook friends."

"But what constitutes a stranger, exactly?" she asked.

Jessica was thinking, of course, of the bartender, and while she was thinking of the bartender, Mitch was briefly trying to imagine his parents having this exact conversation. It was so utterly far-fetched that he couldn't even conjure the imagery necessary to set the scene. It was like picturing them as marines or MMA fighters.

"Good question," he said. "Okay, well, who's someone from your list?"

"My *real*-people list?" she said.

"Yeah. Noncelebs. Everyday people."

Jessica paused to think, which made sense to Mitch. It was a dangerous thing to be talking about, but exciting, too. "Okay. Remember the contractor who fixed the roof last fall?"

Mitch squinted out into the darkness. "The guy with the . . . the *jean jacket*? Really?"

She looked the way she looked when she was pretending not to be embarrassed.

"Don't be a jerk. We're being honest with each other."

"Okay, yeah," he said. "Jean jacket aside, I can see it. He was a good-looking guy."

"I know him," she said. "His name and what he does for a living. But I don't *know* know him. He's not a part of my life in any way. He's not a land mine."

"Yeah," said Mitch. "That makes sense, actually. Okay, he's eligible. In theory. But maybe not him specifically, okay?"

"Okay," she said. "Agreed."

And so, on the fly, "strangers only" was rewritten to the far more cumbersome "nobody that you *know* know."

"What about you?" said Jessica. "Who's someone from your list?"

He squeezed the top of her hand. She was right. This was twisted.

Strange, for sure. But it really *was* fun. "That's easy," he said. "The spin instructor at the gym."

"Which one?" she said.

"What do you mean, which one? Are you kidding? The redhead. Tara. She's a goddess."

"Oh, right," she said. "Yeah, Tara's pretty hot."

RULE NUMBER FOUR: THREE QUESTIONS ONLY

They could thank the film industry for this one.

In every movie ever made in which a man and a woman discuss one of them having had sex with someone else, there's *that* scene. The woman is usually sitting tensely, and the guy is pacing, and there's the unending flurry of questions, each somehow more difficult to answer than the last. They wanted to avoid that.

Three questions each. That was that.

RULE NUMBER FIVE: THIS WAS THEIR SECRET

This was between them, and they would tell no one—not even the Core Four. Especially not the Core Four.

The Core Four had once known everything about Jessica and Mitch's life. The good and the bad. The pretty and the ugly. But times had changed, and the group was all but disbanded now. It was powerless and mostly symbolic, like some Eastern Bloc country during the Cold War.

Jessica and Mitch were on their own. And this was their secret.

RULE NUMBER SIX: NO NAMING NAMES

Five Rules would've been better; cleaner, somehow. But out on the deck, as they both became drowsy, eyes reddening, a sixth and final rule came up, and it seemed, somehow, to be the most important of them all.

Since they'd only be sleeping with people they didn't *know* know, and since they'd be confined to one-off events, they would share only the most general details with each other. No names. No identifiable features. No identities.

"Again," said Jessica. "Massage therapists."

"Right," said Mitch.

"For all intents and purposes," she said, "their names mean nothing."

14

Two days later, Jessica sat in her office across from an eighteen-year-old girl named Scarlett Powers.

Scarlett wasn't the star of a comic book–turned–action movie, as her name might have suggested. Instead, she was a private school–educated drug abuser, possibly a low-level sex addict, a petty criminal, and far and away Jessica's most infuriating patient.

Jessica and Scarlett were in the midst of one of their spontaneous timeouts, in which Scarlett picks at her nail polish and says nothing for an extended stretch of time. The girl had drawn a tattoo on her ankle with a Magic Marker—something tribal and intricate—because, along with being infuriating, Scarlett was a talented young artist.

The temp tat caused Jessica's eyes to wander, for maybe the five hundredth time in the last three days, to her own left wrist.

Despite having scrubbed the delicate skin nearly raw, she could still see the faint lines of the bartender's phone number. He'd written it there after she finished her third glass of free shiraz the other night at Bar Vasquez.

"I'm Ryan, by the way," he told her.

You don't think about how many nerve endings there are on the inside of your wrist until someone who looks like him writes his number there. The sharp little point against her skin felt so intense that she had to bite her lower lip to keep from making an embarrassing sound.

"So, I met a guy," said Scarlett Powers.

Jessica reentered the present seamlessly. Her ability to appear engaged at all times was her greatest skill as a therapist. "Oh? Well, that's interesting. Let's talk about it."

Scarlett crossed her legs. "Okay."

"Now, when you say *met*," said Jessica, "do you mean—"

"Fucked?"

Jessica raised her eyebrows. Swearing, for some of her patients, was just part of the deal. Discouraging it would be like standing on I-95 and politely asking passing cars to maybe please slow down.

"We didn't, actually," said Scarlett.

"Oh?"

"We almost did. Because, you know, they always *want* to, right?"

"Let's not—"

"Generalize," said Scarlett. "Yeah, I know. But sometimes it's easier. Like, generalities save time. That's what they're for. Anyway. Wanna know why we didn't?"

"I don't know, do I?" said Jessica.

"Yes, you do, because it's probably gonna blow your mind."

"Okay. Try me."

Scarlett wiggled in her chair, straightening herself. "Get this. I decided to take *your* advice."

"Wow," said Jessica. She appeared flabbergasted for effect. "I should probably write this down so I know I'm not drunk or hallucinating. Scarlett Powers . . . took . . . my . . . advice . . . for once . . . in her . . . young life."

"Very funny."

"Well, among my friends, I am referred to as the funny one," said Jessica. "Okay. So who is he? A guy from school?"

Scarlett made a face, like, *Seriously?*

"Okay. Older, then? How much older? Where are we on the scale of alarming behavior here, Scarlett? Inappropriately older or *wildly* inappropriate?"

Scarlett folded her arms. She'd come directly from school, and her uniform skirt was pop-star short. "Jeez. You have such little faith in me."

"Do I?"

"He's twenty-five, if you *have* to know. Which is totally legit. I'm eighteen now, remember? That's the one advantage of being held back a year. My jailbait days are over. Twenty-five is, like, motherfucking wholesome."

Jessica made a face, and Scarlett cocked her head with the confidence of a third-world dictator. "See, I can be funny, too," she said.

"We'll call it inappropriate-*ish*," Jessica said. "Which is an improvement, I must say."

"He's got a job, too."

"A bonus."

"*And* he's nice. At least he seems nice, so far."

"A gainfully employed, nice person. This is good news. I'm happy."

"I met him at Jiffy Lube."

Annnnd . . . here we go, she thought.

Jessica pictured a future version of her daughter, Emily, as she almost always did during her sessions with Scarlett.

"Yeah, so, my dad had me take his Benz in for an oil change." Scarlett stopped and laughed. "I don't mean to sound all sexual. Lube. Oil change. Like a euphemism. Like I'm talking about—"

"I know what a euphemism is, Scarlett."

"Right. Anyway, we were making out. Really good kisser, by the way. This thing with his tongue—like, twisty, but not creepy twisty. God, when they're good kissers, it's tough not to be super agreeable, you know. But I was strong."

"Okay."

"So, his hands started to . . . *explore* . . . as guys' hands are wont to do. But then, guess what happened?"

Jessica nodded, easing her along. For a therapist, there's a fine line between encouraging communication and rewarding colorful storytelling.

"*You* popped into my head," said Scarlett. "That's what."

"Me?"

"Yep. *You*, my voice of boring reason. So, I grabbed his wrists, and I said, 'You know, Darnell—' That's his name, by the way. Darnell."

"Got it."

"'You know, Darnell, before this goes any further, let's establish that my sexuality is only *part* of who I am. And I think we should save that part of me for another time.'"

Jessica bit the tip of her pen. "You paraphrased a little, but not bad."

"See? And you say I don't listen."

"So, how'd he react?"

"Well, duh," said Scarlett. "He bolted. Audi 5000. Mahatma Gandhi. Gonzo."

"Oh. Well, that's a shame."

"No shit it's a shame. You shoulda seen him. Like one of those shirtless models at Abercrombie. But then you were right there in my head again, per usual. 'Scarlett, if a guy's gonna reject your ass just because you won't immediately get it on with him in a Jiffy Lube parking lot, then maybe he's not as dope as you think he is.'"

"Again with the paraphrasing," said Jessica. "It's good advice, though."

"Fuck that. Good advice? Whatever. I was pissed at you."

"Why were you mad?"

"I said *pissed*." She hit the word like one of the sharp keys at the end of a piano and retreated back to her nails.

"Come on, Scarlett. No shutting down. The clock's ticking. I don't want to lose this. Keep going."

"You try to make everything so PG-13 all the time," she said. "It's annoying. Like, censorship. *Pissed* means pissed. It's different than mad."

"Okay. Why were you *pissed*? And why were you pissed at *me*?"

A chunk of Scarlett's dark nail polish dislodged and fluttered to the floor. She was silent.

"Can I take a guess?" asked Jessica.

"Will it matter if I say no?"

"Not really."

"Fine, then," said Scarlett. "Go to town."

"You're *pissed* because your instinct is to have sex with every guy who happens to wander by, and going against your instincts is hard, and therefore frustrating. You're not angry with me. You're frustrated. Anger and frustration are very similar feelings—nearly one in the same. This sounds good, Scarlett. *This* . . ." She used her pen to point at Scarlett and then back at herself. "This feels like progress."

Scarlett slumped in her chair. "*This* . . . feels like bullshit."

"Do you have a better theory, then?" Jessica asked. "I'm certainly listening."

"Yeah, I do. My theory is that all of this is bullshit."

"What's bullshit?"

"All of it. The entire premise of this conversation, for starters. Bull. Shit."

"Okay, keep talking. Let's try to be more specific."

"Why should I feel bad because I wanted to have sex with Darnell? Darnell is fucking hot."

"It's not that you should feel bad per se," said Jessica. "That's not the point of this. You need to star—"

"That's more bullshit right there," said Scarlett.

"Is it?"

"Yeah," said Scarlett. "All right, go with me here, okay? For the sake of argument, let's say Darnell is in therapy right now, too. Let's say he's in some pleasant off-white little room like this one, right this very second, and he's talking to someone like you about *me*. You think *his* therapist is trying to make *him* feel bad or unhealthy or crazy or whatever because he wanted to fuck me? I seriously, *seriously* doubt it. Total double standard."

The smart ones are always the biggest pains in the ass, Jessica found.

Scarlett kept going. "I mean, like, I gotta come here, right? My parents and you and, like, *society* think my behavior is . . . what? Wrong? But why?"

"In our collective defense, Scarlett, you've been arrested for shoplifting four times."

"Oh, whatever," said Scarlett. "That's not why I'm here, and you know it. Jacking slutty crop tops from Forever 21? Come on. If my parents hadn't violated my privacy and hacked into my phone, I wouldn't be here in the first place, and you know it."

She was right, of course, although the word *hacked* was a little strong. Scarlett's mom found her phone in the laundry room the previous year and just about face-planted onto the linoleum when she saw her daughter's pictures and videos. Three days later, Scarlett and her parents were in Jessica's office.

"Oh yeah, and breaking news," said Scarlett. "Having sex is dope. It's awesome. I mean, come on, Dr. Butler. Don't you still like doing it with *Mr.* Butler?"

"Scarlett," Jessica said.

"I mean, he's my teacher and all, but he's a decent-looking dude, like, if you're into that high-functioning nerd thi—"

"Scarlett," she said again: a second warning. "Do we need to have yet another discussion about our boundaries?"

The girl rolled her eyes. "I'm just saying, you've got a banging bod for a chick your age. A pretty killer rack, too. And Mr. Butler's not so bad either."

"That's lovely of you to say, but you're not here to talk about my bod—or my husband."

"How *Small*timore is that, by the way?" said Scarlett. "You, my therapist, are married to my English teacher. This town is, like, ridiculous with that shit."

She was right about this, too. For all its neighborhoods and spiraling suburbs and million-some people, Baltimore feels like a college campus where everyone knows everyone. "Let's get back to you, if we can," said Jessica.

"Right." She pointed at herself with her thumbs. "This girl."

Just then, Jessica's iPhone lit up on the armrest of her chair. During sessions, she used the stopwatch app as a timer. She normally put it in airplane mode to avoid calls and texts while she was working, but she'd forgotten that day, and she glanced down just long enough to see a group text message from Amber to the rest of the Wives.

"All I'm getting at is," said Scarlett, "as girls . . . no, as *women*, like, *woman*kind here, can't we just have sex because we wanna have sex? That's what guys do. Proudly. All the fucking time. Just grab 'em by the pussy, right? Can't it be our turn? Hashtag Me Too. Fuckin'-A, right? Did I mention that Darnell's black *and* he's got blue eyes? I mean, that's a pretty sexy combo. Tell me I'm wrong."

"Again, Darnell sounds like quite a catch," said Jessica. "I find this interesting, though, Scarlett. Is that how you're interpreting the Me Too movement? As a license to now do whatever you want?"

"Why not? Nobody's told those fuckers no for, like, thousands of years. They want something, they take it. But if we want something, we're supposed to tell *our*selves no? Like, deprive ourselves. Why? Who says that's gotta be *our* job?"

Jessica thought of Ryan's pen. The sensation against her skin. How casually brazen it was to let him mark her like that in the first place. How exhilarating it felt. "Well," she said, "I wouldn't write it on a protest sign and march on D.C., but you're raising an interesting point."

This caught the girl briefly off guard. "Really?" she said.

"Yes. But when you're here, in this *off-white* little room, we're talking about *Scarlett*kind, not womankind. Deal?"

Scarlett smiled and looked out the office window at the speck of a disappearing Southwest jet on its way out of Baltimore. "Scarlettkind," she said. "I like that."

Jessica's phone screen lit up again, and this time, she looked at it long enough to read Amber's text.

Do you guys have an opinion on chin lifts? Asking for a friend. (Me!)

"Besides," she said. "Womankind has enough to deal with."

15

Later that day, as Mitch stood at the front of his classroom, he thought about beating up his students.

He thought about this a lot, actually, which probably wasn't good. He'd never beaten up anyone, of course, so the violence was just conceptual—borrowed from movies, mostly.

For example, he'd punch everyone in the front row right in the face. Simple, efficient jabs, like Rocky Balboa's, complete with sound effects. The students' heads would snap back, and they'd sprawl to the floor in an orderly fashion, instantly unconscious. He'd go Chuck Norris on row two, disposing of them with a series of vicious round-house kicks. He'd be more tactical with row three, delivering Bruce Lee–style beatings, with death chops and leg sweeps. And, finally, to finish things off, he'd throw desks at the back row. They were surprisingly light for such sturdy-looking pieces of furniture. Perfect for flinging.

The kids never fought back in these fantasies, which made it easier. Instead, they simply disappeared out of the screen like the bad guys in old-school Nintendo games.

With fifteen minutes left in class, the energy had drained from the room, and most of the kids were longingly looking either out the window or at the table at the front of the room, where they were required to leave their cellphones. Mitch referred to it as the "plywood table of distraction," the official keeper of their texts and sexts and kiks and tweets and snaps and whatever else.

Mitch clapped his hands hard, and the students jolted upright.

"Okay," he said. "Enough plot summary. We'll leave that for Goodreads. Here's the important question. The point of all this. What makes this play so special?"

The room, all wood filled and musty, became a sea of blank faces. It was sunny outside, which never helped. Some sparrows sat on the windowsill, flirting with their own reflections.

"Come on, you guys. Let's talk it out. Since this play was scrawled out by hand and bound into book form, millions of other stories have been written. Novels. Nonfiction. Nonfiction novels. Plays. Memoirs. Fanfic. Chick lit. Lad lit. Celebrity tell-alls. Vampire romances. Werewolf romances. Why are we still discussing this play now, in Baltimore, Maryland, in the early twenty-first century?"

"'Cause you assigned it, Mr. B.?"

A smattering of laughter. Kenny Jecelin, a popular, funny lacrosse bro.

"Very true, Kenny. I did. And it wasn't at random. I wrote it on my syllabus and forced you to read it. Why'd I do that?"

"Because you hate us?" said Kenny.

"No, that's not true. I like several of you very much." This got a few laughs, too.

A girl named Britney Christman spoke up in the front row. "I think it'd be a lot easier if it was written in, you know, today's language."

"Fair point, Ms. Christman. You're not wrong. Did you all read it aloud, like I said? It's a play. It's meant to be spoken—performed, actually. Imagine the most fire rap lyrics you can think of, written on a white sheet of paper. Not quite as lit, huh?"

Mitch reveled in the groans that followed this. His students hated–slash–secretly loved when he said things like that.

"I felt like a tool talking to myself," said a kid named Devon O'Leary, and half the class nodded.

"Also fair," said Mitch. He held up his copy of the book. "Listen, I get it. The language is antiquated. Nobody talks like this anymore. They didn't talk like this back then either, by the way. It's a style thing. We'll watch the movie next week. It'll help with some of the nuances."

"The Leo and Claire Danes version?" asked a girl from the middle of the room. It was Scarlett Powers. This gave Mitch pause. Scarlett never spoke in class unless she was called on. Like most of the male teachers at the school, Mitch was a little terrified of Scarlett and her hiked-up skirts and dubious reputation.

"That's the one," said Mitch. "Before he froze to death in *Titanic*, poor Leo offed himself in *Romeo and Juliet*."

"And he got shot in *The Great Gatsby*, too," said Britney.

"Yeah, he did, didn't he? The guy's sacrificed a lot for the adaptation of great literature. He has our respect."

Another collective glance at their marooned phones, and Mitch was pretty sure everyone had forgotten his original question.

"The Leo version is okay and all," said Scarlett. "But the seventies movie version is waaaaay better. Juliet's got huge boobs in that one. I mean, they're seventies boobs, which are different-looking and all, but boobs are boobs, right?"

"Thanks for the insight, Scarlett," said Mitch.

The girl giggled. "If you let me have my phone, I can YouTube it. There's, like, a full-on nude scene."

"That's okay, Ms. Powers. We'll save that for when we're off school Wi-Fi."

Scarlett made a pouty face and put her pen down, and Mitch imagined having sex with her.

Every boy in the class was thinking about this, too—he could tell. But for Mitch it was jarring, and he blinked it away immediately. He never thought of his students like that; he prided himself on it. Since the conversations, though—since their arrangement—sex had gone from something that lingered somewhere in the middle of his mind to something that blinked and buzzed and shook just above his forehead.

Stop it, he snapped at himself.

And then he realized that his students were looking at him. All of them. Even the space cadets in the back row.

"Wait," he said. "What were we talking about?"

The kids laughed, then Devon said, "Why this book is important. I think."

"Yes. Bingo, Mr. O'Leary. Got it. So? Who has an answer? Who has something interesting to say?"

There were seven minutes left. There was still time.

"Forget the difficult language. Forget the funny costumes everyone is probably wearing in your heads. Just think about the story. The plot. The conflict. Millions and millions of books have been written since this one, and we're still assigning it. Why?"

"My mom says it's about the death of innocence," said Britney.

A few nodded.

"Okay," he said. "That's not bad. Pure love is easily corrupted. Young passion burns hottest. You can get some mileage out of that, for sure. But it's more than that. Writers have been killing off innocence forever. Let's dig deeper."

Britney looked annoyed. Mitch figured she'd been saving that one—a mic drop at the bell to ramp up her participation grade. To be fair, though, Mitch wasn't entirely sure what he was hoping to hear. He just wanted to hear something. Something new. Something not cribbed from a ten-second Google search in the hallway before class.

He looked at Scarlett, who was looking at him, then he forced himself to look away. And then his eyes fell on Luke.

Oh, Luke. His ace in the hole, seated at shy attention in the second row, closest to the window, like always. Luke blushed, anticipating what was about to happen. Mitch made it a point to not *always* put his best student on the spot, but sometimes you need a good old-fashioned book nerd to save the day. "What do you think, Luke?" he said.

Luke frowned, accepting his fate.

"Tell us what makes this thing so brilliant."

Luke blushed more deeply now with so many eyes on him. Mitch glanced at the clock.

"I—" Luke started.

Mitch nodded, encouraging him.

"I actually think it kinda sucked, Mr. B."

It was easily the last thing Mitch could've imagined Luke saying at that moment. "Excuse me?"

Luke shrugged. "I do."

"Heck yeah!" said Kenny. "See, even the all-star thinks this book bites it."

"Zip it, Jecelin."

For the first time in as long as Mitch could remember, the entire class was intellectually present. Whatever happened from here, that was a good thing.

"Okay, Luke. You've got our attention. But you know the rules. You can't say something that outlandish and not back it up. You've got about ninety seconds. Explain yourself. What about this—one of the most famous, most read, most discussed works of literature in history—sucks?"

"Well, I don't like how it makes us feel," he said. "As readers."

"What do you mean?"

"The entire time you're reading it, you know what's gonna happen, right? We all know the ending."

"Well, yeah," said Britney. "Duh."

Luke leaned forward, pushing ahead. "We know it's all gonna go wrong. It's gonna be a tragedy. It's . . . it's inevitable. But you care about them the whole time. And you want it to work out for them because they love each other, even though you know it won't. And then you have to watch them die anyway."

Mitch smiled.

The bell rang, and everyone scattered.

16

D o you remember me?

Jessica typed this and stared at it on her iPhone screen. She deleted it, and then she typed it again, and then she deleted it again, because she didn't like how it sounded. Too needy, like fishing for a compliment, like she was just begging him to say something like "How could I not?"

She was at the Under Armour store, downtown, a few blocks from her office. She needed a new sports bra. A water bottle, too, and maybe some new Orioles T-shirts for the kids and Mitch. She couldn't remember the last time she got them something fun "just because."

And then she saw the underwear mannequin.

Headless. Armless. Legless. It was a torso made of gray plaster, perfectly muscled, in nothing but a pair of sleek, skintight boxer briefs. To say it made her think of Ryan wasn't entirely accurate, because she'd been thinking about him nonstop anyway. It did, however, for the first time, make her consider what he might look like in *his* underwear. He was young, and he was gorgeous, so of course this was the kind of underwear he'd wear, right?

The headline above the display read, definitively, YOU'LL NEVER WEAR REGULAR UNDERWEAR AGAIN. She read this a few times in her head, searching for some kind of meaning that wasn't ominous.

YOU'LL NEVER BE WITH YOUR REGULAR HUSBAND AGAIN.

YOU'LL NEVER BE SATISFIED BY YOUR REGULAR LIFE AGAIN.

She imagined them standing face-to-face, she and Ryan. She'd tug at the front button of his jeans, revealing the bold Under Armour waistband like a promise.

Do you remember me?

She held her breath and hit Send.

He could say no. Or he could say nothing. If either of those things happened, she'd just put her phone back in her purse, and that'd be that. She'd shop. She'd buy some things for her family. She'd go back to her REGULAR life. She'd be fine.

When her phone buzzed twenty seconds later, though, Jessica realized she was still holding her breath. She let it out slowly and didn't look at her phone right away. Instead, she held it in her hand and turned to look at her own reflection in a mirror near some hoodies. Music pumped through the store, upbeat and motivational.

Shiraz?

She looked at her reflection again and found that she was smiling.

I guess you don't write your phone number on just anyone's wrist.

She wondered if she should've included a smiley face or something to temper what she'd just written. Her heart raced, pumping blood furiously. She held three Orioles T-shirts in the crook of her arm.

The typing bubble appeared, with its pulsating ellipses, followed by a little buzz in her hand.

Have I caused another moral dilemma?

When she asked him where he was, she expected him to text back that he was at work. That was how she'd put it all together in her head. He'd be at Bar Vasquez, and the place would be empty because it was four in the afternoon. It was only a few blocks from the Under Armour store. She'd walk over and have a drink. She'd have a glass of wine, maybe two, and she'd initiate some small step forward. She'd touch his forearm. She'd hold his gaze. If she was feeling particularly bold, she'd say something like, "Maybe we should meet somewhere sometime."

And that would be enough, thank you very much. Her marriage was evolving, and evolution moved slowly.

But when her phone buzzed again, she read, I'm at home, and she had no idea how to respond. The dynamics had shifted, her plan ruined. No matter, though. Before she could devise a new one, he texted her again.

Maybe you should be here too?

And now she was in a row house in Locust Point, every nerve ending in her body on high alert and humming with pure electricity.

"You're lucky," said Ryan. "I don't usually have shiraz. Not the most robust wine cellar in town, I guess." He nodded to the brushed-metal wine rack in the corner of the tiny kitchen next to the fridge.

The glass in her hand was foggy with dish-detergent residue, but she was relieved to have something to do with her hands. She took another sip and felt warmth. "It's fine," she said. "It's good."

He was drinking beer from a can. He was barefoot, in jeans and a Bruce Springsteen T-shirt with the *Born in the U.S.A.* album cover on the chest.

"Were you even alive when that album came out?" she asked.

He looked down at himself. "Doubt it. The shirt's vintage. My dad's a huge Springsteen guy. Loves him."

She took another sip of wine and tried to remember the year the album was released.

"I'm really glad you texted me," he said. "I mean, I was a little *surprised* you texted me. But definitely glad."

"Why were you surprised?" she said. To her, of course, this all seemed inevitable.

He didn't respond, though. Instead, he looked at her hand. And when she followed his eyes, she arrived at the diamond on her finger, the one she'd worn virtually every moment of her life for years and years. She moved her hand to her hip, out of view. "I guess I felt like being spontaneous today," she said. The *s* got snagged on her bottom teeth, and she flushed. Her old lisp. "Thspontaneous."

"Damn," he said.

"What?"

"That's sexy."

"Three years of speech therapy in elementary school," she said. "It comes back sometimes when I'm—" She didn't finish this, because she wasn't sure exactly how. *Nervous* didn't quite cover it. It was an entirely new sensation. She remembered being a little girl, standing on a diving board at their local pool with her toes peeking over the edge. Her dad bobbing in the deep end, waiting to catch her. *Come on, babes. Treading water's not as easy as it looks.*

This moment felt like that moment.

The tiny kitchen connected to a main sitting room with a flat-screen mounted to the wall, an overstuffed leather couch, and a few Orioles and Ravens bobbleheads. The floor was cluttered with pieces of furniture and odd bits of wood. "So, what's all this? This stuff. Is it broken?"

He laughed. "The opposite, actually. That thing there, that's gonna be an end table. That one over there will eventually be a kick-ass bookshelf. The dark one—that chewed-up-looking thing—that'll be the nicest hope chest you've ever seen. My roommate and I, it's kind of this side hustle we've got going. Our real jobs—I'm a waiter-slash-bartender, as you know, and he works on cars. But we build furniture, too. Reclaimed wood, mostly. It's a thing people are into. Taking all these old things and making them new."

"Oh," she said. "That's neat."

Neat? Who says neat?

He laughed. "The bartender thing pays way better. More tips."

She looked around the first floor. A wooden staircase led up to darkness. "You said you have a roommate?"

"Yeah."

"Is he here?"

"Why?" He smiled, teasing her, the bastard.

"I'm just wondering."

"Nah. He's in and out. Keeps kinda weird hours."

She thought of bending her knobby little-girl knees. She thought of the diving board dipping beneath her feet, and how it felt being launched through the air. She thought of the glorious sensation of falling. "So, where do you sleep?" she asked.

———

Taking his clothes off was the best part. Literally stripping him. It was the thing she'd think about most when she thought of all this. As far as memories went, it'd be more powerful than guilt or regret.

His bedroom was small and narrow but tidy and cool, sparsely decorated.

He kissed her, standing just inside his bedroom door, which he had closed behind him. She stood on her toes to meet his mouth. His hands held her face, then moved to her hair. He ran his fingers through it, grabbing and pulling just enough to angle her head the way he wanted it, and the shock of that simple act of dominance made her moan into his mouth.

She found the hem of the Springsteen T-shirt and pulled up, grazing her knuckles along his stomach. He held his arms up so she could take it off of him, and she took in what she saw—the effortless, youthful perfection of his upper body—and she laughed at the sheer absurdity of how fucking beautiful he was.

"What?" he said.

"Good Lord. How old are you, again?"

He found the top button of her blouse and started working his way downward. "You seem kinda fixated on that. My age." He kissed her forehead and then her temple and then her earlobe, and it felt so good she might have toppled over if he wasn't holding her by her shirt, opening it slowly. "I mean," he said, "at this point, does it really matter?"

Her shirt fell to the floor next to his. He was right; it didn't matter at all.

He pulled the zipper down the side of her skirt, and that fell to the floor, too. The vulnerability of standing there in her underwear wasn't as difficult as she imagined it'd be. This was mostly because of the look on his face. He stared at her—no more fluttering eyes and stolen glances—and she could see how badly he wanted her.

He gently touched the side of her face and her throat, his palms rough against her skin, and ran his hand down her chest and slid it under the top of her bra. He squeezed her—again, gently—and as the tip of his thumb grazed her nipple she made a sound she'd never heard herself make before, like a small, breathless sob.

She meant to undo his belt slowly, to make a sexy thing of it, but she couldn't keep herself together long enough to do anything other than tear into it. Same went for his button and zipper, and there they were: his underwear. She wasn't sure if they were Under Armour, but they fit him like a second skin, like something so much better than whatever regular underwear was. The shape of his penis against the sleek gray fabric was as vivid as a 3-D printing. She touched the tip of it, and his stomach muscles twitched.

It'd been so long since removing clothing had been part of sex.

For years, she and Mitch had treated it like an appointment they were rushing to. This observation wasn't an indictment against him or against them. It's just how you have sex when you're tired, and when you know that at any second you might hear a cry or a shout or, worse, approaching footsteps.

She liked this better.

With her right hand, she grabbed the stretchy elastic waistband and pulled down. And with her left hand, she took hold of him. His body shuddered when she squeezed, and again when she moved her hand up and down.

"Fuck," he whispered.

They kissed again. She closed her eyes and kept hold of him, tugging lightly, until he was fully hard in her hand.

When she felt his hand on hers, she opened her eyes. He was looking again at her engagement and wedding rings—which were, at present, against his cock. His eyes were question marks.

She released her grip and kissed his chin. Then she took her rings off and placed them on his nightstand.

17

It was trash night in their neighborhood, which was a thing for Mitch and the kids. Every week, Emily and Jude helped him gather all the bags from the house, consolidate them into the big can in the garage, and then roll it down their long driveway to the curb.

This particular evening was different in that, along with the regular garbage, the week's trash included the broken pieces of Jessica and Mitch's bed.

The box spring was fine, and the headboard, too. They could eventually be given away. Mitch leaned them against the wall in the unfinished part of the basement where things like that went, their own Island of Misfit Household Objects.

It was the wooden frame that was the issue.

The two long boards that connected to the headboard had splintered into four jagged spears that he had no idea what to do with. They looked like chunks of a mighty tree, felled by lightning in the woods. Mitch carried them while Emily and Jude took turns rolling the garbage can. Needless to say, they had a few questions.

"So, wait, it just, like, *broke?*" asked Jude. "The whole bed?"

"Yep. It was really something."

"Did you save your receipt?" asked Jude. "Can you bring it back to the store and get a new one for free?"

"Well, it's about fifteen years old, bud. Receipts don't really cover you that long."

"Does that happen with beds? Do they just break like that?"

"Sometimes. Kinda the way it goes. Things get old and worn out. Stuff breaks."

Emily seemed more shaken by the damage than Jude. "Did you guys get hurt?"

"Nope. We're fine. Mommy and Daddy are tough."

"Were you jumping on it?" she asked.

He smiled, and loved her wildly for being so young and innocent. "No jumping on the bed, hon, remember? That's how people get hurt."

Emily looked at the ground.

"So, you were just sleeping?" asked Jude. "That's it?"

"Mm-hmm," said Mitch. "Just one of those things."

"Could my bed break like that, too?" asked Emily. "While *I'm* sleeping?"

"No way. We made sure yours was extra strong when we bought it."

Some birds escaped up into the trees and stared at them from above as they walked. The neighborhood was one of the most heavily forested in the Baltimore suburbs, which Mitch supposed was one of the reasons the kids found *E.T.* so scary. Some of the most terrifying moments in that movie take place in the woods, which was pretty much the view from their windows. There were so many places for an alien to lurk.

"Whoa, Dad. Look. Check that out."

There was a Jeep Wrangler in the driveway next door, at James and Ellen's place. It was brand-new and beautiful, and upon further inspection, Mitch saw that Luke was sitting in the driver's seat. When Luke saw them see him, he looked embarrassed.

The kids ran next door while Mitch dealt with the garbage. That was how cool the Jeep was: cool enough to make the kids stop what they were doing and run. Mitch parked the garbage can near the mailbox and laid the pieces of the frame in the grass next to it before joining everyone in Luke's driveway.

"Sweet Jeep, man," he said. "Is it yours?"

Luke hopped out onto the driveway and shut the door. "It's a bribe," he said. "From my dad."

"Well, I recommend you take it." Mitch touched the fender, and then one of the big, shiny tires. The whole vehicle glowed—hunter green and gleaming.

"I thought I was getting a used Toyota Camry."

"This is better," said Mitch.

"Definitely," said Jude. The boy was as smitten as Mitch. He ran his finger over the stenciled lettering along the side of the hood: RUBICON. "You could drive over things with this, I bet," he said. "Like mountains and stuff."

Mitch squeezed Jude's shoulder.

"He left a note," said Luke. "It was here when I got home from school. Like, *surprise*."

There was a piece of paper the size of a postcard pinned under the windshield wiper. Jeep stationery, which was a nice touch.

Hope you like the color. —Dad

"I wanted one of these things so bad when I was your age," said Mitch.

"Really?"

"I used to have dreams about them. That's how obsessed I was. But my parents were convinced that if I got one, I'd roll it immediately and kill myself."

"Why?" asked Emily. "Do they tip over?"

"The old ones did. Not this one, though. It's built way sturdier." Mitch demonstrated this by grabbing the Jeep's roll bar and giving it a good shake.

"It's not exactly my style, though," Luke said. "Right? I mean, look at it. It's like the vehicular opposite of me."

Mitch took in the image of skinny Luke, standing there in baggy shorts and a Han Solo T-shirt next to the jacked-up 4×4. He had a point. The car had "prom king/star quarterback" written all over it. Agreeing with him, though, seemed rude. "Nah. This is *totally* you. In fact, why're you here talking to us? You should be out cruising down Charles Street, waving at college girls."

Luke folded his arms. "That sounds nice and all, but here's the thing. I don't know how to drive it."

"What do you mean? It's just a car."

"It's a stick."

Mitch looked in through the driver's-side window and saw the gearshift. "Oh. Well, that's no biggie. You can learn, right? It's not that complicated."

Luke kicked a tire with the toe of his sneaker while Emily and Jude made faces at themselves in the big side mirror. "He bought me a dope Jeep that I didn't ask for and can't even drive. It's like a symbol for our entire relationship."

While Mitch certainly appreciated the kid's flare for literary analysis, he couldn't help acknowledging to himself that if ever there was a first-world problem, this was it. "Maybe this is his way of trying," said Mitch. "Not for nothing, those custom wheels alone must've cost him thousands extra."

Luke seemed to give this some thought. "Well, I still think he's a jerk," he said. And then he pointed over at Mitch's yard, to the garbage stacked beside the mailbox. "What are those stick things, by the way? They look like weapons."

"Just some old boards," Mitch said. "Stuff from the house."

"I don't think the garbagemen are gonna take them," said Luke. "They usually refuse big things like furniture and stuff, right?"

Mitch hadn't thought of this possibility, and now he felt suddenly helpless. "Well," he said, "I guess we'll see what happens."

And then Emily said, "It's their bed. Mommy and Daddy's. They broke it."

"It happened while they were sleeping," said Jude.

"Yeah," said Emily. "They weren't even jumping on it or anything."

Mitch and Luke looked at each other, and Mitch was pretty sure that Luke was trying not to smile. "She's right," said Mitch. "The Butlers have a strict policy against jumping on beds."

18

"Dad. Hey. Dad. Daddy. Dad. Dad. Dad! Are you awake?"

Mitch woke to a dark figure looming over him—a giant, or a murderer, possibly. But no, it was neither of those things. It was Jude. He looked massive, because their mattress was on the floor.

He considered rolling over and simply ignoring his son. There should be a rule in parenting that you get to do that once every fiscal year. If you skip a year, it carries over—like airline miles or paid time off.

But then he remembered two things: (1) He loved Jude, and (2) Jude was scared. When Mitch was Jude's age, he'd swiped a copy of *Pet Sematary* by Stephen King off his parents' bookshelf, and it basically destroyed his childhood. So he blinked himself awake as best he could and smiled. "Hey, buddy," he whispered. "What's up?"

"I'm scared," said Jude.

"E.T. again?"

The whites of Jude's eyes glowed bright and wide. "Yeah."

"The coloring book, though. I thought we were good. We colored him sitting in a basket and making a Huffy fly."

"What's a Huffy?"

The center of Mitch's brain hurt. "A type of bike from the eighties. Every kid had one."

"Well, I'm still scared. The coloring book didn't help. I knew it wouldn't. I told you. Can I sleep with you tonight?"

"No, buddy."

"Why?"

"It's a bad precedent to set," he said, but he was too exhausted to explain what that meant. He imagined a sixteen-year-old Jude standing at the side of his bed, deep-voiced and stubbly. *Scootch over, pops.*

"But Emily gets to. It's not fair."

"We talked about that. She's little. It's a process. We're weaning her off of us."

"Well, you're not doing a very good job of weaning."

"What do you mean?"

"She's right there."

Jude was right. Emily *was* right there, pressed against him, in fact, and sound asleep. "Oh," he said. "Well, she's sneaky."

Jude twisted his fingers. "I don't want to sleep alone, though. He'll get me if I close my eyes. That's how it works."

"That's not how it works, Judey. I promise. He's only in your head."

"Nuh-uh," said Jude.

Mitch tugged the sheets up over himself. No easy feat; Emily had basically vacuum-sealed herself into the center of the bed. "How about you do me a favor and try something?" he said.

"What?"

"I want you to go back to your room and practice being brave."

"I don't want to."

"I know. That's the brave part—doing something you don't want to do. Something you're *scared* to do."

"How do I do it?"

"Easy. You lie in your bed, and you leave your night-light on, and the hallway light, too, like normal. And when you feel yourself getting scared, you take a deep breath, and you decide you're gonna be brave. You make a decision. 'I will be brave.'"

"But—"

"Do it for like ten seconds the first time. Nice and easy. Then ramp it up. Twenty seconds after that. Count it out. The longer you go, the braver you'll get. A little longer each time."

Mitch was winging it, of course, but somehow this sounded like pretty good advice.

"Okay," said Jude. "I'll try."

"Awesome, buddy. Love ya."

On his way out, Jude stopped at the bedroom door. "By the way . . . where's Mom?"

"What?"

"She's not there."

"Yeah she is. She's right—"

But she wasn't. Next to his sleeping daughter was just an empty space. "Oh," he said. "I guess a lot's been going on since I fell asleep."

When Jude was gone, Mitch touched Jessica's spot in the bed, assessing for warmth, but it just felt like sheets, and he found himself in the difficult nighttime limbo of being too tired to get up and go find her but too awake to immediately go back to sleep. So he grabbed his phone off the nightstand.

The plan was to do a quick run through Instagram—maybe hit Twitter for some political commentary—but he saw that he had a new text message. It was from Alan. It was short and ridiculous.

I'm crazy about this chick.

Mitch rolled his eyes and texted back.

Things are going well then?

The typing bubble appeared. Mitch looked at the clock. It was 11:20 P.M. While the married people of the world were sleeping or dealing with rogue children, Alan was on bachelor time.

Very very well.

The typing bubble persisted, and then some emojis appeared. A water splash, a hand, and an eggplant.

Not sure what that means. Is the eggplant supposed to be your dingle? It's very phallic.

Yes & I think it's weird that you call it a dingle.

I have kids. Dingles & woo-woos up in here.

Noted, texted Alan.

The hand & the splash tho? Hand job? Is that what the kids are into now?

Alan replied with a pointing-finger emoji and a peach.

That's both gross & confusing, texted Mitch.

Alan didn't miss a beat, his text-timing on point.

Which perfectly describes the night I lost my virginity.

Mitch snort-laughed and then touched Emily's head, testing how deeply she was sleeping. He tapped Alan's name on the screen and put the phone to his ear. Alan answered after a single ring.

"Dude, you're calling me? Come on, nobody actually talks on the phone anymore."

"Well, let's try going throwback. We'll use our voices, like legitimate adults."

"Why are you whispering?"

"Emily's asleep. She's in our bed. So, what are you up to?"

"I'm eating a Hot Pocket and watching *SportsCenter*."

"You make divorce sound very glamorous."

"Says the guy who's in bed with his kid."

"Touché," said Mitch. "You're not crazy about her, by the way. It's way too soon for that. Don't be an idiot."

"Oh yeah? How do you know?"

"She's the first girl you've dated in fifteen years. You're just excited. You're not thinking with your head. You're thinking with . . . your eggplant emoji."

Alan laughed, and Mitch put his hand on Emily's back. He could feel her heartbeat, a steady little thud, like the faint drumbeat before the guitar intro in all those Smashing Pumpkins songs.

"Well, I'm breaking all the rules, my friend. She's fucking amazing. Earlier, we worked out together. Went for a run. Then we took a shower together. A motherfucking shower, Mitch. At the same time."

"Wow," said Mitch.

"If I'd have died—been stricken dead right there—I would've been okay with it."

Dual showering is on the long list of things that stop the moment you have a child, like going to movies and concerts. Mitch tried to remember the last time he and Jessica had done it. His mind went blank.

"Dude," said Alan. "Do you have any idea what a twenty-six-year-old girl looks like in the shower? It's like real-life porn."

Mitch remembered now. Pre-kids, of course, in the little row house.

The shower was so small they could barely fit. He thought of licking water off of Jessica's neck. The surge of envy that followed was so strong that he had to close his eyes, and then he wondered whom exactly he was jealous of. Was it Alan, or was it the younger version of himself? "I can only imagine," he said.

"It's not just that, though," said Alan. "I mean, she's hot and cute—but she's cool as hell, too. *Really* cool. You wouldn't believe it. She and her friends—these younger girls. They're actually fun, man. They're up for shit. They *enjoy* things. They get beers at noon on Saturdays, just because. They listen to music. They have . . . fucking belly-button rings. It's like life hasn't beaten them down yet. You know?"

Mitch looked over at the empty space next to Emily, the faint impression of Jessica's shape. "Maybe you *are* crazy about her," he said. "It's cute. Annoying, but cute, I guess."

A bit of silence—some cellular hum on the line between them. Serious moments between the Husbands were rare, but he supposed this was one of them. "I'm actually happy," said Alan. "For the first time in . . . shit . . . years. I'm fucking happy, man. I've finally got something to be excited about."

"Well, I'm happy that you're happy," said Mitch. This was mostly true, but he couldn't help thinking of Luke's comment in class. Could he really root for his friend? Could he care about the outcome, even though he knew, rationally, that the entire operation was doomed to fail? "But just, you know, be careful."

"You keep telling me to be careful," said Alan. "To pace myself. I get it. But maybe it's time for me to *not* be careful. Careful kept me married to a woman I didn't love for almost a third of my life."

"I just don't want you to get hurt," said Mitch. "At your age, you could slip in the shower and break your hip, and that'd be terrible."

Mitch and Alan's serious moment was over.

"I'll be fine," said Alan. "Go back to sleep. It's late. You're a mother-fucking adult, for Chrissake."

19

Jessica had never sexted before.

It sounded downright quaint in this particular day and age, like a lady in a bonnet, clutching her horse as a Model T buzzes by. But frankly, the timing had never quite worked out.

By the time texting was even a thing, she and Mitch had been together a while. And by the time the technology got hijacked for widespread deviance, they were married, and as a married person, sexting never struck her as a terribly necessary thing to do.

Mitch tried once.

He was on a rare overnight trip for work—some conference in D.C. at the PEN/Faulkner Foundation. He texted her just before midnight. She was in bed watching TV, wearing a light-green moisturizing mask and eating a popsicle.

Send me a pic of your legs.

She laughed and texted back. How many drinks have you had, Mr. Butler?

Two appletinis. Heavy on the tini. Lemme see em, woman!

She considered it. She looked down at her loose flannel pajama pants and her gray socks. How easy would it be to kick all that off and find a flattering angle? But she hadn't shaved her legs, and she felt about as sexy as a Microsoft Excel spreadsheet. And, worse, she was just neurotic enough to imagine some enormous folder in the cloud storing a low-res photo of her bare legs, forever and ever. So instead she sent him a picture of her pajamas pants. Enjoy, sucker!

Mitch texted back a moment later, defeated. I should've been more specific.

So now, in the living room, texting with Ryan as her husband and kids slept upstairs, she didn't quite know what she was supposed to do.

Your O face is the hottest thing I've ever seen BTW, he wrote.

My what?

Your O face. The face you make when you have an . . . Oooooh!

Thanks? I assume that's a compliment?

A few seconds passed. The timer on the coffee machine in the kitchen ticked.

I'm getting hard just thinking about it.

Her face turned hot, and she thought of the cloud again. Did people really text these things to each other? Weren't they worried? But then she read his text again and thought about holding him in her hand. How he'd reacted to her touch. How totally in control of him she'd been.

He didn't wait for her to reply. When can I see you again?

She heard something upstairs. Footsteps. It sounded like Jude. She slid her phone under her leg and waited, but he didn't come down. She waited a little longer, just in case. Never, she wrote. I told you that.

I've decided not to remember that.

Jessica did tell him, in no uncertain terms, in fact—as clearly as she could. She explained exactly what this was. Or, more specifically, what it wasn't. She was naked at the time, tangled in Ryan's scratchy, low-thread-count guy sheets. She was feeling a little nauseous. This happened sometimes when she had orgasms, and she'd just had two, the second of which had been among the most intense of her life.

Ryan had been up, walking around the room in his underwear. He had a small fridge beneath his desk, like something leftover from a dorm room. He gave her a Diet Coke, because she wanted something with bubbles.

"This isn't an affair," she said.

"What?"

"I can't have an affair with you."

He smiled, and she wondered how many times in the whole of his young life a female had told him anything that even resembled *no*. "Is that not what we just had?" he asked. "An affair?"

"No." She skimmed through the Rules in her head. "An affair is ongoing. That, just now, was a onetime thing."

"Really?"

She nodded.

He pushed his hair back off his forehead. "You're one hundred percent sure?" he said. "Never ever?"

"Never," she said.

"Well, in that case." He eased himself down onto the bed and moved some sheets aside. He bit the arch of her foot and then kissed her ankle. He kissed her calf muscle next, and then the inside of her left thigh. Her hip.

She watched his mouth on her skin. Kisses turned to licks, and she bit down on her lower lip. "What exactly do you think you're doing?" she said.

"I was inside of you so fast before that I didn't get the chance to do this."

Now, aside from the white noise of the humming Butler house, all was quiet. She went into the dark kitchen and got two Golden Oreos from the cupboard. As she chewed, she looked at the wall that separated the kitchen from the breakfast nook. She and Mitch had talked about knocking it down for years, but there it was, still. Her phone buzzed in her hand.

You there?

She ate another cookie.

This wasn't how it was supposed to go. She and Mitch were supposed to have sex with other people. It'd be fun. It'd be liberating. And then those people were supposed to simply vanish. Gone in a puff of smoke, never to be seen or heard from again. Erased from the record. From cellular contact. From existence. It was all perfectly reasonable.

I'm here.

When his reply came, a few seconds later, she stopped chewing and stared at the little words on her screen. It was so odd to have them directed at her. Completely improbable.

I think I like you. A lot.

"Shit," she said.

Another noise came from upstairs. This time it wasn't Jude. It was Mitch, and he was coming down the stairs. Quickly, like a reflex, she turned her phone off and shoved it under some dishes in the drying rack.

When he appeared in the kitchen, it was clear that he'd come to find her. His hair was sticking up at the back of his head. "What're you doing down here?" he asked.

"Couldn't sleep," she said.

He scratched his stomach. "Too much caffeine today?"

"Probably," she said, which was true. She had too much caffeine every day.

"You want me to put you in a sleeper hold?" he said. "I watched a lot of wrestling when I was a kid. I can knock you right out, Iron Sheik–style."

"No thanks," she said.

They both looked up at the ceiling. Another noise. The smallest one yet.

"Emily," Mitch said.

They listened to the sound of her footsteps and waited.

"Was she still in our bed when you came down?" asked Jessica.

"Yeah," he said. "Racked out."

They kept looking at the ceiling. A thud, then a shuffle—like a little girl walking quickly. The noise stopped, and then there was nothing. The air conditioner clicked on and ran gently, like a faraway train.

"Maybe she went back to her room," said Jessica.

"Maybe," he said. "I just dealt with Jude."

"You did? How?"

"Sleeper hold," he said. "He'll be out till tomorrow. It's really effective."

"Nice," she said. "Want an Oreo?"

"I thought you'd never ask."

As she watched him chew, she decided not to tell him about Ryan. Not now, anyway. Her husband was a handsome guy. He always had been, and he still was. But at that moment, standing in their kitchen beside a superfluous wall in plaid boxer shorts from Target and a stretched-out T-shirt, he looked tired and unmistakably middle aged. Vulnerable in a way he hadn't looked when he was younger. Telling him then just didn't seem fair. So instead, she reached for him and smiled. "Come on. Let's go up. We can eat Oreos in bed till we fall asleep, like sad people."

Mitch looked down at her hand on his arm. "You taking a break from being married to me?"

"What?" she said, startled.

He laughed. "I'm kidding. Look, you're not wearing your rings."

It was one of a hundred little inside jokes, refined over fifteen years. When she took her rings off to cook or work in the yard or do the dishes, he always made this same harmless comment. "Taking a break from being married?" But this time her rings weren't on the windowsill in the kitchen, or in their bathroom beside her sink. They were in Ryan's room, miles away. She'd forgotten them there. Fuck. How could she be so stupid?

"Mitch," she said. "I did it."

"You did what?"

"I had sex with someone."

20

Emily was alone in the woods out behind the house.

She was having a dream. And in that dream, she was cold and wet and lost. She didn't have a jacket to wear, just pajamas, and she was shivering.

She hadn't seen E.T. specifically, but she was pretty sure he was out there, hiding in the trees somewhere, looking for her, which was scary, because the E.T. that existed in the movie—the cute, harmless blob of a candy-eating alien—looked nothing like the E.T. that her brain had concocted.

That E.T. had teeth and jagged fingernails and pale, white, dead skin, and his breathing was like a wet hiss. *That* E.T. was getting closer.

It was the snap that woke her up with a start—a sound in her dream like twigs and branches breaking. Her eyes popped open, and she was looking at her mom and dad's ceiling fan. She was in their room, lying on their floor bed. She'd climbed in earlier, carefully, so they wouldn't wake up and make her go back to her room.

She reached for her mom first, and when she wasn't there, she reached for her dad. When she realized they were both gone, she was terrified.

"Mommy?" she whispered. "Daddy?"

The terror she felt only got worse when she saw the figure in the corner of the room.

Moonlight slipped in through the blinds and reflected off her mom's mirror, which was just enough light to see the E.T.-shaped shadow lurking in the corner. It started to move. It had yellow eyes that glowed in the dark, and it had a long, wormlike neck. "Elliott," it said. "Ellll-lioooott."

That was it. Emily took off running.

The plan was to jump into bed with Jude and burrow in next to him. He wasn't an adult, but he was better than nothing, so he'd have to do.

Jude wasn't sleeping, like she figured he'd be. When she got to his room, she found him sitting bolt upright in his bed with his night-light on, counting. "Twelve, thirteen, four—" He stopped when he saw her. "What?" he asked.

"Can I tell you something?"

"Yeah."

"I saw E.T."

"I think I did, too," said Jude. "Where'd you see him?"

"Mommy and Daddy's room. What about you?"

Her brother looked at the doors to his closet. "Never mind," he said. "It's not important."

"Mommy and Daddy are gone."

"What? No they aren't. I saw Dad just now. I think Mom's downstairs or something."

Emily stood biting her nails. "I think I was the one who broke their bed."

"What?" Jude said. "Dad said it broke by itself."

"No," said Emily. "A while ago. I was jumping on it while Daddy was in the shower, and I heard cracks. The wood part."

"Oh."

"I think that's why it broke while they were sleeping. The cracks turned into big cracks."

"You're gonna be in trouble."

"Don't tell them. You won't, will you?"

"Okay," said Jude. "I won't."

Emily looked at her brother's desk. He had his Legos set out, and she wasn't allowed to touch them. "Why were you counting?"

"When?"

"Just now."

"I wasn't."

"Yeah, you were. I heard you. You were on fourteen, but you stopped. Are you counting things?"

"No," he said. "I'm practicing being brave."

The light from the night-light made the Lego shadows tall against the wall, like monsters.

"How do you do that?"

"It's easy. If something's scary, you just count."

Emily didn't get what her brother was talking about, but she was afraid that asking more questions would annoy him, and he'd tell her to go away. "Can I practice being brave with you?" she asked.

Jude looked at his closet again. "Okay. But if you fall asleep, you have to stay still. You kick too much, and this bed is small."

Emily agreed: No kicking. Jude pushed over, and she climbed in beside him. He had two pillows—one Transformers and one Boba Fett. He gave her Boba Fett, and she balled it up and settled in. "You're sure they're not gone?" she asked. "They wouldn't leave us alone, right? By ourselves?"

"No," he said. "Not till we're older. They're just . . . somewhere else. That's all."

Emily looked up at the stickers on Jude's ceiling. They didn't glow much, because he had so many lights on. "A lot of your stars are peeling off," she said. "They're gonna fall soon."

"I know."

"That one there. And that one, too. And that one."

"I know."

Jude didn't have any stuffed animals in his room. Emily wished she'd grabbed one of hers earlier, but there was nothing she could do about it now. "I was thinking," she said.

"About what?"

"You know how sometimes, when I jump on Daddy, I accidentally hit him in his privates and he gets hurt?"

"Yeah."

"Well, if we see E.T. again, maybe we should kick him in his privates. Then he won't be able to hurt us."

"I don't know if E.T. has privates," said Jude. "They didn't show them in the movie, I don't think."

"Everyone has privates. And Daddy said that boy privates hurt really bad when they get hit."

"Maybe," said Jude.

"Is E.T. even a boy?"

"I think so."

The house made a few house noises, and Emily tried to put E.T. out of her mind. "So," she said. "Should we start counting?"

"Okay," he said. "Yeah."

"Should we start at fourteen? That's where you left off."

"No. Let's start over at the beginning."

"Okay."

"Okay."

"Ready?"

"Yeah."

Jude said, "One," and after a brief pause, he said, "two."

Emily was unsure of herself. She didn't want to do it wrong—go too fast or too slow—but she joined him on "three," and they fell into a pretty nice rhythm. One number after another, their voices in sync, brother and sister.

"Four, five, six, seven, eight, nine, ten . . ."

21

All those goddamn movies.

All those heated conversations between famous actors and actresses.

Mitch thought of dozens of them, but somehow he couldn't think of any quite like this. He considered pouring himself a glass of alcohol—scotch, maybe—but what, really, would that do for him? Drinking steadied some guys. Mitch just got dumber and progressively less co-ordinated.

"Are you all right?" asked Jessica.

Was he? He didn't know.

She was sitting on the kitchen island now, her legs tucked up under her, like she was bracing for something. "Mitch?" she said.

"I'm okay," he said. "It's just . . . that was really fast. I didn't think it'd be so quick. Did you, like, walk down the street, point at a guy, and say, 'Excuse me, would you like to have sex?'"

"Do you really want that to be one of your questions?" she asked.

Right. The Rules. Apparently they were sticking to them. He couldn't remember which number that was, but he had three questions, which, he suddenly realized, was hardly any. "No," he said. "It was hypothetical. Hypothetical questions don't count."

"Noted," she said. "I'll remember that."

He walked in a small circle, and then walked it again, from the sink to the island to the cupboard and back again.

"I take it you haven't yet?" she said.

"Haven't what?"

"Done it?"

"No," he said. "I haven't. I would've mentioned it."

"Have you tried?"

"Wait, do you get to ask questions, too? How does this work? And exactly *whom* would I be trying to have sex with in the last seventy-two hours? I only talk to you and a bunch of teenagers."

"We're just talking," said Jessica. "People ask questions when they're talking. For example, are you breathing right now?"

He let out a breath. "Yes."

"Good."

"No, I haven't tried. I don't really remember how to try. How did I get you to sleep with me?"

"You were very charming."

"I was?"

"Accidentally so," she said. "Which was especially charming."

"It's easier for you," he said. "It's easier for women. You can have sex with anyone you want."

Jessica nodded. "I don't usually go for generalizations like that. But I'm beginning to realize that you're probably right. It's easier for us."

"When did you do it?" he asked. It seemed like a good place to start.

"Today," she said.

"Today? Like, *today* today? What time? No, wait, that doesn't count. But seriously . . . *today*?"

She nodded again.

She'd come home that evening with a sports bra and some Orioles T-shirts. "Jesus Christ. Did you fuck somebody at the Under Armour store? Those dressing rooms are huge."

She laughed.

"Is this funny?" he said. "I don't think it's funny. I actually might throw up in the sink."

"No, it's not funny. But that was a funny question. And you're not allowed to be mad at me, Mitchell. I understand that this is a weird situation. And if the situation was reversed—which, at some point, it *will* be—I wouldn't know exactly how to deal with my feelings either. But this is part of it. We agreed to this. Remember?"

Fuck. She was right. He took another breath.

"And no, I didn't have sex with someone at the Under Armour store. I'm not counting that one, by the way. It's a freebie. You're welcome."

"Thanks." He asked his second official question without thinking about it. "You took your rings off? Why did you do that?"

Her face changed. It went softer—sweeter. "Mitch, it was just a matter of logistics. Rings cause confusion. It's hard to explain."

"And you left them there?"

"Is that question three?"

"Two-B," he said.

"Yes. I know that's gross and shitty. I was flustered. It was all very . . . flustering. You'll see what I mean. Don't worry. I'll get them back. It's not a problem."

Neither of them said anything for a while. He did a few more circles. She untucked her legs and let them dangle freely over the kitchen island.

"Where did it happen?"

"In the city."

"That's not what I meant. Where specifically?"

"A house."

"Fuck."

"Would a hotel be better? A car?"

"I honestly don't know."

He had more questions to ask her, of course. An endless supply of them. And, to his credit, they weren't all about the guy's penis. He wanted to know what he was like. What he looked like. Did he do anything weird? How tall was he? Was he older? Was he younger? Was he a motherfucking Yankees fan? Did he have tattoos? What kind of music did he like? Why did that matter? He didn't know, but it did. Did he have a stock portfolio? Was he foreign? Did he have an accent? Did he work in the city? Who did he vote for in the last election? What was his social security number? Was he married, too? Was he divorced? If so, why? Was he nice to her? Why him? It could've been anyone, right? Why this guy? Did he talk dirty to her? Did she talk dirty to him? If so, what did she say, word for word? Could she type out their entire interaction in Microsoft Word so he could read it? Did he wear cologne? Was he a cologne guy? Did she have an orgasm? If so, how did that orgasm compare to every orgasm she'd ever had with him? To every orgasm she'd ever had in her entire life?

But technically he was out of questions, and none of those questions mattered as much as what he really wanted to know.

"How did it feel?" he said.

She blinked.

"I don't mean specifically," he said. "Not biologically. I know how sex feels."

"What do you mean, then?" she asked. "You're over on your questions, by the way."

"Fuck the Rules."

She hopped down off the island and stood, which meant she was looking up at him. He leaned back against the counter. They were in their spots now—the places where they stood for serious conversations—as if these exact spots had been assigned by the realtors at escrow.

"I mean, how did it *feel*? You know. To do it?"

She looked out the window over the sink. "I'm going to be completely honest with you, okay?"

"Okay," he said.

"That's the point of this, right? This entire experiment? This thing? We're being honest with each other?"

"Yes. We are. Honest."

"And what I'm about to say has nothing to do with you. Okay? You're my husband, and I love you."

"All right."

Maybe he should *throw up in the sink*, he thought. At the very least, it would delay her saying what she was about to say. Of course, he wanted her to say that it was bad. Mediocre at best. Awkward. He didn't know what to do with his hands, and she didn't know what to do with hers. It was a regrettable experience all round, an intellectual exercise more than a physical one, in retrospect, like switching long-distance providers just to see what happens. *It meant nothing.* That was not what she was going to say. He knew that.

"It felt like being alive again."

PART THREE

smallTIMORE

22

Mitch had no idea what in the hell he was doing.

He probably could've guessed that'd be the case if he'd thought it through. But thinking hadn't really been a part of this operation. Not realistic thinking, anyway.

The idea of having sex with other women at age forty, it turned out, was a lot like the idea of summiting a towering, snowcapped mountain in some far-flung country. Great in theory, but not so easy to pull off.

If he'd thought it through, he also could've guessed how much easier it was going to be for Jessica.

No, she hadn't walked down the street, pointed at some guy, and said, "Excuse me, would you like to have sex?" It was more nuanced than that, he assumed, but if he was being honest, she probably could have. She was an attractive, intelligent woman with a lovely body and the slightest, faintest, barely-there-est lisp, and men are stupid, monkey-brained sex monsters. The odds were definitely in her favor.

In the last week, Mitch had made two and a half attempts to engage in conversation with women he didn't know. He was casual about it, because he remembered people always suggesting that, back in his single days. "Just be casual. Be yourself."

The results of being himself, however, were pretty bad.

WOMAN NUMBER ONE

She was at the Ivy Bookshop on Falls Road, looking at a shelf of staff recommendations.

She was in her thirties, he guessed, but she was dressed younger, in ripped jeans, flip-flops, and a T-shirt. Her hair was curly, and a little wild. This seemed like Mitch's wheelhouse—a bookish woman in a bookstore looking at books—and he briefly imagined them together. Not sexually together, though. He actually imagined them reading on a bench in Patterson Park. That wasn't the point of all this, but it was a nice thought anyway.

She bent down and leaned forward to read the handwritten note card above a thick paperback. Mitch noticed that the staff member who'd recommended the book was named Deirdre.

"Not sure I'd trust that one," Mitch said.

She appeared startled, which made sense, of course, because Mitch could've been a murderer or a sex trafficker for all she knew. "Why not?" she asked.

"Well, that's Deirdre up there, and I happen to know that she's a bit of a drinker."

Mitch and the woman looked over at the lady behind the counter. She was sitting on a stool, quietly organizing Harry Potter wrapping paper. He had no idea if she was a drinker or, in fact, if she was even Deirdre. He just thought it'd be a funny thing to say.

The woman with the wild curly hair, however, did not. She smiled politely and escaped to the biographies.

"I'm not a sex trafficker; I'm an English teacher," he wanted to say, but that probably would've made it worse.

WOMAN NUMBER TWO

She was a barista at the coffee shop near Mitch's school.

She had a nose ring, and she looked cute in her red apron, and she had punkish, angular hair that he liked. She was younger than the woman in the bookstore, but he had no idea by how much.

He'd never seen her there before, so he assumed she was new, and he imagined her making him some elaborate coffee drink in her underwear after sex—some crazy thing with nutmeg and finely ground beans from Guatemala. And because he was imagining things, he gave her a shoulder-blade tattoo of an exotic bird and an airy loft apartment downtown, the kind in which artistic people live in movies.

"Hey there," she said. "Can I help you?"

Mitch looked up at the chalk-written menu over the counter. He normally just ordered a simple black coffee, but that wasn't much of a conversation starter.

"I feel like trying something new today," he said.

"Um, okay," she replied.

"Got any recommendations?"

The barista sighed so dramatically that she seemed to partially deflate, and the people in line behind him murdered him with their eyeballs.

"I don't know, dude," she said. "Do you like tea or what? I don't even really drink coffee."

WOMAN NUMBER 2.5

This one got half credit, because their interaction only occurred in his mind.

He was in the frozen foods section at Giant, looking at pizzas, which required his full attention because his children had some pretty strong opinions about frozen pizza. He'd once tried serving them Newman's Own with uncured organic pepperoni, and there'd nearly been a goddamn riot.

A girl in a Towson Tigers T-shirt and jean shorts breezed down the aisle like a gazelle—young and absolutely beautiful. Mitch was old enough to be her father or, at the very least, her super-creepy uncle, so he just looked back at the pizzas and did his best not to stare. He couldn't help but remember a line from an underrated Steve Martin movie, *My Blue Heaven*, and he played the scene out in his head.

Excuse me, miss. You know, it's dangerous for you to be in this section.

Why's that, sir?

Because you could melt all this stuff.

It occurred to Mitch that, instead of trying so hard to have sex, he should be taking a moment to be thankful that he'd ever had sex in the first place.

What was he expecting to come of these interactions, anyway?

He didn't know. But it would've been nice to get something. Anything, really. A smile. A laugh. Any sign at all that maybe he had a chance at this; that in the last fifteen years he hadn't somehow gone and become utterly invisible.

And now he was at spin class, wheezing his ass off and gawking at the instructor, the ripped redhead, Tara.

Alan was supposed to come with him, but he'd bailed at the last minute, so it was just Mitch in a room full of sweaty strangers. They were six collective minutes into a seated climb, and the room was starting to come unglued.

"Who's ready for a little break?" Tara shouted.

"Bad Medicine" by Bon Jovi blared through the speakers in the ceiling. It was the Saturday Morning Eighties Ride, and Tara was wearing pink leg warmers.

"Well, tough shit!" she shouted. "'Cause you're not getting one!"

Tara smiled big and bright, reveling in the desperate-sounding responses. Sweat poured down her face and chest, pooling into a dark spot on her sports bra.

"Eight, seven, six!" she shouted.

Mitch wondered if he might pass out.

"When I get to one, we're standing up, you guys! 'Cause anything worth doing is worth standing up for, right? Right!"

It was classic spin-instructor dialogue. Senseless, but somehow motivational.

"Five, four! And when you stand, add five to your resistance and tell me how much you love it!"

On "one," Mitch and the rest of the room stood on their pedals, and a shock of vivid pain traveled up his lower back. But the new angle revealed Tara's stomach and thighs. Her skin glistened. The track lights over their heads were expertly installed and angled to highlight every twitching muscle on her body, and Mitch thought about her sweat-streaked lips and what they might taste like, all wet and salty.

He wondered, had she ever kissed someone while riding her spin bike? Was that even possible? Did she have a bike at home that she sometimes rode wearing only her underwear?

And then their eyes met.

This sometimes happened in spin class. Tara would scan the room, assessing the pain she was causing, and her eyes would lock briefly on his. This time it felt different, though. Longer than usual. Like something. A moment, maybe.

He was stricken with shyness, of course, but he kept his head up and held her gaze. And, despite the pain and physical exhaustion, he did his best to smile, because maybe that was all he needed to do. Maybe it wasn't about being funny or cool or suave or having a good opening joke about frozen food. Maybe it was just about smiling and making eye contact with another human being.

"Hey, blue shirt!" Tara shouted. "This isn't a spectator sport. Move your ass!"

23

Later, as Mitch drove home from the gym, he reminded himself that Jessica had had sex with someone else.

For the most part, he'd been good at compartmentalizing this fact, putting it in a small metal box and burying it deep in the dark recesses of his psyche. Driving, though, was his weakness. His guard dropped and his brain spun, and there it was—the inescapable fact of it— blinking like a neon sign on some passing bar window.

Jessica was right. He didn't get to be mad at her for this. *This* was part of it. Their experiment. The evolution of their marriage. But that didn't mean that he had to like it.

Behind him, four long pieces of wood rattled in the wayback of his Honda CR-V. It was their broken bed again. He snickered as he imagined his students reacting to this.

That's a metaphor, Mr. B.!

Yeah, no shit, genius.

As it turned out, Luke was right. The garbagemen *didn't* take things like that. Mitch found them on the ground the morning after trash night, next to his empty garbage cans. A bird had crapped on one of the pieces for good measure. They were too long to fit properly in the back of his car, so they poked up over the kids' booster seats. Mitch looked at them now in the rearview mirror and made a mental note to take them to the dump. And then he made another mental note to figure out where in the hell the dump was—if one even existed.

NPR was on the radio. The Saturday-morning host was interviewing a musician Mitch didn't know about his new jazz piano album. As he sometimes did when listening to quiet conversations on NPR, Mitch imagined that *he* was the one being interviewed.

> So, Mitch, what's your advice? What would you say to all the aspiring swingers out there? All the young husbands like you, looking to laugh in the face of thousands of years of marital tradition?

> Well, that's a tough one, particularly because the word "swinger" is so gross.

> It is, isn't it? There isn't really a word for it that isn't gross, is there? Maybe that's a sign that you're a fucking idiot, and that this entire thing was a huge, huge mistake.

Were you allowed to say "fuck" on NPR?

The jazz conversation ended, and a guy with a British accent started reading international news.

The light at the intersection up ahead turned red, and Mitch eased to a stop next to some teenagers. Three boys—high school kids, his students' age. They hung their arms out the open car windows to catch some sun. They were listening to rap music. Mitch rolled his windows down, too, and nudged the volume up on NPR, because at that moment, he felt an overwhelming need to give them a firsthand look at what each of them would someday become.

Halfway to death. In a sensible, fuel-efficient compact SUV. Listening to public radio.

As he drove up the street toward his house, Mitch saw something he wasn't expecting: his next-door neighbor's BMW, in the daylight.

It was parked in James and Ellen's driveway, and as he passed, Mitch saw James. He was standing next to his car looking at his own house. If Mitch wasn't mistaken, James appeared to be pensive.

Mitch pulled into his driveway and got out. He put his head down and made for the front door, trying to appear oblivious. It didn't work, though, because James was waving at him. "Hey there, Mitch!" he said.

"Hey, James."

For the entire time they'd been neighbors, this had usually been the extent of it in terms of interacting. At most, maybe there'd be something harmless about the weather or tree fungus or the Orioles, so Mitch was surprised when James said, "You got a second?"

"Yeah. Sure."

Mitch diverted through the grass and found himself shaking James's hand, as if they'd just met. James wore a pair of jeans and a nice tucked-in Ralph Lauren polo, and Mitch felt self-conscious in a sweat-soaked T-shirt and biking shorts. James's teeth looked less aggressively white in the sunshine, despite his deep tan.

"You get a workout in?" asked James.

"I did," said Mitch. "Spin class."

"Nice. Good way to start out a Saturday, huh?"

"Gotta keep it tight," Mitch said, because he wasn't good at small talk. The two men took a moment to stand silently in the driveway, nodding at the pavement.

"I'm not sure if you've heard, but Ellen and I . . ." He trailed off.

"Yeah. Jess and I were sorry to hear about it."

James frowned. Luke's new Jeep was parked up near the garage. It hadn't moved since arriving the week before.

"Awesome Jeep, by the way," Mitch said.

James regarded the shining 4×4. "Not bad, huh? I'm pretty sure Luke still thinks I'm an asshole, though."

Mitch did some more nodding.

"I've gotta teach him to drive it, still," said James. "It's a manual. The clutch is giving him trouble."

"They can be tough," said Mitch.

With the topic of the Jeep thoroughly explored, the two men had run out of things to say, and Mitch was planning his escape. And then James said, "Marriage isn't easy, is it?"

"No argument there."

"Luke's always spoken very highly of you, Mitch," said James. "He really loves your class."

"That's nice to hear. He's a wonderful student. My best one, actually. Don't think I'm supposed to rank them, technically. But he is. Good babysitter, too."

"It's funny," said James. "English was always my weakest subject. The reading and writing. Never really my thing, you know?"

Mitch heard this often as a teacher, usually from fathers. He used to interpret it as an insult—a knock on his masculinity—but over time, feeling that way got to be exhausting. "Well, it's not for everyone," he said.

James nodded. "I think this . . . this *transition* . . . might be rough on Luke. I'd look at it as a personal favor if maybe you checked on him from time to time. You being his favorite teacher and all. Plus, you see him every day. I'm just gonna have . . . well, every other weekend or so. We're still ironing all that out."

The nerve of this fucking guy, Mitch thought. Still, he was struck by his neighbor's sudden vulnerability. James's expression was set and stoic, like they were exchanging stock tips in the driveway, but Mitch could see it in the other man's eyes.

"Glad to," he said. "He's a great kid."

James thanked him and opened his car door. Mitch noticed a box of neatly rolled neckties in the passenger seat. There must have been twenty-five of them, arranged, apparently, by color. As James climbed in, he said, "I know I'm gonna be the bad guy here. I've accepted that. It's just the way it is, right?"

Mitch had no idea how to respond, so he just nodded and looked over at his own house. He'd never seen it from this vantage point before, and it looked different. Smaller, somehow—a trick of lights and angles.

"But shit, man," James, said, "since when is it a crime to want to be happy?"

24

She saw him before he saw her.

It always feels like an invasion of privacy when that happens—when you see someone who doesn't know they're being seen.

He passed a shoe store, a mall kiosk that sold drones, and Banana Republic, and then he walked into the food court. He was as beautiful as he'd been when she left him at his narrow house in the city a week ago. He wore a V-neck T-shirt, jeans, and canvas sneakers. Someone else would look like a slob in things so simple, but on him it was perfect. His sunglasses even hung on the V of his collar, tugging it down at his chest.

"Jesus," she whispered.

She was sitting at a table near the Chinese place where no one ever goes. Two Chinese ladies stood behind a counter of steaming food with nothing to do as a line formed next to them at Subway.

Ryan stopped and scanned the expanse of tables. When he saw her, he smiled.

Jessica had it all figured out. It was efficient and effective. She was meeting Amber at Nordstrom in fifteen minutes, on the other side of the mall. She'd come here first, meet Ryan, and that'd be that.

"This seat taken?" he asked.

"No," she said. "All yours."

"I haven't had a date at the mall since junior high," he said.

There was zero chance that Amber would come to the food court, what with all the gluten and non-kale there, but Jessica ran her eyes over the crowd anyway, just in case. "Well, this isn't exactly a date," she said.

He drummed his fingers on the table. "A girl and a guy at the food court? Sounds like a date to me. Can I buy you a Whopper? That Burger King over there's the shit, according to Yelp."

She laughed, despite herself. "Stop it."

He leaned forward on his elbows. "When you smile, you get these little crinkles next to your eyes. Did you know that?"

"I believe those are called laugh lines," she said.

Of course, *lines* came out wrong—a *th* crept in before the *s*—and she flushed. Ryan sank back in his chair and put his hand over his heart. "Fuuuuuck," he said. "You're not playing fair with that."

"Sorry."

"Don't apologize. I could listen to it all day."

She remembered lying naked next to Mitch one night in college. They were in the little apartment he shared with Terry and Alan senior year. He made her stick her tongue out so he could hold it between his lips and try to suss out whatever imperfection caused those *s*'s to occasionally go so wonky.

"I was stoked when I got your text," he said. "I was like, maybe this isn't a onetime thing after all. Then I saw that . . . well, you were all business."

Jessica shook her head. "I just don't understand this," she said.

"What?"

"You could have any woman in this . . . well, this entire mall. That's for sure. Why me?"

He laughed and looked around. In fairness, the options in that particular food court at that particular moment were pretty limited. "Shut up," he said. "It's not like that."

"I'm not kidding," she said. "We've been vague about our ages here. I get that. But I'm too old for you. If we took a walk around this place together, people would look at us and wonder what our story was. 'Is she his sugar mama? Is he a male prostitute?' No offense."

He laughed again. He was enjoying this. It actually did feel like a date.

"Fuck 'em," he said. "All I know is, the second I saw you that first time, when you were with . . ." he trailed off and started again. "Is it so hard to believe that I think you're gorgeous? And that the first time I saw you I wanted nothing more than to be touching you?"

She would've teased him for that—such a panty-dropper of a line, like something from a commercial for male body spray—but he seemed to genuinely mean it, and she remembered the ease of being his age, of being desired and desirable and naïve enough to think that that's all that matters.

"Plus," he said, "you look smart. Your entire aura. I have a thing for smart women. If you put on a pair of glasses right now, I'd pass out. Honest to God."

"You're sweet," she said. "But sorry. I've worn contacts since high school. Glasses give me vertigo."

"Sigh," he said.

She was aware of the time passing—of the tables filling up around them. "So, you have them, then?" she said.

He reached into the front pocket of his jeans and set her rings on the table between them. It seemed somehow vulgar to slide it immediately back onto her finger, but what choice did she have? That was where it belonged.

"Done and done," he said.

Neither of them spoke for a moment. She looked around again, hoping not to see Amber or anyone else she knew there in the city of Smalltimore. She hadn't a clue what she'd say if she did. And then Ryan noticed the empty Chinese food place nearby. "That makes me kinda sad, you know?" he said. "Look at those poor ladies. They have to stand there and watch all those assholes wait in line for shitty Subway. Kinda feel bad for them."

Goddammit, she thought.

Because, if she'd never been married. If she were divorced. If she were a widow. If she were anything other than what she was, and if there were no Rules or consequences or reality, maybe she'd let him buy her that Whopper after all. *Fuck 'em.*

"I'm not a bad person, you know," she said.

He smiled. "Who said you were?"

"We have an arrangement."

"A what?"

"Oh God," she said. "I hate how that sounds. My husband and I. We have . . . We're trying something. It's sort of an experiment."

He sat back in his chair. "Really?"

She nodded.

"People actually do that?"

"Apparently," she said.

"Well, your husband's an idiot. If you were mine, no way I'd share you."

He was trying to be sweet. She knew that, but it hurt anyway. "I should go," she said. "I'm meeting a friend."

It seemed like he might touch her hand, but he didn't. "This is the second time you've said goodbye to me forever, you know," he said.

"For real this time."

Ryan looked at her in a way that showed pretty clearly that he didn't believe her. And then, instead of leaving straightaway, he stepped up to the counter at the Chinese place and ordered food. He looked back at her and shrugged.

And that's how she left him. On her way out of the food court, she looked back just in time to see the two ladies smiling as they heaped his sweet-and-sour chicken into a Styrofoam takeaway container. Jessica spun the wedding rings on her finger as she walked, reacquainting herself with their weight. That was when she saw Kate Upton. She was over the Hallmark Store, hanging from the wall on the second floor. Wearing the smallest nightgown ever, she smiled down at Jessica from above.

This was all her fault.

25

Nordstrom was having an insane dress sale. They did it every year.

Winter dresses, mostly—getting rid of seasonal inventory—but there were deals to be had on spring and summer stuff, too, and Amber claimed to need absolutely everything. A full-fledged restart.

"Work dresses," she said. "Going-out dresses. First-date dresses. Third-date dresses. Hoochie dresses. Fun dresses. Serious dresses. Dresses to wear when I'm on my period. I can't live in tank tops and yoga pants anymore like some antisocial mole-woman. This girl's back in the game."

Jessica leaned against a SPRING DRESS EVENT sign. "That sounds exhausting," she said.

"And expensive. Forget the national debt. If I ever *do* have kids, this'll be what they're paying off when we're all dead."

Technically, Jessica was shopping, too, but less aggressively than Amber, so she was playing the role of Amber's Sherpa. There were currently five dresses slung over her arm, and she was lugging a large iced coffee, too.

Amber looked at her watch. "When did Megan and Sarah say they were coming? *Did* they say there were coming? I get lost in the text chains sometimes."

"They've got kid stuff," said Jessica. "They said to get started without them."

"Right."

The Wives had never shopped together when they were all married. They had a book club, which was really just a wine club. And they'd experimented with a restaurant club a few times, too, but there were always too many conflicts to make a consistent go of it. Now that they were 75 percent single, they stopped making up activities and just hung out when they could. "I mean, this is bullshit," Megan had said last year at the final official meeting of their floundering book club. "Why do I have to pretend to read *Anna* freaking *Karenina* just to see you guys?"

Amber held a floral thing up to herself. "What do you think?" she said. "For garden parties and stuff."

"You get invited to a lot of garden parties?" Jessica asked.

Amber pouted into a mirror. "No. When I was younger, I imagined there'd be garden parties."

"For me it was galas," said Jessica. "I thought there'd be tons of them. And those New Year's Eve parties where everyone dresses like it's 1920. It's a pretty dress, though."

Amber draped it over the other dresses on Jessica's arm. "We'll throw it on the pile," she said.

They milled for a while. Amber picked up more dresses, seemingly at random, and held them up to herself for comment, and Jessica glanced incessantly toward the mall entrance.

"Why do you keep looking out there?" Amber asked.

"Do I?" Jessica asked. "Sorry."

"You're distracted today. I need you focusing on me."

"God, you're so high-maintenance. No wonder you're divorced."

Jessica hated admitting it to herself, but she was still thinking of Ryan, and now she wondered: Did he take his Chinese food home, or was he sitting on some mall bench out there eating off his lap? Or, more likely, had he sauntered into the Gap and seduced some poor girl folding jeans, just to spite her?

"So, Alan's seeing someone," said Amber, quite suddenly.

"What?"

"Yep." Her face was resigned, emotionless. She was standing at a rack of nautical-inspired floor-length evening dresses.

Jessica had been waiting for this. Mitch had showed her some texts from Alan the previous week, but she wasn't sure what the exact protocol was for the friends of the recently divorced. How does it work? What do you share? What do you hide? More specifically, do your friends want to know about their ex-husbands' hand jobs? "How do you know?" she asked. "Are you sure?"

"You know this city. Everybody knows everybody. Plus, he posted something on Instagram, the idiot. We agreed to unfriend and unfollow each other across all social media. Smart, right? But my brother saw it and ratted him out. You can't escape this shit."

"How do you feel about it?" Jessica asked.

"Are you being a therapist or a friend?"

"Is there a difference?"

Amber ran her hand over some velvet thing with a silly built-in belt. "Well," she said, "I feel shitty."

"That's normal."

"Yeah, but shittier than I thought I'd feel. I always figured I'd meet someone before he did, you know. I mean, I don't love him, we established that, but that doesn't mean I don't wanna beat him. Right?"

Jessica totally understood this.

"And you know what really sucks?" said Amber. "Well, besides all of it?"

"What?"

"Alan's more attractive now than when we met. Significantly. It's unfair."

Jessica understood this, too. Fifteen pounds, three forehead wrinkles, and graying temples had combined to make Mitch far more handsome than the skinny twentysomething she'd married. It was yet another line item on the long list of humankind's biological injustices.

"What about you?" Jessica asked. "Have *you* met anyone?"

"You mean future dick-pic candidates?"

"Yeah."

"No. I dipped my toe in a little with the apps. Did some research. But they were mostly gross."

"Really?"

"They all brag about their algorithms or whatever—like, these matchmaking formulas—but it's all just a bunch of people trying to get laid."

"Well, it kinda seemed like that was what you were looking for the other night," said Jessica. "Something physical."

"I was all talk. You know how I get when I drink shots." Amber looked at her own reflection again, posed with her hand on her hip. "Truth is, I'm just a girl standing in front of a mirror, asking for a boy who isn't an Internet sex fiend."

"Well put," said Jessica.

As they moved through the store, the quality of merchandise steadily improved—less novelty crap—and Jessica noticed a little black dress hanging on a tucked-away rack. It was from Anthropologie—short and form-fitting—and a thought fluttered in and out of her head, like a passing butterfly, of wearing it for Ryan. His eyes moving over her body. Him whispering, *"Fuuuuuck."*

"And—surprise, surprise—she's younger, too," Amber said. "That's not helping me feel any less shitty."

"Who?" Jessica asked.

"Her. Alan's girl. Whatever her name is."

"Oh. How young?"

"Who the hell knows? Every chick under thirty-five might as well be nineteen." Amber tugged at the skin beneath her chin. "Young enough to not have any of this. That's for sure."

"Stop it. Your chin is fine."

"I'm starting to look old," she said.

"No you're not. You look great. The lighting in these places is always terrible."

"Fine," said Amber. "I'm starting to look like the stage just before old. If I was an actress, I'd be playing the younger, hotter actress's quirky older sister or gynecologist or something."

Amber was an advertising and PR writer by trade. She was always saying things like this—too concise and clever to argue with.

The store was filling up fast. Women clustered in groups around them, working through the racks together.

"You wanna see her?" Amber asked, pulling out her phone. "My brother took a screenshot and sent it to me."

No, Jessica didn't, not particularly, but then again, of course she did. Either way, the girl on Amber's iPhone screen was just a girl like any girl. Midtwenties, leaning next to Alan, grinning and loopy eyed and unwrinkled.

"Hot, right?" said Amber.

"Eh," said Jessica. "Her freckles are cute, I guess."

"Do you lie to all your patients, Dr. Butler?"

"Amber, she's just young. That's all. When you're that age, you can fool anyone into thinking you're hot."

"Do you think they're having sex?"

Jessica said she didn't know, which was a harmless enough lie, like telling Emily that her macaroni sculpture was the most beautiful thing ever.

"She's probably one of those horrible monsters who pretends to like watching baseball and giving blow jobs."

A mother and her teenage daughter were shopping nearby. Their eyes went wide, and Jessica nudged Amber toward a clearing in the crowd. "Look on the bright side," she said. "Statistically speaking, there's a decent chance she has HPV."

Amber smiled. "That's sweet."

"Which one are you trying on first?" she asked.

Jessica sat in an uncomfortable chair, looking at Amber's feet at the bottom of the changing-room door.

"Garden party," Amber said.

Her jeans fell to the floor, and she kicked them out of the way. She stepped into the floral dress, and then there was silence. Jessica could hear Amber breathing.

"How is it?" asked Jessica. "You like?"

"I'm too tall."

"You always say that. Open up. Lemme see."

Amber opened the door and stood barefoot and pigeon-toed, a little hunched. The material clung to her legs, but not in a good way, and it was cut far too short from shoulder to hip.

"Yeah," said Jessica. "You're too tall."

"Did the designers all get together and decide to abandon me?"

"Well, that one did."

She shut the door again and started over. Jessica could read Amber's emotions just by seeing her feet. They were set firm, shoulder-width apart, the way you might stand if you were expecting to be slapped in the face.

"By the way," said Amber, "Megan and Sarah really got in my head the other night."

"What do you mean?"

"Their little tough-love speech. What if I don't *want* to date fifty-year-olds?"

"I'm sure they were exaggerating," said Jessica.

Amber tried on something else—the navy blue one, from what Jessica could see. "Okay," she said. "This one's for work." The door opened, and there she stood again. The right length this time, but shapeless. "Thoughts?"

"You look like the branch manager of a bank in 1987."

"Right? Who puts shoulder pads in dresses anymore?" The door closed, and Amber worked her way out of the second dress. And then she said, "I wish I would've talked to that waiter."

Jessica looked up at the door. "What waiter?" she said, but, obviously, she knew. There was only one waiter.

"You know, the hot one. You guys were trying to get me to go throw myself at him, but I was too nervous."

"Oh. Him? Really?" Jessica was surprised at the intensity of her instincts—at the ownership she felt.

"Well, he was absolutely gorgeous. And he was taller than me, too. Not a bad combination."

"He was . . . kinda young, though, right?"

"Well, Alan has no problem going after young, pretty things. Why should I? If I find a dress that doesn't make me look like either a horse or Murphy Brown, maybe we'll head there for another Wives' night.

Or ladies' night. We should probably stop calling ourselves the Wives, by the way. I've been thinking about that. For accuracy's sake."

Jessica felt a surge of preemptive jealousy.

"By the way, why aren't you trying on anything?"

Jessica sipped at the last of her iced coffee.

"You need to buy *something*, so I don't feel bad for buying *everything*. That's how this works. Didn't you see anything you like?"

"No," said Jessica. "Not really." But that wasn't true at all. "Well, actually."

Amber's forehead and eyes appeared over the changing room door. "Yeah?"

"Maybe," said Jessica. "Hold on a sec."

"Atta girl," said Amber.

Jessica went back out into the store and grabbed the little black dress off the rack. Then she hurried into the changing room next to Amber. "Okay," she said. "I got one."

"Nice," said Amber. "What color?"

"Black," said Jessica.

"Classy."

"It probably won't even work," said Jessica. "It's ridiculous."

"I'm trying on the red one now," said Amber. "The strapless one. I like to attend events with the full knowledge that my boobs might pop out at any moment, so this should be perfect."

Jessica took off her jeans and pulled her thin sweater over her head and stepped into the dress. Even before she had it on, as she tugged it up over her knees and hips, she could tell it was different from anything she owned. And then she looked at herself. She stood on her toes, pretending to be in heels. She pulled her hair out of its loose tie and let it fall over her shoulders.

"You show me yours, and I'll show you mine," said Amber.

They stepped out of their dressing rooms at the same time.

"I'm too tall for this one, too, but—whoa." Amber took a step back, looking at Jessica.

"It's short," Jessica said. "And it's tight."

"Yeah. It's both of those things. But . . . wow."

"I really don't need it," said Jessica.

Amber reached down and straightened the hem at Jessica's mid-thigh. "You aren't looking to get pregnant, are you?" she asked. "'Cause this is the kind of dress that gets a girl *really* pregnant."

Before they could laugh at this, they heard a sound a few dressing rooms over. A woman. She was muttering something.

Amber pointed. "Did you know there was someone in there?" she mouthed.

Jessica shook her head no.

"Fuck this," the voice said. Then the door opened, and out walked a short-haired woman who Jessica recognized instantly. The woman stopped when she saw Jessica and Amber standing there barefoot in expensive dresses. It was Jessica's next-door neighbor.

"Ellen," she said. "My God. Hi."

"Hey," said Ellen. "Small world."

Amber said hello and introduced herself.

"Ellen's my neighbor," said Jessica.

"Oh, that's cool."

Ellen was clearly upset. Her eyes were puffy, like she'd been crying. She wore jeans and an oversize long-sleeved Maryland Terrapins T-shirt.

"Are you all right?" asked Jessica.

Ellen looked at Amber and then Jessica, tentative. "James left today," she said. "Like, *left* left. Gone."

"Oh," said Jessica. "I'm sorry, Ellen."

"And he's screwing a thirty-five-year-old who isn't even that pretty. And every dress in this goddamn place makes me look like a transvestite."

And then, timing be damned, a saleswoman appeared with an armful of plastic hangers. "How're you ladies coming along in here?"

"Um, we're gonna need a minute," said Jessica.

When she was gone, Amber asked Ellen how tall she was.

"What?" asked Ellen.

"Like, five-five? Five-six? Something like that, right?"

"Five-five," said Ellen. "Yeah."

"Perfect." Amber pointed at herself. "You wanna try this thing on? I think it'll look great with your coloring."

Ellen took in the expanse of Amber's exposed shoulders. "You think? It might be a little aggressive for me."

"Oh, stop it," said Amber. "That's the point. These things are all just costumes anyway."

Amber put her regular clothes back on, and then she and Jessica waited while Ellen tried on the red strapless dress.

"Nordstrom should really get a liquor license," said Amber. "Can you imagine how much money they'd make?"

Jessica agreed.

"So, are you gonna buy that dress," asked Amber, "or are you just gonna lounge around the dressing room in it?"

"I don't think so," Jessica said. "If I bought it, it'd just be one of those things I have but never wear."

"That's practical," said Amber. "And very lame."

When Ellen came out of the dressing room, Jessica and Amber stood up.

She looked like a different person. Yes, her skin was pale and chalky, deprived of sunlight and moisturizer. Her toenails had been utterly ignored, and her hair was, at best, a miscalculation. But she looked good.

"Nice," said Amber. "Look at you."

"Yeah," said Jessica. "It fits you perfectly. It's like it was made for you."

Ellen clearly believed them, or at least wanted to. Her eyes brightened; she even smiled. "I think I like it," she said.

"Hey, there you guys are. We've been looking for you for twenty minutes."

The three women turned to find Megan and Sarah. They were holding Starbucks cups and wearing sneakers.

"You guys came," said Amber. "Did you bring the kids?"

"Hell no," said Megan.

"God bless babysitters," said Sarah.

And then they both noticed Jessica's dress at the same time.

"Damn, Jess," said Megan. "You trying to get knocked up again or what?"

"That's what I said," said Amber. "Look at her boobs in that thing."

"Mitch is a lucky guy," said Sarah.

"Relax." Jessica crossed her arms—aware, suddenly, of her cleavage. "I'm not buying it."

"The hell you aren't," said Megan. "Jesus, I'll buy it for you."

"All right," said Jessica. "Maybe."

"I can't stop looking at your boobs," said Sarah.

"Okay, that's enough." And then Jessica noticed how uncomfortable Ellen looked standing there among them. That was the power of the Wives' friendship. It could leave others feeling left out. "Sarah, Megan, this is my neighbor. She lives right next door. This is Ellen."

Sarah and Megan said hello.

Then Amber said something that reminded Jessica just how happy she was that these three wonderful, messed-up women were in her life. "Ladies," she said. "Ellen's one of us."

26

Jessica and Mitch rarely had sex on Sunday nights.

They were typically worn out from the weekend—from two days in a row of nonstop parenting—and anxious about the coming week and all the logistics and hassles and responsibilities it would entail. Consequently, it was a night reserved for sweatpants and streaming episodic television and dozing off three pages into one of the countless books stacked up in their respective to-be-read piles.

And while that particular Sunday was no different on the surface, Mitch found that there was an edge to their sexlessness. What usually felt organic—like an unspoken agreement between two tired adults to just chill the fuck out—now seemed forced. It didn't help that they hadn't laid a hand on each other since Jessica had told him about . . . well, it.

He looked over at her.

She was lying beside him, propped up on a pile of throw pillows, which she'd leaned against the wall behind them. The charm of their floor bed had worn off, and not having a proper headboard was really annoying.

"Did you buy anything good yesterday?" he asked.

"Just a dress," she said, not looking up from her book.

"Yeah?" he said. "What's it look like?"

"Like most of my other dresses, basically. It was on sale. Amber wasn't gonna let me out of there without buying something."

He rolled onto his side and faced her, and then he took the book out of her hand and set it on the floor. She looked surprised, but not, he thought, in a bad way, despite its being Sunday.

"Hello," he said.

"Hi," she said.

Mitch kissed her, and her lips felt like they always felt, and she kissed him back like she always did. And then their kiss deepened, and their tongues touched and he slid closer to her. When you've been married for fifteen years, you don't typically make out for the sake of making out. This sort of kissing is the thing that happens before doors are secured and sweatpants come off. But when their lips parted, the energy stalled out, and they just looked at each other.

"We didn't think about this, did we?" he said.

This meant a lot of things, but mostly it meant that they'd have to have sex again at some point after their *evolution,* and it would feel different. He didn't have to explain that, though, because, apparently, she was thinking the same thing.

"No," she said. "We didn't."

"I'm jealous," he said. "We didn't think about that part either. The jealousy part. Is that hardwiring, too? Like a caveman instinct? Like, I'd smash a rock over his head if he was here, steal his rudimentary tools."

"Probably," she said. "I'd be jealous, too. I *will* be."

He looked at the television. *SportsCenter* flickered; he wasn't paying any attention to it. These guys in uniforms had defeated these other guys in different uniforms. Etcetera.

"Amber knows about Alan's new girlfriend, by the way," she said.

"Oh?" he said. "Did you tell her?"

"Didn't have to." She told him about Amber's brother, the Instagram detective.

"Well, I guess that was inevitable," he said.

"She feels jealous, too."

"Really?" This surprised him, frankly. Of all The Divorces, Amber and Alan's seemed to be the cleanest—the poster child for modern-day uncoupling.

"Amber wanted to be first," she said.

"Ah."

"Jealousy is a normal human emotion," she said, "but it's a complicated one. She'll meet someone, and when she does, she'll have her turn. She'll feel better about all of it."

"Mm-hmm," he said. She was being clinical again—fiercely reasonable, like always—and he understood what she was getting at. Mitch was jealous for lots of reasons, not the least of which was the fact that Jessica had gone first.

"Have you had . . ." She paused here, maybe because what she was about to ask was such an incredibly, debilitatingly odd thing to ask a spouse. "Have you had any luck?"

He gave her a brief progress report—a quick run-through of his two and a half attempts at human contact. For the sake of honesty, he spared no self-deprecating detail.

"For the record," she said, "when I was in college, if a handsome older man had told me I was hot enough to melt all the stuff in the frozen food section, I'd have thought he was hilarious."

"Really?" he asked. "That's good to know. I'll try to do some shopping this week."

The TV remote was marooned between them, half-tucked under the bed sheets. She found it and turned off the TV. "Listen," she said. "I've been thinking about something."

"Yeah?"

"Yeah," she said.

Mitch was certain that she was going to suggest they call it off. They'd reached the end of their evolution. And in the three seconds it took her to continue talking, he vacillated between annoyance and relief. But then she got up and told him to hold on. She left the room, and he found himself alone looking at the blank television. The floor bed provided an unpleasant vantage point, and their bedroom looked cluttered and haphazard.

When Jessica returned, she was holding her laptop. She fell into bed beside him and hit the power button. "I did some research today," she said.

"Okay," he said.

"Apps," she said. "The Internet. Apparently that's how people have sex now."

The site that she went to wasn't for dating; that much was instantly clear. It wasn't one of those sites that advertised on TV with testimonials and success stories. The word *discreet* appeared three times in the opening blurb. It was a hookup site.

"How did you find this?" Mitch asked.

"Google doesn't judge," she said.

She'd opened a profile for him already, apparently. The name at the top threw him off. "Wait," he asked. "Who's Will B.?"

"That's you," she said. "What? You think we're going to use your real name?"

"Ah, right," he said, and then he watched as she filled out his information. Long walks on the beach and a mutual love of literature weren't the objectives here, so the space for personal details was limited to the basics. He was five-eleven, but she wrote six feet. He had brown hair and an athletic build. That part was more of a stretch than his height, but he let it go for the sake of advertising.

She opened the photos folder on her computer. "I like this picture of you," she said. "It's nice. You look good."

He squinted at himself. It was technically him, but indistinctly so, shot from a distance on the National Mall down in D.C. the previous year. It could've been him. It could've been anyone, really.

"My hair's lighter now," he said.

She touched a tuft of it over his right ear and smiled. "Grayer, you mean?"

When all the boxes were filled and his online profile was complete, she moved her computer from her lap to her knees and angled it toward him. "That's it," she said. "You're ready."

"Am I?" he said.

"Mitch," she said.

He'd thought about the Internet, of course. How could he not—the ease, the anonymity? It seemed somehow, though, like cheating—

like cheating at cheating. And worse than that, he now realized, was the fact that it might actually work. There was safety in being rejected by women who were minding their own business in bookstores and coffee shops and frozen-food sections. A woman on a hookup site, though, would actually *want* to hook up. That was part of the deal, presumably, and lying there next to Jessica now, he found the prospect of actual sex less appealing than potential sex.

"Do you remember *The Dark Knight*?" he asked. "The Batman movie with Heath Ledger?"

"What?"

"The scene in the hospital, where the Joker's talking to Harvey Dent. The guy's just had half his face melted off."

"All right."

"In that scene, the Joker compares himself to a dog chasing cars. But the thing is, he doesn't know what he'd do if he actually caught one."

Jessica squeezed the sides of her laptop. "You wanna know why so many women think men are idiots, Mitch? This is why. Right here."

"No," he said. "I'm actually making a point. I promise. What I'm saying is, what if I don't really *want* to catch a car?"

She closed her eyes and then opened them again slowly. "Mitch, it's too late for that."

He didn't say anything. Admittedly, as far as epiphanies went, this one was arriving a little late.

"You're just nervous," she said. "I get it. I was nervous, too. It's scary. But we can't go halfway on this. We're doing this together. We have to."

She was right, and Mitch knew it. If they turned back now, they'd be screwed. For the rest of their lives, it'd be something she did and he didn't do.

He looked at the computer screen in her lap. A beautiful blond girl in underwear and a tight tank top looked back at him from the website, biting her lip. She was a model, of course, not an actual user of the site, but he set this fact aside for a moment. "Okay," he said.

"Okay," she said.

He grabbed his grind-guard mouthpiece from his nightstand. "But can we at least acknowledge, for the record, how weird this is?"

The computer cursor hovered over the Post button. "Relax," she said. "You're just a married man going online under a fake name to find sex. What could possibly go wrong?" And then she tapped her finger.

Will B. was live.

27

Over that weekend, a freshman girl named Misty Crabtree tried to kill herself.

Along with her normal daily dose of Ritalin, she swallowed an entire bottle of Advil; so, on Wednesday, Luke's fourth-period English Lit class with Mr. Butler was replaced by an all-school assembly to "come together" and "have a heart-to-heart" about the dangers of depression.

Principal Michaels kicked things off.

She didn't say Misty's name aloud—a privacy thing, probably—but everyone knew why they were there. The news had spread instantly across text and social media, so by Monday morning everyone knew what the deal was. At least a dozen memes had already been created and circulated, one of which included some Jedi-level photoshopping of the recommended-daily-dosage language on a bottle of Advil.

1–2 pills every four hours as needed. Or entire bottle if Daddy won't buy you a pony.

"Young people today," said Principal Michaels, "are facing a legitimate health crisis. It's a crisis that has all of us here at school—your teachers and faculty—very, very concerned."

She went on from there. Luke was having trouble concentrating, though, because he was sitting next to Scarlett Powers.

This was how all-school assemblies worked. You went to your regularly scheduled class, got your attendance taken, and headed to the gym from there. You weren't technically required to sit with kids from that specific period, but that was usually how it ended up, and now Luke used the miracle of peripheral vision to look at Scarlett's thigh, which was currently a mere inch from his own.

At least twice a day, some teacher—usually female—told Scarlett to roll her skirt down immediately, but then she'd just roll it back up five minutes later, thank God, and now very little was left to Luke's vivid imagination.

He saw his female classmates' thighs all the time, of course—gym class and sports and all that. Most girls shaved from the knee down, he noticed, but not Scarlett. Her thighs were as smooth and hairless as anything on earth, and Luke was left desperately trying to will away what he feared was going to be a pretty obvious boner.

"It hardly counts, right?" Scarlett said.

Luke was startled to find that she was talking to him. She barely even bothered trying to whisper.

"I mean, come on. Advil? That's JV-team shit. You'd have better luck killing yourself with a bag of gummy bears."

He looked around to makes sure no teachers were looking. "I know, right?" he whispered.

He felt like a dick for making a joke. It wasn't that he didn't get the gravity of the situation—of why they were all there, packed into the gym. But it *was* Advil, after all, as Scarlett pointed out, and there was a Magic Marker tattoo on Scarlett's ankle. *Scarlettkind*, it read, in intricate cursive. It was mostly faded, but he still found it hot as hell.

"Of course, this is a school—and you're all students," said Principal Michaels. "But I like to think of us as one very large, very tight-knit family."

"Oh God," said Scarlett.

"And when one member of that family is hurting or struggling or otherwise in trouble, it impacts all of us."

Scarlett leaned her shoulder into Luke's and made a whacking-off gesture with her loosely cupped hand. He was afraid of getting in trouble—of being guilty by association. And he was also imagining what it'd be like to get a hand job from Scarlett Powers. The combination of these disparate thoughts was nearly more than the fly of his uniform khakis could handle.

"It's like *Romeo and Juliet*, you know," she said.

"What?"

Her breath smelled like coffee, but he didn't mind.

"Come on, pay attention. Lit Suicide 101. If you're gonna kill yourself, *kill* yourself, right? Go all in."

"Oh," said Luke. "Yeah."

Mr. Butler's face appeared. Teachers were sprinkled in among the students like prison guards, and Mr. Butler sat a few rows down. He turned and gave Luke and Scarlett a look. "Come on, you guys," he whispered, and Luke did his best to create a facial expression that appeased his favorite teacher without looking super lame in front of Scarlett.

"And now I'd like to introduce you to our very special guest," said Principal Michaels. "Dr. Aarav Gambir joins us today from down the street at Hopkins, and he's here to talk about how we can all look out for one another."

Most of the students in the gym made a go at polite applause; even Scarlett, although hers seemed sarcastic. Dr. Gambir was an Indian man in his forties, Luke guessed. He wore a crisp white shirt and an Orioles tie, and when he spoke, he didn't have an accent like Luke was expecting. "Thanks for having me, Patty," he said.

"Patty?" said Scarlett.

Luke looked down at the back of Mr. Butler's head.

"Did you know her name was Patty? Next time she's bitching me out, I'm gonna be like, 'Shove it, Patty.'"

Mr. Butler turned around again. "Seriously?"

"It's pretty easy to tell when someone's depressed, right?" said Dr. Gambir. "The power of simple observation is all it takes."

Students looked at one another. Some nodded.

"If someone's depressed, they *look* depressed. They listen to sad music. Power ballads from the eighties, maybe. They're all pale, because they don't want to go outside. Generally speaking, if you're depressed, you put out a pretty standard, run-of-the-mill 'I'm sad' vibe, right?"

There were a few more nods, but mostly there was caution. The students sensed what was coming. The old lecture-hall switcheroo.

"Well, actually, no," he said. "Not at all, in fact. Right now, suicide is one of the leading causes of death for people your age. And when it happens, who can guess what the friends, parents, and loved ones who are left behind almost *always* say?"

No one guessed. It was an all-school assembly. Raising a hand and saying something would've been either an act of stuntman bravery or social . . . well, suicide.

Dr. Gambir cleared his throat. "I . . . never . . . saw . . . it . . . coming."

He looked around the gym, from one wall to the other and back again.

"Depression looks like a lot of things. But more often than not, unfortunately, it looks *totally* normal."

The A/V team's monitor, which was behind Dr. Gambir, started showing a diverse montage of faces, one after the other. Different ages, races, genders. Frowns, grins, scowls, blank stares.

Dr. Gambir went on. "And here's the scary thing, guys. And this is why I'm here today—to drive this point home. As a community, we need to check in on the people we love. Even the people we just *like*, in fact. Because sometimes, just before someone reaches a crisis point, just before they're about to make a decision that they cannot undo, depression looks like this."

The montage stopped now and held on the single image of a woman smiling. A pink blouse. A pretty necklace. Nice teeth.

"She looks happy, doesn't she?" he said.

"I'd tap that," whispered Scarlett.

"She doesn't look depressed at all, right? You could look at her and say, 'Oh, she's fine.' She looks like she's got all the energy and optimism in the world. Well, that's the point. The fact is, suicide requires a great deal of energy. Like, a tidal wave of it. So, as counterintuitive as it seems, depressed people are often at their worst just when they appear to be at their best."

Scarlett whispered something snide, but Luke didn't hear her, because now he was thinking about his mom.

For the last few months, her sadness had been like furniture or a major appliance—something Luke was so used to that he barely saw it anymore. She slept in nearly every morning, arriving downstairs in her pajamas and robe. But since his dad left the previous weekend—like, *officially* left—she'd been up every morning, dressed and ready, asking him about his homework and flipping through the A.M. talk shows. That very morning, in fact, she offered to make him pancakes.

"Pancakes?"

"Yeah, why not?"

"It's Wednesday."

Luke looked at the smiling middle-aged woman on the screen. And he kept looking at her until her image was replaced by a pie chart of statistics. He thought of the pills his mother took—of the orange cups lined up in the cabinet in her bathroom. He knew nothing about medicine, but any one of them, with their clinical, unpronounceable names, had to be stronger than Advil. Right?

I . . . never . . . saw . . . it . . . coming.

When Dr. Gambir was done talking, the screen went dark, and Principal Michaels thanked him and announced a new crisis hotline that any student could call at any time, day or night.

The fifth-period bell rang, and a thousand teenagers stood up at once.

"Well, I don't know about you, but I feel a lot less like killing myself," said Scarlett. But Luke was already gone. He sidestepped and dodged his way through his classmates and found Mr. Butler.

"What's up, Luke?"

"I think I need to go," he said.

"What? Are you sick?"

"No. I just need to leave, just for a little while. Like, half an hour. Tops."

"Where do you need to go? You're in school."

"I have lunch fifth period, then study hall. I won't miss anything."

"You're a junior, Luke. Only seniors can leave campus on free periods. Them's the rules at Shawshank."

"Yeah, I know. But—"

"What's the deal?" said Mr. Butler. He looked around, then leaned in. "What's going on?"

Luke looked back at the screen, now blank. "It's my Mom."

"What about her? Something wrong?"

"I just think I need to check on her."

Mr. Butler looked at his watch. He wasn't just Luke's teacher. He was more than that, and he got it. "You sure?" he said.

"No," said Luke. "I don't know. That's the thing. I just have a bad feeling."

Mr. Butler sighed, trying to decide. And then he said, "Okay, go."

28

t was an eleven-minute bike ride from school to Luke's house. As he pedaled up Charles Street, he imagined her dead.

Dead dead. Gone. Eyes open, lifeless, staring up at the ceiling. In the bathtub, maybe, the water spilling over the lip and pooling in slo-mo. Or possibly sprawled out on the floor in some flowing outfit, like he imagined Juliet would be.

He hopped the curb next to the mailbox and skidded to a stop in the driveway. Then he leaned his bike against the Jeep's fender.

When he opened the door, he knew right away that she wasn't dead.

Everything was fine. Better than fine, actually.

Sunlight shone through the windows, and the entryway felt airier than it had in months. He set his backpack down next to the stairs and took in the smell of food cooking, which he followed into the shock-ingly clean kitchen. A casserole of some sort was bubbling in the oven. Above that, lined up on the countertop, a dozen chocolate chip cookies sat cooling on a rack.

"Holy shit." He touched one. It was warm and soft.

"Luke?" Her voice came from the bedroom. "Luke, is that you?"

"Hey, Mom. Yeah, it's me."

"What're you doing home? Are you okay?"

The truth was ridiculous, so he said, "Mr. Butler let me leave for my free periods. I had two in a row."

"Well, that was nice. Come in here for a second, would you? I wanna get your opinion on something."

Her voice had a tone he hadn't heard in a long time. Bright and vivid even, fully alive. On his way to her bedroom, he passed his dad's study. Well, *former* study. It still looked odd, all hastily emptied, like someone had grabbed shit at random during a fire. Some left-behind office supplies were strewn across his desk, along with a few shards of broken glass from the ship in a bottle his mom nuked a few weeks ago.

"I was gonna surprise you with dinner," she said. "You spoiled it." She stood in the middle of her bedroom in workout shorts and a T-shirt. An exercise video played on the flat-screen.

"Sorry. But it smells great."

"You used to love it when you were a kid, remember? Cheesy chicken casserole."

"Right. Yeah. Um, awesome." The bedroom, like the kitchen, was sparkling and orderly. "You cleaned."

She laughed. "Yeah. I got tired of the drabness. Drabness is contagious. We needed some lightness in here."

"It's . . . awesome." He realized this was the second time he'd paused before saying "awesome." It made him sound suspicious, which, of course, he was. "You did all of this today?"

"Yep. Never underestimate the power of a triple-shot caramel macchiato. I put my head down and let 'er rip."

"And you made cookies?"

"Well, they're the ones from Graul's that come in the tube. I just laid the dough out in little globs on the tray. No biggie."

"Yeah, but still."

"Anyway," she said. "Your opinion. I need it."

"Okay. On what?"

She held up one finger and disappeared into her closet. "Okay," she said. "I did some shopping this weekend. Scored some new dresses." She came out in something with blue and white stripes. "What do you think?"

He took an involuntary step backward. The fabric revealed the shape of her hips, and maybe half an inch of cleavage. "Shit. Mom?"

She laughed. "Is that good? Is swearing good?"

"You look different."

"And I'm gonna do something with my hair, too. Sort of a spiky thing. I need to frame my face better."

"Right."

"Do you like the colors? I feel like the stripes are flattering."

"It's great."

"Okay, but how does it compare to these?" She went into her closet again. When she came back, she held three other dresses on fancy hangers. A red one, a black one, and one with a print. She looked at him, waiting.

"Is that snakeskin?"

"Well, not *really*. It's just a design. Is there one you like better than the others?"

Luke looked at the dresses. He had no idea. Not a clue. Who was this woman? "Maybe the red one?" he said. "Red is good."

"I agree," she said.

"Are you, like, going somewhere? Do you have plans?"

"No," she said. "Well, nothing specific. Not yet. I just thought, Why not make myself *available* for plans? I've been wallowing. I've been watching my own feel-sorry flick over and over."

"You've been watching what?"

"Nothing," she said. "Never mind. Your father is gone, Luke, and he's not coming back. I just thought it was time to make some changes. He got to make changes. Why not me?"

"Yeah," he said, even though what he wanted to say was, *So . . . you're not going to kill yourself, then? I can cross that off the list of things I need to worry about?*

"The red, then? It's your favorite?" She held it up to herself.

In seventeen years of being alive, he'd never assessed his mother like this. "Yeah," he said.

"Me too. Which is great, because I got some shoes to go with it. And they're perfect."

"Can I have some of those cookies?" he asked. "Or are they for dessert?"

"Sure. Why not?" She set the dresses on her bed. "Oh, and I have some bad news."

"What?"

"Your dad called this morning. He's in New York for the rest of the week. He can't make your driving lesson."

Luke bit the inside of his lip, pissed at himself for being surprised. "Is he there for work? Or is he with . . ."

She told him she wasn't sure, but he could tell she was lying.

"I wish I could teach you how, honey. But I've never driven a stick in my life."

"I know," he said. "It's not your fault. I'm glad you're feeling better, Mom."

"Luke?"

"Yeah?"

"It's just gonna be us now. We need to get used to that."

"I already am," he said.

"Ellen and Luke," she said. "You and me against the world."

29

When Mitch pulled into the driveway the next evening, the kids hopped off their boosters, and they all got out of the car.

"You seriously need to do something about those wood boards, Dad," said Jude.

"Yeah, Daddy," said Emily. "They're spiky. And they're broken."

They'd whined the whole way home from aftercare about the pieces of bed frame poking up between their heads. They weren't wrong per se. There were few good arguments for driving around with jagged planks in your car, but Mitch had a strict personal policy against showing weakness in front of his children, like how the government doesn't negotiate with terrorists.

"It's on my list, guys," he said. "Get your backpacks."

They pulled their book bags out of the back seat, along with the typical armfuls of take-home papers and art projects.

"What's that noise?" asked Emily.

They heard a rev, a grind, and then a screech. A combination of sounds like a dying animal.

Jude pointed next door. "Look. There it is."

He was right. Luke was in his driveway, sitting in his Jeep again. The sound they'd heard was him stalling the engine. Through the rolled-up window, Mitch heard a muffled "Fucking, fucking fuck!"

"Oh," said Mitch. "Well, that's not good."

"He said eff three times, Daddy," said Emily.

"Shoosh, baby."

He didn't invite the kids to follow him, but they did anyway, because they were kids, and their babysitter swearing in the driveway next door in a dope new Jeep was infinitely more interesting than whatever else they had on their schedules for the rest of that day. When Luke saw them approaching across the yard, he appeared to try to shrink to the point of invisibility.

Mitch tapped the door. "Hey, dude," he said.

Luke rolled the window down. "I hate this car," he said.

"Not going well?"

His knuckles were white against the steering wheel. There was an iPad on the passenger seat, running a YouTube video on how to drive a manual transmission. A man with a British accent was saying, "The friction point is key. When you find it, you'll most certainly know it."

"What're you doing, Luke?" asked Emily.

"I think he's trying to drive," whispered Jude.

"Oh. But the car's not on."

"You're not helping, guys," said Mitch.

Luke looked straight ahead. "Can you please tell me what in the hell the friction point is?"

Mitch loosened his tie and clapped his hands. "All right, kids. Come around. We're getting in."

Emily and Jude were thrilled as they climbed into the small back seat. The khaki-colored interior was clean and cool, and it smelled brand-new. "Do we need our boosters?" asked Jude.

"Put your seatbelts on, guys. We're just gonna be in the driveway for a few minutes." He reached back and helped Emily buckle up.

"This roof isn't like a real roof," she said. "It's like a pretend roof."

"It's a ragtop, honey," he said. "It's all part of the Jeep experience."

"Are you sure you want them in here?" asked Luke. "I'm clearly awful at this."

"Sure. I trust you, basically." Mitch turned off the yapping Brit and set the iPad at his feet before belting himself in. "Okay, Luke, where're we at here? How far have you gotten?"

"Not very far," he said. "I can't make it go. It's the stupid clutch. It doesn't work right." He looked on the verge of tears.

"How long've you been at it?"

"Half an hour. My dad was supposed to be here, but he's . . ." The rest was lost in scowls and teeth grinding.

Fucking James, Mitch thought. *Where the hell are you, you asshole?* It didn't matter, though, of course. All that mattered was that he wasn't there. Mitch remembered when his own dad taught him how to drive a stick, back in the day. "It's not as hard as you're making it, bub," he'd said. "The car knows what it wants."

"It keeps stalling. I've killed it like fifteen times. I'm gonna put it in neutral and push it into a river."

"Okay, that's a little dramatic. Why don't you fire it up? We'll give it a go."

Luke pressed the clutch in and turned the key. Everything rumbled to a start.

"Your mom's good, by the way?" Mitch asked. "Everything okay?" He'd been wondering about her since Luke bolted after the assembly the day before. The kid had looked genuinely spooked.

"Oh, yeah," he said. "It's fine. False alarm. She made cookies."

"Cookies?" said Emily.

"Not now, hon," said Mitch. "Our buddy Luke here is concentrating. He needs to be totally focused. Okay, now pop it into neutral and let off the clutch for a sec."

The Jeep rolled a lazy inch and steadied into an idle.

"The friction point," said Mitch. "It's a cool term, right? Like a book title or something. Kinda angsty. It's the exact spot when the clutch is out and the engine needs gas. It's when stuff happens. Every friction point's different, depending on the car. You just gotta find it, and, when you do, you hit it. That's the trick to this whole thing."

"Okay," said Luke.

"Now, put it in gear, then let off the clutch, and let's see what happens."

"It's gonna stall again. That's what's gonna happen."

"You're right. But this time, pay attention to exactly *when* it stalls. *That's* the friction point."

Luke lifted his left foot slowly. The Jeep lurched ahead, tossing them all forward against their seatbelts, and then died. A sickly little whine came from the engine.

"Is it supposed to do that, Daddy?" asked Emily.

"Um, should we get out?" asked Jude.

"See, man, right there. That jolt, right before it cut off. Time that. Right when you think it's about to die, give it some gas."

"Okay."

"Heads up, though," said Mitch. "I learned on my cousin's Nissan Sentra twenty-five years ago. This is a brand-new Jeep Wrangler. Much more powerful engine. If you hit it too hard, this thing'll take off like a rocket. We don't want that."

Luke nodded with grim determination and turned the key again. He held the wheel, ten and two, shoulders hunched. This was way too much car for him, Mitch knew, like handing Emily a bazooka, but all he could do here was help. It wasn't that different than teaching, really. You give them some tips, share some experience, and send them, woefully unprepared, out into the cruel, stupid world.

The Jeep started to shake; the engine muttered.

"Okay, there you go. Give 'er some gas."

Luke lifted his left foot. His skinny calf muscle flexed.

"Easy now."

The tachometer shot up, and the engine roared.

"Little less."

They rolled five feet, and the car died again.

Luke slapped the top of the steering wheel. "See?"

"No. That was good. You had it. You just got tentative at the last second. It's not as hard as you're making it. The car knows what it wants, Luke." Mitch smiled at his dad's words coming out of his own mouth. "One more time. Come on. You got this."

The engine turned over again. And, again, the Jeep shook just on the cusp of death as he released the clutch. This time, though, Luke timed it right and gave it just enough gas to save it from stalling. On gleaming custom wheels and trail-rated tires, the Jeep rolled along the pavement.

"Yes!" said Mitch. "See, man? You did it."

"We're driving," said Emily.

Luke grinned. The houses in the neighborhood were set back from the road, so each driveway was long and straight. Still, though, they made it to the mailbox in just a few seconds.

"Okay, that's good. Stop it here. We'll work on reversing."

But Luke didn't stop. Instead, he took a hard left turn out of the driveway and headed up the street. Mitch looked at his own house as they passed it and then watched it shrink in the distance. Emily and Luke smiled in the back seat. Booster seats be damned, they were on an adventure.

"All right, then," said Mitch. "I guess we're going for a ride. Hold on to those handle things, kids."

The rpms spiked. The Jeep wanted second gear.

"Okay. Time to shift, Luke."

"Really?" he said.

"Yep. They put five gears in this thing for a reason. Let's do it."

It was perhaps the roughest first-to-second-gear transition in the history of suburban driving. Luke gave the Jeep too much gas, and it lurched ahead again, like something released suddenly from a cage. But then it settled, and Luke let out a long breath.

"You're like an old pro at this," said Mitch.

"Thanks," said Luke. "I think I got it."

"Hell yeah, you do."

"Go faster, Luke!" called Jude.

Emily agreed. "Yeah. Let's race!"

For a few blocks, stuck in noisy second gear at just under twenty-five miles per hour, they drove on, and everything was fine.

30

"I heard about the girl at your school."

Scarlett Powers made a face like she didn't know what Jessica was talking about.

"The girl who tried to commit suicide, Scarlett."

"Oh, that. Yeah. She'll be okay. She just did it for attention, obviously. Mission accomplished, I guess."

"I think you're smart enough to know that that's a pretty enormous understatement."

"Yeah, but . . . *Advil*?"

Jessica made a strategic decision to let that go. She didn't want to spend the final moments of their session debating what did and did not make a teenager's suicide attempt legitimate. "You've never thought about doing anything like that, have you?"

Scarlett smiled a sideways smile. "Come on. You know me better than that."

And Jessica did. Scarlett was self-destructive, and she had an addictive personality, and she'd likely struggle with both of those things for the rest of her life. But she wasn't depressed. "Well, do you want to talk about it? Mr. Butler said some of the kids were pretty shaken up."

"I like how you call him '*Mr.* Butler,'" said Scarlett. "It's, like, very sub. You don't call him that at home, do you?"

Jessica ignored this, and Scarlett looked out the window. Rain clouds. A 70-something-percent chance of showers, according to everyone's iPhone. Spring in Baltimore. "Well, you clearly want to talk about something," she said. "You're being evasive. You're always evasive when something's on your mind."

Scarlett leaned forward and then back again, shifting. "Am I?"

"I've been at this a while. So let's maybe save each other some time. Why don't you put that 770 verbal score to good use?"

"Fine," said Scarlett. "I recently had a setback." She put air quotes around *setback*.

"You're using the terminology. I'm impressed. Okay, what kind of setback? Drugs? Stealing? Sex?"

Scarlett was still looking out the window. She smiled. "Yes, please."

Jessica waited.

"Darnell," she said. "Jiffy Lube. I went back. And this time . . . well, you weren't in my head handing out advice."

She noticed that the girl's ankle art was faded almost entirely now. "Well?" she said.

"Well what?"

"Tell me about it."

"You, like, want details? Who did what? I'm happy to share, perv."

"No, Scarlett. I don't want details. Was the experience positive or negative?"

"Well, we woke his roommate up because we were being so loud," Scarlett said. "So I'd call that pretty positive, wouldn't you?"

Jesus. This girl. It was like talking to a jaded, grown-ass woman. She could hang with the Wives drinking wine and wisecracking about penises. "*Emotionally* speaking, Scarlett. After it was over. On your way home. The next day. Now. How did you feel about it? How *do* you feel? About yourself?"

Scarlett went quiet, but Jessica could see that she wasn't evading; she was thinking. "We've been over this. How you feel *while* you're acting out is one thing. It hardly counts, because usually what you feel is euphoria. Like, a thrill. A hit of a drug. But when the thrill's gone? When that euphoria fades? Your feelings *then* are far more telling."

And now it was Jessica who was shifting in her chair. Sometimes at work she'd actually listen to herself. In this case, she might as well have shooed Scarlett out of her office and replaced her with a giant mirror.

Jessica's own ongoing emotional inventory had turned up only the slightest traces of guilt; virtually nothing. That was something to be concerned about in and of itself. But even more disturbing was how often she found herself thinking of Ryan. Weeks ago, spying on Mitch through a restaurant window, she'd doubted that a man could think about sex every seven seconds. But since she watched Ryan walk out of the food court, how many times had she thought of him? The way he'd felt inside her. His mouth on her. Him in her hand, helpless and near agony. And it wasn't just sex. She thought about his silly woodworking business. His Springsteen T-shirt. How effortlessly he'd made those Chinese ladies happy at the mall.

"I don't know," said Scarlett. "I actually felt pretty okay."

Jessica gave Scarlett a doubtful look. "Let's talk about attention for a moment, shall we?" she said.

"Okay," said Scarlett.

"Is that part of the draw for you? Attention from Darnell? From men in general?"

"Oh, fuck that," said Scarlett. "What am I, a toddler?"

"No, you're not. And neither is your classmate. The one you say was just looking for attention. Is her need for attention any different from yours?"

"Well, yeah. Totally." But then she went quiet, because she was smart enough to know that Jessica was on to something. "Okay, fine," she said.

Jessica wrote the word *attention* in her notebook, for no good reason, and underlined it.

"Is it bad that I get, like, a rush when I know that a guy wants me?" asked Scarlett. "When there's nothing to interpret? When he just thinks I'm hot as fuck, and that's all that matters?"

She thought of Ryan's face as he took her clothes off—of the utter lack of ambiguity in his expression. "This isn't about good or bad, Scarlett," she said. "Remember?"

"Oh, stop it," said Scarlett. "That's therapy talk."

"No, it's not bad. It's natural. Desire is part of sexuality. Being desired."

"Truth," said Scarlett.

"But here's the catch. You have to want it, too."

Scarlett smiled. "You know what?" she said. "You're right."

"Am I?" Jessica put her legal pad down. "You've never said that, Scarlett. This is a first."

"No, for real," said Scarlett. "It's the sequel to Me Too. Hashtag I Want It Too. Let's do a manifesto together and send it to *HuffPost* and get famous."

Jessica looked at her phone. The clock on the screen ticked away. "Well, I haven't been published in a while."

Their session was over, essentially. Just a few seconds left. But Scarlett wasn't quite done yet. "Listen," she said. "I know you want me to say that I feel tortured, and having sex with dudes means nothing, and it's like some attention-delivery device or whatever."

The iPhone screen flashed 0:00.

Scarlett rubbed at the ghost of a pretend tattoo. "But what if that's not the case this time? What if it's different?"

"What do you mean?"

Scarlett looked flustered. In fact, unless Jessica was mistaken, the girl was blushing. "Darnell was really sweet to me. He asked me if maybe I wanted to be his girlfriend. Like, go steady or whatever. Can you believe it? God, my parents would shit."

Her phone kept flashing its zeroes. Jessica did her best to keep her expression still as she pondered this terrible, terrible idea. "Just be careful, Scarlett," she said.

When the girl was gone, Jessica looked out her office window. The rain had arrived, transforming the city below into a glossier version of itself. She turned off the timer on her phone and then checked the fake email account she'd created to see if any new women wanted to have sex with her husband.

31

Eight hours later, Mitch sat alone at Tark's, a restaurant in the northern suburbs.

It was the last place he'd expected to be on that Friday night, particularly by himself. The week had wound down as usual—his classes, his service as the faculty sponsor of the school's literary magazine, his trips through the pickup line at aftercare to get the kids. But when he walked in the door, he found Jessica at the kitchen table looking at her phone.

She said hello to the kids and asked them about their days, like she always did. They hung their backpacks on the banister and ran upstairs to change.

"Pizza tonight?" Mitch asked. "Or we could try that new Thai place by Nacho Mama's. I hear they give you, like, fifty fortune cookies." He was already thinking about how nice it'd be to put on his sweatpants.

It was as if she didn't hear him, though. "Guess what?" she said. She looked up at the ceiling, making sure the kids were fully out of earshot. "You've got a date tonight."

———

Tark's was a pretty decent bar and grill next to a doctor's office and some faceless office buildings. He hadn't been there in years, and he found that he was the only person in the whole place who wasn't part of a plural. It was all couples and groups, and it was an older crowd than downtown.

Since marrying Jessica, Mitch had sat like this in bars and restaurants waiting for her more times than he could possibly count. But now he was waiting for someone else—a stranger—and he couldn't stop fiddling with his ring finger.

"I know it sounds unseemly and all, but you're gonna want to take that off," Jessica had told him earlier, pointing at his ring. The kids were in the other room enjoying some screen time. "It's just too complicated otherwise. Trust me."

He twisted it a few times before taking it off.

And then she helped him pick out his outfit. Jeans and a nice button-down and his teaching blazer, because that was what she'd told the online woman he'd be wearing. When he looked at himself in the mirror, all dressed and ready, he thought of Alan. All he needed was one unbuttoned button and a neckful of cologne.

Once Mitch's profile was up, the matches had come in pretty steadily—five right away, then a handful more over the course of the week. Jessica monitored them, categorizing and eliminating, until she'd settled on a woman named "El."

"Look," she said. "I like her." She'd handled all text correspondence, pretending to be Mitch, which was even more unseemly than his ditching his wedding ring, but there were so many things wrong about all of this that it hardly mattered anymore.

"Yeah? You think?" He looked at the small, grainy picture of the woman she'd picked for him. According to her info, she was forty-five, a little older than him, and up for an adventure. Like Mitch's picture, hers was indistinct, but seemingly attractive.

"El," he said. And then he said it again, "El. You think it's her real name?"

Jessica tilted her head. "I don't know, *Will*. Does it really matter?"

"Jesus," he said. "Could this be any fucking weirder?"

The bartender came by, and Mitch ordered a Jack and Coke.

The Orioles game was on mute above the bar, but he had trouble focusing on what was happening. His hands were shaking, he felt hot under his jacket, and he kept asking himself one unanswerable question after another.

Was he nervous, or was he excited? How did one actually initiate sex with a stranger? Would it happen organically, or would it require saying something like, "So, should we have all the sex now?" Statistically speaking, what were the odds that this was all a ruse by an online psychopath? Was he about to be murdered and have his skin made into a lampshade? Would this entire night eventually be dramatically re-enacted on *Dateline NBC*?

"Mitchell?"

He looked up, and there was a woman standing next to his barstool. She wore a blue-and-white-striped dress, and she was smiling. Her hair was short, blondish, kinda spiky, and she had on a lot of makeup. She was familiar. Mitch knew her. He was sure of it.

"It's me," she said.

He squeezed his drink. "Hi there."

The woman laughed. "God, Luke was right. I guess I really *do* look different, huh? Maybe that's a good thing."

"Excuse me?"

"Mitch, it's me. Ellen. Your next-door neighbor, you dope."

"Ellen?"

She waved to the bartender. "Hey there. Can I get a cosmo?"

Ellen took her first drink down with purpose, barely pausing to breathe, and for a while, even though she'd sidled up onto the stool next to his, they didn't talk much. Mitch was too busy being on the verge of panic, because in a moment, a woman in a red dress was scheduled to arrive. That woman would not be his wife. How would he explain this to his next-door neighbor?

"Are you meeting Jessica?" she asked.

"No," he said.

Ellen waited, and he realized that more information was required.

"She's at home. With the kids. I had a parent-teacher thing at school. Needed a drink after three hours of one-on-ones with angry moms."

Ellen's face sank. "Shit. Was that tonight? Was I supposed to be there? I didn't get an email."

"Oh, well, no," he said. "It wasn't mandatory. Just conferences for parents of kids who're . . . having trouble. Luke's definitely not in that category."

He was, indeed, a terrible liar, but it worked, and Ellen relaxed. "Thank God. That'd be just like me, right? Spacing on my first official week as a single mother."

He looked at the half-empty bowl of sweaty peanuts on the bar in front of them. "Yeah," he said. "I was sorry to hear about you and James."

She nodded. It was one of those "it is what it is" gestures that people make when their lives have been flipped over like a Monopoly board.

"What about you?" he asked. "You meeting a friend or something?"

Ellen turned shy. "Not exactly. More of a date. Well, kind of. I'm not sure what you'd call it, exactly."

"Yeah? Great. Good for you."

"Getting back on the horse, right?" She laughed. "Horse. What am I even talking about? Isn't it funny how utterly ill prepared we are sometimes to talk to other human beings?"

"Nah," he said. "You're fine." He clinked his glass against hers. "To horses. Or whatever."

In the years she'd been their neighbor, Mitch had talked to her only marginally more often than he'd talked to James, which wasn't very often at all. He liked her well enough, though. Once, a few years back, she got locked out of her house in the rain and had a glass of wine with

Jessica and Mitch in their kitchen while she waited for the locksmith to show.

"I'm meeting him here," she said. "It's an Internet thing. All the kids are doing it, right? I figured, why not?"

She flagged down another drink, and Mitch glanced at his watch again. El was ten minutes late. Maybe she wasn't coming. Or maybe she was already there, watching him from a distance in her red dress and wondering who this other woman was.

"Can I be one hundred percent honest with you about something?" Ellen asked. "Since we're neighbors and all."

"Okay," Mitch said.

"I had a drink before I got here. Two, actually."

Mitch saw a woman in a pink dress. Pink wasn't red, though. Another woman wore something that could possibly be described as burgundy. "Well," he said, "it's Friday, right?"

"I'm nervous. This whole thing is terrifying. How do people do this day in and day out? If this is single life, honestly, I'm gonna lose my mind."

"Don't be nervous," he said. "You look nice. That dress is great. I dig the stripes."

She looked down at herself. "Thanks. It's flattering, right? I just got it. Tonight's the maiden voyage." She made a little sound like a ship's horn. "Okay, more honesty. I changed into this at the last second. I had on this red thing at first. Serious vamp dress. It was so tight I could barely breathe. But I totally chickened out. I was like, Do I wanna show up to my first new encounter with a man in twenty years looking like some middle-aged prostitute?"

The mingling noises in the bar all faded to a dull hum in the background as Mitch stared at the cubes of ice floating in his drink. "Did you say it was red?" he asked.

Ellen nodded. "*Very* red. Like a fire truck."

He looked back at the door one last time. El wasn't coming, of course. El was right here. El was Ellen. He picked up his drink, took it down in two gulps, and ordered another one.

"And you wanna hear something that's *really* pathetic?" she asked.

"I'd love to," he said.

"I've been reading a book. Self-help. I know how cliché that sounds, but, well, it got me out of the house, right? Here, look." She unzipped her purse and showed him the cover. *Light Your Own Fire: Why Feeling Better Is Up to You.*

Mitch probably would've rolled his eyes at this a month before—hell, maybe an hour before. But as he sat there, thoroughly married and on an unwitting hookup date with his next-door neighbor, he knew that he was in no position to judge anyone for anything.

"It goes on and on," she said. "Blah, blah. These kindsa books always do. But the crux of it? It's so simple. Stop letting other people be in charge of your happiness—of your self-worth. If you're sad, then, guess what? It's up to you to get *un*sad."

Her drinks were starting to add up. Mitch could see that. The alcohol swirling in her system gave her words a dose of heartbreaking sincerity.

"Sounds like good advice," he said.

"A self-help book that actually helped. Who knew?" She looked at the hostess stand. The first signs of worry were starting to show on her face. "Come on, Will," she whispered. "Where are you at, buddy?"

Mitch felt sad for her. And then he felt sad for himself, too, and for Jessica, and for the Husbands and the Wives, and for everyone there at Tark's, and for the world at large: for humanity in general.

Fifteen minutes later, her fourth drink mostly gone, all hope lost, Ellen tugged at the shoulders of her new dress. "Janice Perkins can kiss my ass," she said.

"Who's Janice Perkins?"

"The author of this dumb fucking book, that's who."

"It's not dumb," he said. "Like you said, you're out. You're dressed up. It's a win, right?"

"If you had any idea how uncomfortable this bra is, you wouldn't call it a win."

"Maybe he was nervous, too," said Mitch, trying. "This Will guy. You know, maybe he's scared to get back on his own horse. Like you said, this stuff is scary."

She tried to get the bartender's attention but failed. "I don't know," she said. "Do men really think like that? Do men actually have feelings?"

He finished his Jack and Coke and smiled as best he could. "Believe it or not," he said, "they do."

As he drove back toward his neighborhood—*their* neighborhood—the incongruity of Ellen's presence in the passenger seat of his car was so vivid that he kept glancing over at her as if she wasn't quite real.

To the best of his recollection, a woman had never sat there who wasn't his wife. She positioned her arm on the door differently than Jessica did. She crossed her feet on the floor mat in a way that Jessica didn't. Ellen was shorter than Jessica, so her head touched the headrest differently.

"Thanks for driving me," she said.

"Oh. Yeah. It's on the way. Obviously."

They both tried to laugh.

"So, what's all that stuff in the back?" she asked.

He could see the pieces of wood in the rearview mirror, cracked and splintered and jagged, bouncing as they drove.

"Is it a . . . bed frame?"

"We're getting a new one," he said. "The garbagemen wouldn't take it, so I put it back there. I need to take it to . . . wherever you take things like that."

He braced himself for a follow-up question, but it didn't come. Instead, she touched her window absently with her knuckles—in a way, again, that Jessica never did. "I was gonna Uber home," she said. "Responsible, right?"

"Very," he said.

"Or maybe I was gonna let *him* drive me home. Because, you know, maybe that's how the night would've played out. Maybe we'd've gone to his place for a nightcap. I was kinda winging it, I guess."

NPR whispered through the car stereo, something about birds migrating across Delaware. He lowered the sound until it was just wheels on pavement.

"I guess that was the point, though, right?" she said. "The fact that I didn't know what was gonna happen. That I was open to whatever. Now that I think about it, that was the most exciting part of it, you know. The possibilities."

A mile up, he turned onto Buckingham Road. They were only a few minutes from their respective houses when she asked him to pull over.

"Are you okay? Are you sick?"

"No. I don't know, exactly. I just need a second."

He steered off to a small, U-shaped run of gravel and stopped some twenty feet from the road. On Saturday and Sunday mornings, a truck from an organic farm up north parked there and sold fruits and vegetables, but it was clear now. He shifted to park, and Ellen folded her hands in her lap and looked out the windshield. Some insects floated drunkenly out ahead of them, catching the light from a street lamp nearby.

"Ellen?" he said. "You okay? You good?"

"You're not wearing your wedding ring," she said.

He touched the absence there—the dent in his skin.

"I noticed in the bar earlier. I didn't know you and Jessica were having problems."

"We're not," he said. "Well, not exactly. It's . . . not straightforward."

A truck rumbled by, shaking the ground. "I understand. It happens slowly, right? Then it happens all of a sudden. One day you're arguing about whether or not to paint the first-floor powder room, the next day you're smashing some stupid ship in a bottle in his home office."

The car felt stuffy. He turned on the AC, and the air hummed.

"I have a question for you," she said.

"Ellen," he said. "Just—"

"You're Will, aren't you? You're my date."

"Yes," he said. "And I'm sorry. I didn't figure it all out until you said that thing about your dress. I didn't know if I should say anything."

She sighed, then laughed. "It's actually a relief. I thought I got ditched. I was scared maybe he saw me and took off."

"You didn't," he said. "And *he* didn't."

"Our profile pictures," she said. "Neither of them look very much like us, do they?"

"Not really, no."

"That's probably a sign," she said. "For both of us."

Ellen had stumble-walked her way to his car through the parking lot when they left together. But she sounded perfectly coherent now—downright levelheaded.

"A sign of what?" he asked.

"That we're not ready for this. I mean, we're ready enough to go online and fill out the questions. That's something. But we're not ready enough to actually do it. We're in transition."

Mitch was just going with it now, because this was all beyond explanation, even to himself—a misunderstanding on top of a misunderstanding overlooking a deserted suburban access road. He reached down to shift into drive, but she put her hand on his hand.

"What did you think when you saw me?" she asked.

"What do you mean?"

"You didn't recognize me at first. For a few seconds, I was just a woman in a bar."

"Oh, right."

Her seatbelt was off. Her body was turned to his. Her dress was tight against her chest. "Were you attracted to me?"

In truth, the answer was no. Mitch wasn't attracted to her or unattracted to her. He was too nervous to be anything. He couldn't tell her this, though. She'd bought a dress. She'd changed her hair and put on makeup and called an Uber. She'd read a book. She'd allowed herself to be excited, and none of this was her fault. "I thought you were lovely," he said.

Ellen smiled. "You did?"

"Of course. Yeah. Totally."

She touched his hand, stopping him again from putting the car in drive. She'd let her uncomfortable-looking heels fall to the floor of the car, and now her legs were curled up under her. The bottoms of the windows were beginning to fog against the cool April air outside. "Maybe we could help each other," she said. "You know, help each other get through the transition part."

He looked at his dashboard, all the gauges and lights and numbers.

"The fact that we know each other—that we're not strangers— might make it less scary."

And then she kissed him.

Her lips were different than Jessica's. Add that to the list. They were drier and fuller. The blur of her face was different, too, just centimeters away. When she removed her mouth from his, she opened her eyes slowly and rested her forehead against his forehead. "That felt good," she said. "I've missed that."

"Ellen," he said. "I think—"

"Shh," she said. "Don't talk. I wanna feel that again."

32

Luke had seen Scarlett's Instagram before.

The boys at Ruxton Academy were very familiar with their female classmates' social media accounts.

A lot of the girls at school put it all out there online. They posted grids full of bikini pics every summer from pool chairs and beach houses: a never-ending montage of sunburned skin and hips and midriffs. They stuck their tongues out and wore halter tops and made blow-job eyes at their phones. They pretended to make out with their girlfriends and licked giant ice cream cones suggestively.

Scarlett's Instagram, though—in fact, her entire online persona— was pretty frustrating.

As he scrolled down, there were close-ups of her pen tattoos and sketches from her notebook. A grim reaper drawing. A deer with enormous black eyes. There was a whole series of pictures of a beat-up pair of red Chuck Taylors set against different backdrops. Band posters. Vintage movie artwork. A boomerang of raindrops splashing off a puddle in a parking lot. A dying flower drooping next to a flower in full bloom.

The shots that actually *did* feature her weren't much more revealing. They were always of her alone, because she didn't really have any girlfriends that Luke knew of, and she was never smiling, either. He stopped on a photo of her in a baggy sweater with her hair tied up in a bun. She'd pulled the woolly neck up over her mouth, so it was just her nose and her eyes. Midway down, he found one he'd seen before, a selfie, in which she rolled her eyes. There was a lake behind her, and an out-of-focus sailboat. It showed her from the mid-chest up, and he could see just enough to know that she was wearing a swimsuit— possibly a bikini. One of the straps had slid slightly askew, revealing a faint tan line.

Since experiencing the full impact of Scarlett's attention at the suicide assembly—as bored as she'd seemed—his mind kept coming back to her. She'd busted him staring at her several times since then, which was embarrassing. Once in the hallway. That was Thursday. He played it off with a wave, which seemed reasonable, since she'd talked to him and all when they were sitting next to each other, but she'd just frowned at him. That very afternoon, she'd caught him looking at her foot in Mr. Butler's class. Her legs had been crossed, and one of her Sperry boat shoes dangled from her toes. When he moved up from her shoe to her face, he found that she was looking at him, like, *Why are you staring at my foot, you fucking weirdo?*

He checked his bedroom door.

This was just force of habit; his mom was out. She was in her red dress earlier, and then she was in her striped dress, all flustered and nervous, the Uber sitting out in the driveway. "Don't wait up!" she'd told him, laughing as she dashed out of the house.

He untied the drawstring at the waist of his shorts and focused on Scarlett's lips in the lake picture.

Luke had kissed exactly two girls in his life, the first of whom hardly counted, since it'd been eighth grade and a dare. Kissing Scarlett would be an entirely different sensation, he imagined, like the difference between flying in an airplane and being launched into the atmosphere aboard the space shuttle.

And then Luke saw headlights through the gaps in his blinds.

It was just a car—not a huge deal—but on a Friday night, their block was usually still and quiet, so it was unusual enough to stop him from doing what he was about to do.

The car moved along at a normal clip, but then it slowed. And then it pulled to the curb one house down from his and stopped all together.

It was Mr. Butler's Honda CR-V. The headlights went dark.

Luke pulled his shorts back into place and went to the window. There were two people in the car, talking. He could see their silhouettes through the windshield. Mr. and Mrs. Butler, he assumed. When the passenger door opened, Luke leaned closer to the window, and he saw a woman step out. She looked back and said something. The headlights came on again and the car pulled away from the curb. Luke recognized the dress. The striped one. It definitely wasn't Mrs. Butler.

The security alarm beeped.

He went downstairs and found his mom taking off her shoes in the entryway. She tried to set her purse on the hall table, but she missed, and it fell to the floor. "Fucking A," she said.

Luke flipped on the light, and she looked up, startled. "Luke, Jesus," she said. She'd spent an hour on her makeup earlier, making sure it was just right, but it was different now, smeared at her mouth.

He thought of how happy she'd looked before, laughing on her way to the Uber. She didn't look like that now. "Are you okay?"

"I'm fine, Luke," she said.

"Why were you with—"

She stopped him, though, her voice sharp. "I'm going to bed," she said. "Turn out the lights and lock things up, okay?"

33

J essica heard the front door open.

She listened as Mitch climbed the stairs.

The fact that he was stepping so carefully—like he was trying to be quiet—was actually funny, as if somehow she might be asleep instead of sitting up in their floor bed waiting for him to come home.

Oh, sorry, dear. I must've dozed off while you were out having sex with the woman I found for you on the Internet.

Before he left for his date, Jessica had kissed him. You'd think she'd have gone all out, like she was kissing a marine on his way to fight some endless war, but it was as standard and absentminded as any goodbye kiss she'd ever given him.

He didn't come to their room right away, because he never came to their room right away. He followed the path he always followed. Jude's room first, because it was closest to the stairs. He spent a minute there, and then he went to Emily's room. All the while, Jessica sat wondering what exactly she wanted him to tell her.

Yes, I did it. We're even.

No, I didn't. Because I couldn't.

And then there he was, standing in the bedroom doorway. His jacket was off and his shirt untucked. He looked tired, but no more tired than he always looked at this time of night. She read his face, searching for meaning.

"Hey," he said.

"Hi," she said.

"How was your night?" he asked.

Jessica laughed. "Mitch, I don't know if this situation really calls for small talk."

"That's fair," he said.

They stood looking at each other—her waiting, him not talking—and for Jessica, all the doubt she'd felt was erased. She didn't know why, exactly, but she was suddenly sure. Right or wrong. Even or not. It didn't matter. Jessica wanted him to tell her that he hadn't done it.

"Just a minute," he said. He grabbed a pair of shorts and a T-shirt from the top drawer of his dresser. "I'll be right back."

In his closet, standing among his clothes and shoes, Mitch looked in the mirror.

He slid out of his jeans and took his socks off and then looked at the mirror again. Pantsless and barefoot in an untucked oxford shirt isn't a great look for a guy his age, so he looked away as fast as he could. He thought about what had just happened, and about what he was going to tell Jessica.

He stepped into his mesh sleeping shorts, and then he took his shirt off. The wound on his right shoulder—reopened now—was pink and tacky with blood.

The second time Ellen kissed him had been far more intense than the first time. Her hands got involved. They gripped his thighs and then slid over his crotch. Somehow, she was able to maneuver herself over the center console between them, and before he fully understood what was happening, she was planted between him and the steering wheel, straddling him.

"Grab my breast," she told him.

"What?"

"My boob, Mitch. Like this." Ellen took his hand and pulled it onto the rough fabric, and she moaned.

His back and head pressed against the driver's seat—he had nowhere to go. "Ellen," he said.

She lifted herself, moving her breasts over his face. The hem of her dress slid up, and he could feel her against his jeans. He said her name again, but she ignored him, unbuttoning the top three buttons of his shirt and burying her face in his chest.

He didn't want this, because this was ridiculous. This felt wrong. She was Luke's mother, and he was married, and they were in their forties, and the fucking road was right there. But before he could articulate any of this, a lightning bolt of pure, glowing pain shot through his shoulder, and he screamed.

Ellen jumped back, blasting the horn. "What?" she said.

"Ouch," Mitch said. "Fuck."

"What is it? Are you okay?"

He touched the source of the pain and absorbed another quick strike. He hit the dome light, which turned the car closing-time bright, and they both squinted. In the rearview mirror, he saw the bite mark, beside his right collarbone, ridged and angry-looking, left there by two perfect rows of teeth.

"Jesus Christ," she said. "Did I do that?"

No, Ellen didn't. Jessica did. The night this all started—the moment before their bed snapped and they fell to the floor. Jessica bit him as she came. "No," he said. "Old injury."

Ellen smiled. "Whew." And then she kissed him again.

This time, though, he was able to turn away. "Ellen," he said.

She looked surprised, and then hurt. Mitch's hand was still on her breast.

"We can't," he said.

"Really?"

"Yes."

"But you said I was lovely."

"You are, Ellen," he said. "But I just can't do it."

———

Mitch stepped out of the closet in his pajamas. Jessica had come out from under the covers and was sitting cross-legged at the center of the mattress, waiting for him.

"I'm just gonna brush my teeth really quick," he said.

And maybe he would've gone on like that, finding things to do—household errands to tend to. *I should shave. I should see about that wobbling ceiling fan. I should really go file our taxes.* But Jessica wasn't having any of it. "Mitch," she said. "Did you do it?"

Mitch knew that she didn't want to hear that El was Ellen. She didn't want to hear that he couldn't do it. If she did, she wouldn't have sent him out into the night by himself in the first place. So Mitch decided to tell her what he knew she *did* want to hear.

"Yes," he said. "I did."

34

"If you think about it, sex when you're married is a lot like going to spin class."

The Husbands fell silent.

Mitch, Doug, and Alan stared at Terry. They were five minutes into a discussion about Tara, the redheaded spin instructor. They all belonged to the same gym, and she'd become something of a folk hero to them. Doug heard a rumor the week before from the guy who made protein smoothies that Tara was gay, which, for the Husbands, was both intriguing and devastating.

"I can kinda see it," said Doug.

"I'd *like* to see it," said Alan.

"She could beat the shit out of any of us," said Doug.

"I'd literally *pay* to have her beat the shit out of me," said Alan.

And then, apropos of nothing, Terry had said that thing about sex and spin class.

"What?" said Alan.

"Go on," said Mitch. "I'm genuinely interested to hear the second half of that."

Terry reveled briefly in the undivided attention, and Mitch assumed that he was about to say something offensive. Terry was the most crass of the four, a characteristic that had only intensified since his affair and subsequent divorce. The lying and betraying, sneaking and conniving had somehow managed to sharpen his already-jagged edges.

Terry cleared his throat and smiled. He was wearing a Metallica T-shirt—skeletons, guitars, and lightning bolts. "Yeah. When you're done, you're always glad you did it, right? But, sometimes it's just a hell of a lot easier *not* to go to spin class, you know."

Doug and Alan laughed.

"Did you just come up with that?" asked Mitch. "You could probably rewrite it as a haiku."

"Oh Christ," said Terry. "Stop being such a geek. And no. I saw it on a meme, I think. Online somewhere."

"That's what I hate about the Internet," said Alan. "Every time I have a brilliant thought, I have to stop and think, Is that mine, or did I see it on Twitter?"

This was the general trajectory of their conversations—random and bouncy, yet somehow continuous—the result of four men who'd known each other long enough to make transitions unnecessary. In the last two hours, they'd discussed their spin instructor, the removal of back hair, The Divorces, the Orioles' inability to develop pitching, the creeping power of Internet porn, the Wives, and now, marital sex.

Mostly, though, they'd talked about how much they hated IKEA.

They were in Terry's apartment downtown, putting together what appeared to be the world's shittiest bunk beds, which Terry's sons would be sleeping on every Wednesday night and alternating weekends. They'd torn into the boxes with no clear strategy, so there was cardboard, plywood, brushed metal, and bubble wrap everywhere, and enough poorly labeled nuts and bolts to reconstruct a World War II fighter plane.

"Fucking IKEA," said Terry.

"What do you think SVÄRTA means, anyway?" asked Doug. "Who names these things?"

"I think it's Swedish for 'Americans are dipshits,'" said Alan.

The sum total of their work had produced a wobbling, crooked mess that looked like scaffolding that had been torn off an abandoned building. Terry tossed a piece of wood onto the floor. "This thing's gonna collapse and kill my kids in their sleep, isn't it?"

"Seems like a safe bet," said Alan.

"Yeah," said Doug. "Inviting us here has basically made us accessories to gross negligence."

"Why is this even necessary?" asked Alan. "Don't they already have beds?"

"They most certainly do," said Terry. "But they wanted *bunk* beds."

"Those little shits," said Doug.

"You could've gone to a *real* store, you know," said Alan. "One that sells preassembled furniture with pronounceable names."

"Fucking tried," said Terry. "The boys insisted on this thing. Their idea of heaven is running around IKEA eating meatballs and picking out shit for me to put together."

An Oriole hit a single, and they watched him take a wide turn around first on Terry's insane television.

"I blame my dad for this," said Terry. "He has tools. A big fucking workbench. All that shit. Why didn't he teach me things?"

To a man, the Husbands shared some degree of physical incompetence, a fact that was perfectly exemplified by Doug, who dropped his IKEA-issued wrench for the tenth time that night and then called it a "Stupid, stupid whore."

"What do you expect, dude?" said Alan. "You're too jacked for tools that small. You've lost your fine motor skills."

"It's all that fucking CrossFit," said Terry. "You gotta tone that shit down, man. You look like you should be bullying Ralph Macchio."

They watched baseball for a while and continued to pick on Doug for being in such good shape, which was more entertaining than the Orioles. It was only April, but the poor team already seemed doomed. The young centerfielder blew an enormous pink bubble with his gum.

Alan's phone vibrated on the coffee table, and he practically leapt for it. He'd been distracted all night, checking it every thirty seconds. Mitch watched his face come to life when he looked at the screen. He quickly texted something back.

"Is that . . . ?" asked Mitch.

Alan grinned. The phone vibrated again, and he texted back.

Nearly two decades ago, Mitch had watched this very same guy take a deep breath and walk across a crowded house party to talk to the lanky, complex-looking giantess who he'd eventually date, marry, and divorce. And now he was tapping on a little screen talking to a girl in her twenties. *The modern-day Circle of Life,* Mitch thought, *complete with a soaring Elton John vocal.*

"Hey," said Terry to Alan. "Less texting, more working. This thing isn't gonna fucking construct itself. That much I promise you."

"Sorry," said Alan, although he made no move whatsoever to stop doing what he was doing.

"Who're you texting, anyway?" asked Doug. "Your girl?"

"Maybe," said Alan.

Terry tore open a bag of tiny washers, which rained down on the floor like summer hail. "Proud of you, buddy. Back in the game." He punched his own palm a few times, which, as far as Mitch could tell, symbolized sex.

"You guys, shut up," said Alan. "I'm working on something here." There was another buzz, and then he held his phone up in triumph. "There it is. Check this out."

The Husbands abandoned their IKEA posts and gathered around Alan's outstretched arm. Terry put on his reading glasses. For a moment, they didn't know exactly what they were looking at.

"Is that . . . ?" said Terry.

"What is it?" said Doug.

"Is it a boob?" asked Terry. "Am I looking at tits here?"

"No, it's not a boob, you Neanderthal," said Alan.

"Wait, no, it's a shoulder," said Mitch. "That's definitely a shoulder."

"Yeah," said Alan. He sighed like a lovestruck fourteen-year-old on a ten-speed. "She's got all these freckles. I'm obsessed with them. Look. Aren't they sexy?"

In a delightfully PG-rated move, Alan's new girlfriend had sent him a close-up of her own freckled shoulder.

"Oh, right," said Doug. "Look at those. They *are* sexy. Not for nothing, though, she should probably have a regularly scheduled appointment with a dermatologist."

"They're on her chest, too," said Alan. He swiped his thumb to the left and there was a second picture. Another close-up—probably

PG-13 on this one. Little brown freckles between two clavicles, the shadowy hint of cleavage at the top of a sundress.

"Man," said Doug. "The female anatomy, right? It's just the best. Undefeated. Bravo."

"Whatever," said Terry. "We're adults. I'm not gonna eye-fuck some girl's shoulder. Call me when you get nudes."

"Why are you so dead inside?" asked Mitch.

The Husbands went back to work, but their enthusiasm for Project SVÄRTA had waned considerably. And then it fell apart altogether when Alan got yet another text and suggested that it might be time for a break.

"No way," said Terry. "We're nowhere near done yet. Look at this piece of shit."

Mitch saw something in Alan's smile, though, and knew something was up. "Why?" he asked. "What'd she just text you?"

Alan shoved a few half-built pieces of SVÄRTA aside. "Well," he said, "she's with three friends down at Ale Mary's in Fells Point. And she's asking if they can come over."

There was silence, except for Jim Palmer, the broadcaster on TV. "That's a nice pitch," he said. "Right at the knees."

"Hmm," said Doug. "That definitely sounds like more fun than this."

"Fuck," said Terry.

He went into the kitchen and came back with four beers. The Husbands opened them together, as they'd done countless times, in bars, at O's games, in one another's houses, at the beach, on road trips, in backyards, in parking lots, at concerts, and at a million other places.

"My kids are gonna kill me," said Terry.

35

They were reading a story about a bear in the forest whose hat gets stolen by a rabbit. It was a delightful book, and the simple fact that it wasn't *Go, Dog. Go!* made it that much better. Jessica found herself reveling in the beautiful silliness of it.

"How do you think the rabbit stole it in the first place?" asked Emily.

"I don't know," said Jessica. "Maybe he snatched it while the bear was sleeping." She pointed to a line of words on the page, which meant it was time for Emily to read. There was a drawing of the bear talking to a turtle that stood next to a rock.

"Have you seen my hat?" read Emily.

When the book was over—the hat found, the rabbit dealt with—story time transitioned into cuddle time, and Jessica and Emily lay together in silence for a while, Emily's head resting on Jessica's shoulder.

"If E.T. comes into my room tonight, it's okay, because Jude taught me how to be brave."

"Yeah?"

"Yeah."

"I'm pretty sure he won't, honey, because he's not real, like we've talked about. But how would you be brave?"

"By counting."

"Counting?"

"Yeah."

"Oh. Okay."

She scanned the clutter on the surfaces and in the corners of the room. All kids are hoarders, but Emily was reality show–worthy, and Jessica promised herself that she'd do another purge at some point that spring. Out with everything but the essentials.

She felt her iPhone buzz in her back pocket. Mitch, probably. She didn't look, though. He was with the Husbands for the night, and frankly, she was relieved to have him out of the house. Their time together since Mitch's date with El had been exhausting. She never could've guessed how much energy it would require to appear perfectly fine and downright cool with the fact that he'd had sex with another woman.

"Your shirt looks pretty awesome," said Jessica.

Emily was in her new Orioles T-shirt, which she'd insisted on wearing to bed, even though it wasn't jammies. It needed to be washed, of course, because, along with being hoarders, kids are hopeless slobs.

"Mm-hmm," said Emily, drifting. "Can we read *Go, Dog. Go!*?"

No, God. No! Jessica thought. She had a recurring fantasy in which she opened the back door and tossed *Go, Dog. Go!* out into the pitch-black suburban woods.

"Not tonight, sweetie. Tomorrow. You're nearly asleep."

"Well, can you tell me the dog story about you and Daddy, then?"

"Why do you wanna hear that old thing?" She eased her arm out from under Emily's head. She'd be asleep in ninety seconds.

"'Cause I like it."

Jessica slung one foot onto the floor. When your kid is on the cusp of sleep, exiting their room is a delicate operation, like backing away from a bomb. "It was our first date," she said. "Your daddy picked me up in an old Honda he borrowed from your uncle Alan, because he didn't have his own car yet."

"Lame," said Emily. She always said "Lame" at this part of the story, and giggled.

"He didn't have any money then. None of us did."

"Where'd you go?"

"We went out for pizza near Hopkins. The place isn't there anymore. It's an LA Fitness now, but it used to be a weird little pizza spot."

"What did you eat?"

"Taco pizza."

"Gross."

"It actually was, kind of, but I didn't tell your dad that."

Emily's eyes were closed. "Why not?"

"Sometimes you know something will hurt someone's feelings, so you don't tell them." Jessica thought about the three-question rule. Of all their thrown-together guidelines, that one was both the most infuriating and essential, because she knew that all the questions she wanted to ask Mitch were ones she'd never want to answer herself.

Emily pulled her comforter up and rolled onto her side: her go-to knockout position. "What happened when you were done eating?"

"We talked for a long time. The people at the pizza place started mopping the floors and putting chairs on the tables so we'd get the hint."

"Yeah. Did you?"

"We did. When we went back out to the street, there was a car parked near Uncle Alan's. It was crooked, up against the curb, and the engine was on. Someone had left it running."

"What was in it?"

Even when she was about to be out cold, Emily kept up her end of the story, delivering her lines well. Jessica's lines were mostly the same, too, like muscle memory.

"That was the weird part," she said. "There was a dog in the car all by itself. A big yellow Lab. And it was sitting in the driver's seat. It even had its paws up on the steering wheel, like it was about to drive off."

"That's funny," Emily whispered.

"I know. We stopped to look at it. We would've taken a picture, but we didn't have camera phones back then."

"What did Daddy say?"

It was Emily's favorite part of the story—Mitch's silly quip from twenty years ago, the one that cemented his status as the funniest guy Jessica knew. Alas, Emily would have to wait until next to time to hear it, because she was fast asleep.

Jessica checked on Jude next. He was also asleep. Beneath his peeling constellation of sticker stars, she turned off his reading light and left as quietly as she could.

The blinds weren't usually open in the upstairs hallway window, so when she walked past it en route to her room, she noticed Luke outside again, on his stump. She shook her head and moved on, heading toward her room, where she flopped down on the bed. At that particular angle, stretched out on her back, her iPhone dug into her rear end, and she remembered the text message.

There wasn't a name, because she hadn't saved this particular number as a contact. It didn't matter, though. She'd memorized it weeks ago, when she watched it being slowly written on her wrist.

36

The Orioles won, somehow.

The shortstop hit a walk-off home run in the ninth, and the Baltimore crowd went wild. The shortstop's teammates threw water and sunflower seeds on him when he touched home plate. A few minutes later, when the shortstop was being interviewed on TV, one of the outfielders jumped into the shot and hit him in the face with a pie. Some of the pie got on the reporter, but she didn't care, because everyone was so happy.

The Husbands would've been thrilled about all of this if they'd been paying any attention at all. They weren't, though.

The game had been relegated to a muted background blur, and "Gin and Juice" by Snoop Dogg shook the speakers. Before that, "Jump Around" by House of Pain played. And, right before that, "Gangsta's Paradise" by Coolio. Terry had a music collection like no other, complete with crates full of vinyl and four looming CD towers, saved from college, and of course a thoroughly modern digital archive. At the moment, though, it was all about the nineties hip-hop station on Pandora.

Terry, Doug, Mitch, and Alan—the Husbands—were drinking and full-on dancing, just the four of them, as they waited for their guests. At first, they'd just stood there, swaying, beers in hand, the four of them, to "California Love" by Tupac and Dr. Dre. But then they'd started cutting loose, because, well, it was funny, and it made them forget how old they were.

Terry dragged the doomed SVÄRTA and all its boxes and misfit parts and pieces into the kids' room, so there was plenty of space. The Husbands shouted "Biatch!" along with Snoop and laughed.

And then came the knock at the door. They were expecting it, of course. Terry had just notified his doorman, Gilberto, that guests were on their way. Still, though, all four men froze.

Terry turned the volume down with an app on his phone. To Mitch's surprise, he didn't say something Terry-like, like "Game time, motherfuckers." Instead, he looked suddenly worried. "Wait," he said. "You think we should change the station?"

"What? Why?" asked Alan.

"These chicks. Were they even alive when this music came out?"

The Husbands did some quick back-of-the-envelope math and determined that, yes, the girls standing out in the hallway were, in fact, alive in the 1990s.

"Still, though," said Doug, "Terry's got a point. Does it make us look old?"

There was another knock at the door.

"I think it's our faces that make us look old," said Mitch. "And . . . time."

"By the way," said Doug, "have you considered a daily moisturizer? I'll email you a few links."

"Thanks," said Mitch.

"Relax," said Alan. "It's just music. You guys, seriously, don't embarrass me."

Alan's shirt was tucked in now, his top button open again. Doug and Terry had stepped it up, too. Doug had done a quick fifty pushups to make his arms look even more ridiculous, and he'd borrowed some hair product from Terry's bathroom. Terry, tapping into his home-field advantage, had changed out of the Metallica shirt into a nice polo and some darker jeans. All three of them, Mitch realized, looked better than he did.

This is what being single requires now, he thought. *You have to con-*

stantly be on high-alert. You have to have the ability, in a matter of min-
utes, to go from half-assedly building IKEA furniture with a bunch of
dudes to entertaining women.

Alan went to the door. The sound of female voices came from the
entryway. And when Alan returned, four girls were with him. Their
youth, vivid and glowing there before them, had wattage, like Christmas lights. "Guys," he said, "this is Jenny."

Jenny.

It was the girl from Alan's phone, all freckled and blond, in three
dimensions, and it dawned on Mitch that until that moment he'd never
heard her actual name. "Hey, Jenny," he said.

Terry and Doug said hello, too.

She was shorter than Mitch had imagined her to be, particularly in
the context of a decade and a half of seeing Alan with Amber. She
looked nervous standing in her sundress and nice flip-flops, but she
smiled through it and tossed her jean jacket onto the couch. "Hi, guys,"
she said. "What's up?"

"And these are Jenny's friends," said Alan. The three girls behind
Jenny smiled. Jenny introduced them as Kristen, Abigail, and Molly.

Abigail stepped up in front of the other girls. She had jet-black hair
and smoky eye shadow. She nodded her head along to the music. "Vintage rap," she said. "This stuff is dope. Turn it up."

The Husbands all looked at the ceiling, because that was where
"Funky Cold Medina" by Tone Loc was coming from. Mitch couldn't
speak for the other Husbands, but he was pretty sure each of them was
asking the same question silently in his own mind: *Did she say* vintage*?*

made this for you.

An instant later, an image appeared. It was a delicate-looking end table made of lightly shaded wood.

It's a complicated feeling when something you tell yourself you don't ever want to happen happens, and you're left knowing that you've been lying to yourself.

Jessica sighed.

That's lovely. But you shouldn't be texting me.

She hoped that wasn't too harsh. Apparently not, because Ryan totally ignored it.

What are you doing right now?

She imagined this happening on a normal Saturday night. She and Mitch would be sitting on the couch downstairs having a civil debate about what show to stream, or whether or not they should open a bottle of something. He'd notice that she got a text, and he'd notice her reading it. "Who's that?" he'd ask. But on that particular Saturday night, Mitch was gone.

I'm alone. Going to do some reading.

He's not there?

She felt heat blooming like some prickled flower on her skin—her lower back and palms.

No. He's out.

He. Her husband, the pronoun.

What are you wearing?

None of your business.

Something sexy?

She looked down at her long-sleeved T-shirt and Lululemon pants and her chipped toenails.

Not at all.

If you're wearing it then it's sexy.

I suppose lines like that work well for you.

As she watched the text-bubble bubbling, she chastised herself for how well it *had* worked on her. Everything. All of it, from his first glance at her breasts weeks earlier at Bar Vasquez until this exact moment.

Send me a pic.

Jessica smiled. This was harmless. Mitch had had sex with someone. She had had sex with someone. There were no Rules against this.

A pic of what?

Be creative.

She took a total of nine pictures before she got the one she wanted. None of her face, of course, because as foolishly as she was behaving, she wasn't a fool. She focused just below her breasts and down to the waistband of her stretchy pants, which she slid down strategically—low enough to reveal the soft V shape at the very bottom of her stomach, but high enough to cover her faint C-section scar. She looked at the picture for a moment. Her belly and hips, admittedly, weren't the features she was most confident in, but taken lying on her back with the overhead light dimmed, the image on her screen looked objectively quite sexy. She hit Send.

OMFG!

Jessica laughed.

Stop it.

Ur so damn hot.

She didn't respond, and for a while, he didn't either. Jessica lay on her bed, phone in hand, clothes back in standard wearing position. She wondered if they were done talking. Perhaps she even hoped they were, because, again, it was harmless. But then her phone buzzed, and a photo of Ryan's chest and stomach appeared, and air escaped her lungs.

See look. I have a stomach too.

She looked at the digital version of the chest she'd run her hands over, and the abdominals she'd bitten. A headless underwear manne- quin turned to flesh.

You should work out more. You're getting fat.

LOL

So, we've established that we both have stomachs.

Yes we have.

She ran the bottoms of her feet along the soft comforter. Her bed- room door was open, so she got up and closed it. She wiggled out of her pants, discarding them on the floor near her closet, and got back into bed to find another text message. Still harmless enough, right?

Your turn.

It only took three tries to get this one right. A photo of her black underwear.

Damn

She hated emojis, but she sent him one with a smiley face and tongue hanging out. And then she texted, Your turn, and waited.

Jessica didn't bother lying to herself this time. She knew what she wanted, and it wasn't a picture of *his* underwear. Ryan knew this, of course, and when the photo arrived a moment later, more air escaped.

She thought of Megan and Sarah complaining about their phones being inundated with these images. Looking at it now, though, her lower lip held firmly between her teeth, she was certain it was the sexi- est thing she'd ever seen. It wasn't just that it was hard. She could find a million of those if she wanted to. It was that it was hard for *her*.

Hello you, she texted back, and then she grazed her right nipple over her T-shirt with the tip of her finger.

You're alone right?

I am.

And so am I.

We've established that we are both alone.

She wondered if this was how it went. *Sexting*. Despite being totally accurate, it was such a stupid word. Regardless, there was no turning back now. She wondered if they'd take turns? Would she tell him to do things to himself and then be told to do things to herself?

Then he texted her back.

Come over.

38

So many things change.

Knees go bad and temples go gray. Dad bods appear one day in the bathroom mirror with zero warning. The world gets warmer, and thousand-year storms batter pristine landmasses. Priorities shift, net worths expand, and children are born. There's progress, and then progress is replaced by proud anti-progress. Net worths are halved, apartments are rented, and custody is negotiated.

But so many things don't change at all.

Like, for example, the effects of alcohol and music.

For the first fifteen minutes after Jenny and her friends arrived, it could've been a junior-high mixer in Topeka, Kansas: boys on one side, girls on the other. But then the orange crushes that Alan made for the girls broke the divide, and it became a party.

"That's the thing, though. This nineties stuff. It's fun and all, but it's kinda just bullshit party rap, isn't it?"

That was Kristen, talking shit about their music. She wore a short gray dress and a pair of Vans, and she had a small orange-and-red Baltimore skyline tattooed on the pale skin of her right inside biceps. The song in question was "Hypnotize" by Biggie Smalls, and Terry was deeply offended.

"What the fuck are you talking about, lady?" he asked. "You've just committed sacrilege."

"No, I mean, no offense to the OGs and all that. They paved the way. But they weren't exactly saying much, were they?"

They listened to a lyric in which the singer admitted that he liked being called "Big Papa." Terry gave Kristen a big thumbs-down, but she sipped her drink and stood her ground. "I mean, listen to it. It's all about hooking up and drinking. That's it. Getting bitches and being stupid."

"And those are bad things?" asked Doug.

Kristen lifted her sweaty glass. "No, not necessarily. But it's pretty lightweight. Here, give me that. I'll show you. You have Spotify on this thing or what?"

She took Terry's phone, which he'd been using to hop around from song to song, and started tapping away with her thumb. Mitch instantly liked her. She was clearly the edgiest of the four girls. "Now, see?" she said. "*This* is what I'm talking about."

The Notorious B.I.G. cut out, and a Kendrick Lamar song came on, all bass and anger.

Mitch recognized it. It was called "Loyalty." He'd downloaded the album after the rapper won the Pulitzer for music so he could talk about it in class. Doug, Terry, and Alan knew it, too, and everyone embraced the tonal and generational shift in the room. The Husbands switched from beers to hard alcohol, which they poured together at Terry's decked-out rolling bar. The girls kept at it, too. Occasionally, someone yelled, "Shots," and things eventually fogged over in Mitch's head.

Alan and Jenny held hands as they danced. He kissed her neck, and she squealed and laughed, and then they made out.

"Get a room!" yelled one of the girls.

"Loyalty" ended, and another song from the album came on. Then another song after that. The girls were in charge of the music now, and with each passing song it got louder. A$AP Rocky. Childish Gambino. Drake. Mitch was in the middle of all of it—the swirl of dancing and flirting and laughing and joking and musical smack-talking. And then he noticed a phenomenon. It was subtle at first, but it became increasingly obvious with each passing song. The people around him were coupling up.

Alan and Jenny were already together, of course, what with the making out and all. But it was happening with the others, too. Molly was the most athletic-looking of the girls—lithe in her dress, like a pole vaulter—and Mitch felt the gravitational forces in the apartment pull her toward Doug, whose shirt, thanks to the pushups, now appeared a full size too small. A similar tug occurred between Terry and Abigail, who were mixing drinks and discussing the view of the lit-up Domino Sugar sign over the harbor.

That left Kristen and Mitch.

They were two lone satellites in this tiny man-made galaxy of slowly colliding planets. She looked at him and looked away. Clearly she'd noticed what was happening, too.

And then Jenny briefly pulled herself from Alan's grasp to shout, "Hey, Mitch. You're an English teacher, right?"

Mitch admitted that he was.

"Awesome!" she said. "'Cause Kristen's a writer."

Of course she is, Mitch thought.

39

Jessica rang the doorbell and put on her old glasses. The world blurred for a second, then cleared when he opened the door.

"I didn't think you'd really c—" he stopped and smiled. "Nice glasses," he said.

"You like them?" she asked.

"Smart women," he said, sighing, and Jessica nearly took off her jacket right there on his stoop. She didn't, though. She told herself to be patient. He reached for her and pulled her into the house.

She hardly remembered the previous thirty minutes—all harried and thrown together in her head. She'd checked the kids again and then gone to the window that overlooked Luke. He was startled when she called his name.

"Oh. Mrs.— Hi."

"What're you doing right now?"

"Now? Well, I'm . . ." Instead of finishing his sentence, he held up a book. "You know, at first, I just sat out here to avoid my dad," he said. "But it's actually a really good reading spot."

"Can I ask a favor?"

"Okay," he said.

Jessica looked over at James and Ellen's house, mostly dark. She wondered if Ellen was in there. "Can you do some quick babysitting?"

"Um, Mr. Butler isn't there?"

"No," said Jessica. "He's out."

She slid into her new black dress and looked at herself in the mirror. And then she dug the glasses out of the back of the junk drawer on her side of the bathroom and hid herself with the longest jacket she could find. When Luke arrived, he had more questions about Mitch, which was weird, like he was suspicious, but Jessica was probably just being paranoid. "I won't be long," she told him. "It's just an errand. I forgot something."

Her hands shook as she sat in the car. She checked the time, started the engine, and then checked the time again. She told herself to relax. Mitch never came home early when he went out with the Husbands, and there was no reason to think that he would tonight. Like always, he'd surely stumble up the stairs at 2:00 A.M. after chugging water and tearing into whatever he could find in the kitchen. She had plenty of time.

Ryan's little house was the same as before. It smelled like sawdust and paint thinner. The end table from the photo he'd sent her was next to the sofa.

"Can I take your jacket?" he asked.

As she removed her coat, she took in the expression on his face— that stupid, spacey look, as Scarlett would've called it—and she smiled. She could get addicted to that look.

"My . . . God," he said.

"What, this?" she said.

When he kissed her there in his entryway, she leaned back against the door and pulled him close. His hands were on her body, a frenzy of sensation. She pulled away and touched his face. She'd never seen him *not* scruffy, but he was even scruffier now, to the point that his stubble had turned soft. He bit her throat gently, and she closed her eyes.

"Oh, wait," he said.

"What?"

"My roommate's here."

She looked over his shoulder. The room was empty.

"In the basement, I think, with his girlfriend. She's kind of annoying. We should go upstairs."

She pulled the hem of her dress down. One of her sandals had come off in the excitement, and she slid her foot back into it.

He kissed her again, quick this time. "Come on," he said. "Let's go."

40

"I'm actually not a real writer," Kristen said.

"Oh?" said Mitch. "What does that mean?"

"I'm actually a third-grade reading teacher."

"That's awesome."

"I write a little, though, like, on the side. Nights. Weekends. When I'm not totally exhausted. I haven't published anything, though."

"Well," said Mitch, "every published writer spends a good bit of time being an unpublished writer. Part of the gig." He'd heard a writer say this once, and he wondered if he'd repeated it right—if he'd arranged the words correctly. He must have, because she smiled.

"I'm gonna tell my mom that the next time she reminds me how much dental hygienists make."

He leaned in to hear her, and she leaned in to be heard, and she smelled lovely. Not Starbursts, like Jenny, but good nonetheless. Some other candy, maybe. They were talking in Terry's kitchen now—a study in barren stainless steel—but there were speakers mounted everywhere, so it was still loud, and Mitch had lost track of how many drinks he'd had. Everyone else was out in the TV room taking turns playing music from their respective eras. Mitch and Kristen were tucked away a bit, but they could still see their friends through a cutout in the wall over the sink.

"Both my sisters are hygienists," she said. "They have cars and houses—like, *real* houses. I live in a one-bedroom with that ho over there." She pointed to Molly, who at present was next to the flat-screen, showing Doug her impressive right calf muscle.

Doug nodded, chin in hand. Over the noise, Mitch heard him say, "So, you're a toe-striker when you run. That's how you get all that definition."

"Can't hardly blame her," said Kristen. "If I had legs like her, I'd be showing everyone my calves, too."

Mitch glanced down at the girl's short legs, which were perfectly nice as far as he could tell. The Vans on her feet had *Wonder Woman* logos on them, which made him laugh.

"You have nice teeth, by the way," she said.

"I do?"

"Family business. It's my curse. I'm conditioned to notice every-one's dental situation. And you look *exactly* like an English teacher, too, by the way. It's kinda scary."

"I've been told that," he said.

"It's not a bad thing. I like English teachers."

"I was gonna wear my tweed blazer, but it's warm tonight. Seemed like overkill."

Kristen smiled. "Good call."

He'd forgotten what this felt like. The rush of being this physically close to a girl he barely knew—and making her smile. "So, what?" he said. "Short stories? Novels? Nonfiction? Flash fiction? What do you write on nights and weekends?"

"Essays, mostly," she said. "If I get enough of them, maybe I'll try to, I don't know, get an agent or something. That's what writers do, right? Get agents?"

"I have no idea," he said. "Sounds right, though."

"I have seven essays that I don't totally hate. Fifteen pages or so each. Which feels maybe halfway there."

"I'd love to read them," he said.

She looked up. "You would?"

He said yes but found himself suddenly brokenhearted with the knowledge that (a) he never would, and (b) he was only saying this because he found her attractive.

She tucked some hair behind her ear—just a simple thing he'd seen girls and women do a million times—but he found himself considering what it'd be like to bite her there, lightly, just above her star-shaped earring. Maybe she'd sink into him. Maybe she'd like it and go all dizzy and dumbstruck.

"I could send them to you," she said. "I don't know if they're good yet. They probably aren't. I want them to be. I'm trying to make them good."

For nearly twenty years now, when students pre-apologized for their writing, he told them to stop it—to own their work, dammit. Amateurs apologize, not writers. But he let it go this time. Partly because he wasn't her teacher, but mostly because he could see how much she cared.

Someone yelled "Shots!" again from the TV room.

It was Jenny. She stood over four shot glasses full of perfectly clear liquid, holding a saltshaker and a little lime-shaped squeeze bottle of juice. "And this time," she said, "we're taking it up a notch."

Kristen and Mitch stepped back into the TV room, and they, along with Abigail and Terry and Molly and Doug, stood watching, because everyone knew what was coming. Despite their age differences, they'd all been on spring break. They'd all been too drunk in bars, in summers past. They'd all made questionable tequila-related decisions, and they'd all woken feeling shitty and full of regret.

Jenny stood on the tips of her toes and slowly licked Alan's neck.

"It's *Girls Gone Wild* in this place!" shouted Terry, and Molly shook her head. Kristen shrugged up at Mitch and smiled.

"That's right, ladies," Jenny said. "Body shots." She sprinkled salt in the crook of Alan's neck and held her shot glass up for the crowd. Then she licked the salt off Alan, took the drink down, and squirted lime juice into her mouth, straight from the bottle. When it was over, Terry stood stunned-looking, like the victim of a slow-moving hit-and-run, and Jenny set the shot glass upside down on the bar. "Your turn, bitches!"

Abigail looked at Terry, and he smiled. "I'm not scared," he said, and when she licked his neck, he grinned and said, "Wait, wait . . . a little to the left," and everyone laughed.

Molly, the athlete, took her time with the whole thing when it was her turn, making a show of it for her friends. She wrapped one toned leg around Doug's waist—no easy feat—and had her way with him and her drink.

And then they were all looking at Mitch.

As drunk as the Husbands were, he could see conflict in their eyes, like each of them was thinking, simultaneously, *Are you really gonna do this?* and *You're not really going to do this, right?*

Jenny, Abigail, and Molly showed no such signs of inner turmoil. "We're waiting!" said Jenny.

Kristen looked up at him. Another shrug. She walked around the couch and passed her friends to get her shot and its accoutrements. When she returned to Mitch's side, she said, "Maybe this'll make a good essay someday."

The sensation of the girl's tongue on his neck took his breath away. And then it took it away a second time when she licked the rough salt off his skin. She put her hand on his chest both times, flush against his heart, supporting herself as she stood, like the other girls before her, on her toes. When Kristen swallowed the shot and the little blast of lime juice, she batted her eyes up at him and bit her lip, and that nearly took his breath away, too.

It took Mitch a second to recover while the Husbands laughed and applauded. And then it took him another second to realize that his hand was in his pocket—his left one. It'd been there this entire time: when the girls arrived, while he chatted with Kristen, while she used him as a human salt lick.

Maybe he'd put it there on purpose, maybe not. Either way, the result was the same. His ring was hidden from view. He was taking a break from being married.

41

He undressed her this time.

As frenzied as everything had been downstairs, coming up to his room reset things, and he moved more slowly.

"This dress is hot," he said, "but it's stupid. I don't think you should be wearing it." He reached around and pulled the zipper down from the nape of her neck, and then he went to his knees as he guided her dress down over her hips and legs. He kissed her stomach, and she squeezed the top of his head and twisted his hair.

The light stubble of his chin brushed against her belly, and he looked up at her. "I just realized," he said. "You know that I don't even know your last name?"

"It's Butler, but that's not imp—"

The rest of this was lost when he bit her gently. He stood up and smiled. "Nice to meet you, Jessica Butler." And then he told her that her bra was stupid, too. "Even worse than that dumb dress."

In just her underwear, it was cooler in his room than last time, and goosebumps rose on the bare surface of her skin. He rubbed her arms with the palms of his hands. "You're cold. I could adjust the AC."

She kissed him, though, to stop him from being like this.

In her pre-Mitch life, Jessica had slept with a total of five guys. Some of those guys were crazy about her, and some of them simply wanted to fuck her. The ones who were crazy about her acted like Ryan was acting now: lovely and sweet and gentle and concerned. But that was not why she was there.

She sat on his bed and looked up at him. "Why are you wearing so many clothes?" she whispered, and then she watched him strip down to his boxer briefs. She lay down on her back, and he settled gently on top of her.

Anticipation was loud in her head, like blood rushing.

"Did you see the end table I made you?" he said into her neck.

"What?"

"I set it out so you'd see it."

"Oh," she said. "Yeah. It was nice."

"I never used that color stain before. I think it turned out really coo—"

She bit his lower lip and grabbed him over his underwear to shut him up. She rolled onto her stomach, and he kissed her between her shoulders and down her spine. As he pulled her underwear down, she closed her eyes and he kissed her lower back. He took a handful of her hair and pulled, which was exactly what she wanted him to do.

She imagined the possibility of years and years of this.

Forget reality and jealousy and an infinite number of unanswerable questions. Her happyish life with Mitch could continue on, and every once in a while a beautiful stranger would make her gasp. It'd be like some French movie, explicit and subtitled. The full evolution of a marriage.

Her iPhone had been cast onto the floor next to the bed, atop her dress. She opened her eyes at the exact moment that its screen lit up. It was a text from Luke.

Are you coming home soon Mrs. B???

The messages flowed from there, one text after another popping onto her screen.

Jude started freaking out.

And then Emily started freaking out.

I don't know what to do.

Never seen them like this.

They keep asking where you and Mr. B are?

"Are you okay?" Ryan asked.

She rolled over and pulled a blanket over herself.

"Jessica?"

"My kids," she said.

"Your kids? You . . . you have kids?"

She nodded and watched his face transform; she watched the desire fade.

"Yes," she said. "And they need me."

42

There aren't a lot of buzzkills as thorough and deadly as a mirror.
As Mitch stood in Terry's bathroom looking at himself, though, he was somehow able to set aside the papery skin under his eyes and the mother-of-pearl of his teeth and the fact that he looked, quite clearly, forty and drunk.

Jessica had told him that having sex with someone else made her feel alive again, and as rap music thudded along on the other side of the bathroom door, Mitch got it. The look Kristen gave him in the TV room, her saliva still damp on his skin, had made him feel just that.

Alive.

The barista, and the bookstore woman, and the girl from Towson U, and even Ellen straddling him with her tongue in his mouth . . . those weren't actual temptations. They were pratfalls—moments of slapstick in his ham-fisted middle age. This was different. He took a breath and put his hand on his chest, where his heart was working double time. He took another breath, and then another, willing it to slow down. This was a calming trick he'd taught himself when he was a student teacher, years ago, and was nervous facing rooms full of bored-looking students.

He put his ring in his pocket and gave himself one last look in the mirror.

When he opened the door, there was music and laughing, and his intention was to rejoin it—to find Kristen and see where things went. But on his way down the short hallway that led to the kitchen and TV room, he passed Terry's kids' bedroom. He could've walked right by, but he didn't. Instead, he stopped to look at the half-built SVÄRTA, which was piled like a shipwreck in the corner beside two small desks, one for each of Terry's boys. There was a chest of drawers and two soon-to-be-replaced single beds, crisply made. Terry's oldest, Will, was Jude's age, and his youngest, Trevor, was a few months older than Emily. The sparseness of their room here at their dad's apartment was jarring. There was a crayon drawing of a purple and black raven on one of the desks. On the opposite bed, a stuffed monkey lay on its side. It still had the price tag stuck through its ear. There was a kid-sized baseball mitt at the foot of the other bed—stiff and rigid, obviously never used. That was it.

Together, the effect of these random things caused a silence in his head powerful enough to drown out everything else.

It was a chillingly lifeless space, like a room in an institution for wayward boys, and he thought of Jude's and Emily's rooms at home, cluttered with Legos and chapter books and life. With discarded art projects, Hot Wheels, fidget spinners, and Beanie Boos arranged just so. He thought of Jessica and Emily painting Emily's room together the previous winter. It was a project for the women, they insisted, barring Mitch and Jude from helping. Jessica wore a bandana as a headband, and Emily painted her bright-pink initials on the white primer.

Mitch had seen the kids no more than four hours earlier. But now he missed them so intensely that he had to grip the molding around the doorjamb because his knees felt so weak.

When he got to the kitchen, it was empty, and he stood next to the refrigerator and thought about what he was going to say to his friends and to these girls he'd just met, to Kristen. He could see all of them from where he stood, clustered together. The Husbands were laughing, dancing like goofballs, because that was the only way they knew how. The girls were dancing, too, and they were all barefoot now, their flip-flops and strappy sandals cast aside, except for Kristen, who still wore her *Wonder Woman* Vans. He silently wished her the best—the best in her writing, in being a third-grade reading teacher, in life.

And then he put his ring back on and left.

43

"Just hold up a sec, okay?"

Ryan was walking and putting on his jeans at the same time. It looked like dancing, and he nearly fell.

She grabbed her shoes off the floor.

"What's the deal?" he asked.

"They're afraid of E.T.," she said. "My kids."

"What? *E.T.* E.T.? The alien?"

"Yes. It's this whole thing."

He laughed and zipped his jeans. "So they're not, like, hurt? They're not dying? They're scared of a fictional character, and so you have to leave?"

"Yes."

He put his hand on her hip, pulling her back to him, away from the door. He put his other hand on her breast and kissed her neck. "A few more minutes of being scared won't kill them, you know. Right?"

"Ryan, I have to go."

"You're fucking serious?"

She pulled away, and he stepped back, and she could see by the look on his face that he genuinely didn't get it. Someday, maybe, he would. He'd have a kid, and that kid would be scared and calling for him, and he'd think back to this moment. But for now he was just some dude in a row house. He might as well have been from another planet.

"Fine," he said. "At least let me walk you out."

"You don't have to. My car's just around the block."

She shut his bedroom door and headed for the stairs. On the first floor, sawdust grit hit the soles of her feet, and she held the banister to put her sandals on.

Ryan came down after her. "Stop it. Didn't you watch *The Wire?* We're in Bodymore, Murdaland, here."

It would take her twenty to twenty-five minutes to get home, depending on the stoplights, and she thought of Emily and Jude not knowing where she was, and it made her feel sick to her stomach. She didn't belong here. This entire thing was a mistake.

Halfway to the front door, she was startled to see that there was someone else there, standing in the kitchen. Shirtless, like Ryan, he was black, and he had shockingly blue eyes. Both of which were now fixed on her.

"Oh shit," he said. "Sorry, guys. Didn't know anyone else was here. We're making nachos if you want in."

Even in her current state, Jessica could plainly see that he was gorgeous. Behind him, facing the open refrigerator with a hand on her hip, stood a girl with mismatched underwear and messy hair. She was skinny and pale, and even from behind, Jessica could see that she was younger than all of them. There was a mole on her back. Her shoulder blades protruded like budding sparrow's wings. Jessica noticed all of these things at once, but it was the girl's right ankle that made her stop walking. A blotch of faded black pen ink, like a bruise.

"Darnell, what the hell?" the girl said. "Did you seriously not get me my root beer?" Then the girl turned around. And when she did, she saw Jessica. "Holy . . . fucking . . . shit."

It was Scarlett Powers.

Ryan held Jessica's coat. Darnell held a bag of Trader Joe's corn chips. Neither of them moved.

Scarlett looked at Ryan and then back at Jessica. "Wow, though, Doc. That dress is hot as shit."

44

M itch might've beaten her home.

And how would that've gone, exactly? Him walking in the front door to find his wife gone and his frightened children huddled on the sofa with Luke from next door.

But that's not what happened.

For Jessica, every traffic light glowed green—an unbroken string of them—from Locust Point down Key Highway, around the Inner Harbor, and onto 83. As for Mitch, as he left Terry's apartment and got off the elevator in the lobby, instead of making a beeline for the door, he stopped to watch highlights of the Orioles' dramatic victory on the small TV that the doorman, Gilberto, kept at his desk.

"Four hundred and twenty-five feet," said Gilberto. "A bomb!" He mimed the shortstop's perfect swing.

"No shit?" said Mitch. "A walk-off?"

And then, instead of immediately calling an Uber, even though he wanted so badly to look in on his sleeping kids, he decided to hit the all-night convenience store at the end of Terry's block for a soda. Some caffeine would clear his head for the ride back to the suburbs, and more important, when he kissed Emily's and Jude's foreheads in their rooms, maybe he'd smell like a fountain drink instead of beer and tequila.

"Hashtag parenting," he said to himself, aloud. A couple walking together nearby looked at him, probably wondering if he was insane. "Good evening," he told them.

Consequently, Jessica and Mitch pulled into the driveway at almost the same time: first Jessica in her car, then Mitch in his Uber.

"Looks like you have a friend, sir," the driver said.

Mitch looked up, confused. He'd been zoning out in the back seat on the way out of the city and into the burbs, playing on his phone and fielding texts from the Husbands.

Dude, where'd you go?

Did you ghost us?

Mitch "The Phantom" Butler.

He hadn't even realized the car they were following was Jessica's until that moment. He finished the last of his soda and dropped it in a small trash bin that hung from the seat in front of him. "That's my wife," he said.

Jessica had more time to prepare herself than Mitch did.

She'd watched the Uber in her rearview as it followed her up their street, knowing, somehow, that it was him.

She pulled into the garage and thought about what she was going to say—how she'd explain all of this—as the headlights lit up the driveway behind her. She wondered what would happen if she told him everything. Just one long, rambling release of truth, starting with the feel of Ryan's number being teased across her wrist at Bar Vasquez and ending with nearly being taken from behind half an hour ago in the city. After all, that was one of the Rules, right? Not a formal one, but probably more important than any of the others. Total honesty.

His Uber backed out and pulled away, and then it was just the two of them there in the driveway. He flipped his wrists gently at his sides, the universal sign for "What the hell's going on?" Mitch didn't know where she'd gone, of course, but he knew enough. There were so many questions to ask that he couldn't decide which one to start with. Instead, all he could think to say was, "Jesus Christ, look at your dress."

"Mitch," she said.

He waited.

"We're gonna go inside, okay? Luke's in there with the kids."

"Luke?" He looked next door and thought of Ellen, over there in that dark house somewhere.

"Yeah," she said. "I'll explain everything, okay? I promise. But for now let's just go inside."

She was walking away from him, toward their front door. "Or maybe you don't," he said.

"What?"

He thought of Kristen's tongue on his neck, of the casual intimacy of leaning into each other like they had. He thought of hiding his ring, and of Ellen pressed up against him, and of dream Jenny in her cross-country outfit and running socks. He didn't want to tell Jessica about any of it. And he sure as hell didn't want to hear about her night— about where she'd been and who she'd been with, dressed like that. "What if we just go inside, and that's it?" he said.

"What do you mean?"

"What if we just tuck the kids in and pretend none of this ever happened? All of it. The whole thing."

Jessica stepped out of her heels right there in the driveway and stood barefoot, her costume removed. "Don't ask, don't tell," she said. The floodlight behind her lit up an elaborate spiderweb over the garage, like a piece of Gothic artwork.

Mitch nodded.

"Okay," she said.

She picked up her heels, and Mitch followed her into the house.

PART FOUR

THE FRICTION P•INT

45

Scarlett Powers was smiling.

She was an intimidating girl on an ordinary day, but sitting there in Jessica's office, legs crossed, uniform skirt hiked, she looked positively frightening.

"Sooooooooo," she said, long and slow. "How ya doin'?"

Jessica held her writing pad in her lap, squeezing the edges. This was their first session since Ryan's kitchen. She'd been dreading this. It was going to be awkward, obviously; the entire situation was endlessly embarrassing. But more than that she dreaded what she knew she was going to have to do.

She'd played their moment at Ryan's house over and over in her head. Scarlett standing there in her underwear. Ryan and Darnell frozen to the point of utter stillness, like the dug-up remains of some ancient people wiped out by sudden plumes of volcanic ash.

Jessica cleared her throat. She picked up her pen and then set it back down on her pad. "Scarlett," she said.

"At first, I seriously thought I was hallucinating," said Scarlett. "I was like, am I dreaming this? Did Darnell drug me or something?"

"Scarlett," she said again.

"So, you and Ryan? You're *doing* it? He's like, what, your side piece? How did that even happen?"

"Scarlett, this is a very unusual situation."

She snorted. "Ya think?"

"Yes, I do."

"It's actually kinda funny, you know, from my perspective, if you think about it. The tables have turned pretty hard here, Doc. I mean, we have *you* slut-shaming *me* nonstop for, what, like ten months? Like some kinda nun in a convent. And then I find you with JBF hair at my boyfriend's house. You gotta admit, it's pretty validating."

"I haven't been slut-shaming you," said Jessica. "Scarlett, is that honestly what you think I've been doing?"

"Don't get me wrong. I don't blame you. God, look at the guy. I mean, how could you say no to something like that? Girl's gotta do what a girl's gotta do. Hashtag I Want It Too, right? Like we said."

"It's not like that," she said. "It's not what you think."

"It *is* a little sad, though. Mr. Butler and all. I feel bad for him. He's, like, the only teacher in the whole school that doesn't make me wanna gouge my eyeballs out from boredom. This oblivious guy, going about his daily English-teacher life, while his wife gets raw-dogged by, like, the hottest guy ever. What if he finds out?"

Jessica gripped the arm of her chair. She imagined Scarlett raising her hand in Mitch's class. *Mr. Butler, I don't really have a question. It's . . . more of a comment.*

Scarlett read her perfectly. "Relax. That's not what I meant. I'm not, like, gonna tell him. This is . . . this is your shit. He doesn't have to know. None of my business."

Jessica didn't relax, though, and she was fairly certain she never would. Information was like a virus, and this girl was patient zero, wandering carelessly through Smalltimore, talking to everyone she saw.

"So anyway," said Scarlett. "What's Ryan like? Is he sweet? I always imagined the two of them running this game, like, two hot guys with a revolving door of vag parading in and out, all day and all night. But I think they're both a lot more down-to-earth than that, you know. Surprisingly."

"Scarlett, listen to me," she said. "In therapy—in this business—for things to work, there need to be boundaries."

"We're talking about boundaries again? Come on. I think we're well past—"

"You're absolutely right," said Jessica. "Well, *well* past boundaries. That's what I'm trying to tell you. There's a reason I don't talk about Mr. Butler in here. Or my children. Or . . . well, anything, really. My private life. Because if you know too much about me and my life, it compromises us. And you and I having connections, links to each other outside of our working relationship, also compromises us."

Scarlett's smile faded for the first time since she sat down. "What're you saying?"

"I'm saying that, in light of recent events—"

"Are you dumping me?"

"No. It's not like that. This isn't something you should take personally. I've made a list for you. Some really good therapists that I think you'll—"

"But *you're* my therapist."

"Scarlett."

"You're the fucking voice in my head. Who's gonna tell me when I'm being a fucking idiot?"

"Well, in fairness, Scarlett, you rarely seem to listen to that voice."

"Yeah, but I like that it's there."

Jessica wasn't expecting this. This sullen, infuriating girl looked genuinely hurt. Worse, for the first time since Scarlett became her patient, she looked like the kid that she actually was. "I'm touched that our time together has meant something to you. I've also enjoyed having you as—"

"Can't we just, like, erase it? The other night? You saw me in my undies. I saw you with some guy. No biggie. That's life."

"Unfortunately, that's not how it works. You can't just pretend something didn't happen."

Fuck, Jessica thought. She was doing it again. The patient as mirror. The night before, she and Mitch had made fajitas. The night before that, they'd played Connect Four with the kids. They'd ordered a new bed online. They'd pretended nothing had happened.

Honey, use your napkin.

Pass the shredded cheese, please.

Should we stick with a queen, or should we try a king?

"So, that's it?" Scarlett said. "You can't keep it in your pants, so I get screwed? I get ditched? Like, what, disposable fucking Scarlett, as usual."

"I'm sorry. I didn't want it to be like this. You didn't do anything to deserve this."

"You know what?" Scarlett said. "Maybe I was wrong before. Maybe Mr. Butler *does* need to know about this. I mean, it'd be kind of a dick move on my part to just sit there in his class talking about plays and shit while you're off—"

"Scarlett," Jessica said.

"What?"

"He knows."

"What?"

"Mitch knows."

"He knows? Like, *knows* knows?"

"Yeah."

As Jessica said this, it didn't feel like a lie. And, in some ways, it wasn't. It was more complicated than simple truth or untruth.

"Goddamn," said Scarlett. "What the fuck's wrong with you people?"

46

The school billed itself as "college preparatory."

The deluxe laminated recruiting brochure, which Mitch helped update and edit every other year, used that term no fewer than a dozen times. The curriculum, environment, extracurriculars, workload, even the sprawling, leafy campus itself, surrounded by woods, were all designed to emulate some of the best universities in the country.

The same went for the faculty. They were high school teachers, but the understanding was that they were to conduct themselves more like college professors. Which was why, on that particular Friday afternoon, his classes done for the week, Mitch found himself sitting in office hours.

The school year was winding down—the students largely checked out—so it was a slow day. Mitch was on his laptop chatting with Alan on Facebook Messenger.

Alan: I'm going to tell her that I love her.

Mitch: Do you think that's a good idea?

Alan: It's what I feel.

Mitch: You've been drunk a lot since your divorce. Are you thinking clearly?

Alan: Clearer than ever.

Alan included two emojis: a heart and a peach, which symbolized love and . . . maybe a butt? Mitch briefly flashed forward and imagined the utter absurdity that would be Jenny and Alan's wedding. There'd be a modern, broken version of the Core Four, scattered about in nice clothes, avoiding eye contact with one another. There'd be twenty-somethings galore begging the DJ to cut it out with the vintage rap already. Kristen would be there in a dress. She wouldn't wear *Wonder Woman* Vans to a wedding, he guessed, but her shoes would definitely be something interesting, and she'd be looking at Mitch like he was a dick the whole time. Jenny's parents would be doing their best to smile, despite being heartbroken, because the last thing they wanted for their lovely young daughter was some divorced guy with a fresh coat of cologne and a shitload of baggage. Mitch laughed to himself in his silent little office on the third floor of the English Department.

Jessica and Mitch were done evolving.

At least he thought they were. They hadn't formalized it, but that was what he'd chosen to believe, based on their driveway conversation from the previous Saturday night. When they'd walked into the house, the kids were watching late-night cartoons with Luke, who'd looked very confused. The kids' faces were streaked with dried tears. From Jessica and Mitch's floor bed that night, lying in the dark, Mitch considered saying, "So, 'The Relaxed Marriage' is done, right? Now we're on to the sequel, 'The Closed Marriage?'" It didn't seem like a moment for Cheever jokes, though, and frankly, he didn't want to ask—in case she gave him anything other than an immediate and resounding yes. What if this was what she wanted? An open marriage. It was far more comfortable to assume that it wasn't.

Sure, the metal box in which he kept the image of her with another guy had sprung open a few times that week and melted his face off, like the lost ark in the first Indiana Jones movie. But honestly, isn't that adulthood in a summary? Constant feelings of pure, overwhelming dread?

Alan: I see my future with her.

"Jesus," Mitch said, and then, since he was indulging in flash-forwards, he allowed himself a moment to consider what a life with

Kristen would be like. He imagined going to concerts and making out in public, because these seemed like the kinds of things one would do with a much younger girlfriend. Although what the hell did he know? Either way, honestly, it sounded exhausting and just plain wrong.

Mitch: If you have babies, will those babies naturally call you grandpa?

Alan: Ha-ha-ha

Mitch: You know, because you're so old.

Alan: I get it.

Mitch's office door was open, and there was a knock. When he looked up, Luke stood at the threshold, a huge backpack slung over one shoulder. He wasn't smiling like he usually did. Luke had been different all week, less engaged in class, less friendly to Mitch.

"Luke," he said.

"Hey, Mr. Butler."

Mitch noted that it was *Mr. Butler,* not *Mr. B.* "Hold up a sec," he said. "Let me get rid of someone."

Mitch: Gotta go, you lovesick asshole.

He snapped his laptop shut.

Luke hesitated to sit down.

That had been his plan—to walk in and sit down immediately and just start talking—but now he wasn't sure of himself, so he just hovered there by the door. "Are you busy?" he asked. "I could come back."

"I couldn't be less busy if I tried, Luke," said Mr. Butler. "Sit."

Luke did, dropping his backpack on the floor with a thud like a small house collapsing. "Why were you with my mom the other night?" That was what he had planned to say. He'd practiced it on the walk up the stairs to the English Department, along with: "Why was she in your car?" and "Why was she upset when she got home?" But he took too long, and Mr. Butler started talking.

"So, *1984.* You through it yet?"

"Twice," said Luke.

"Show-off. Ominous, right? The classics *always* feel relevant. You could read that thing aloud on CNN and it'd sound like it was written yesterday."

Luke didn't say anything. Neither of them did. Whistles blew faintly through the walls from the soccer fields, a few hundred yards away. Now was his chance to talk.

"Listen, Luke," said Mr. Butler. He put his hands to his chin like he was praying, and then he touched his desk. "The other night."

Luke hadn't thought of this—of Mr. Butler bringing it up first. He waited.

"I want to thank you," said Mr. Butler. "For stepping in there and helping out with Jude and Em."

"What?" asked Luke.

"Saturday. For babysitting."

Luke thought of Mrs. Butler's dress. "Oh," he said. "Right. Yeah, no big deal. It was nothing."

"Well, it was appreciated. Really. I don't . . . I don't think that sort of thing will be happening again."

"Cool. So, why—"

"I've actually been meaning to talk to you," said Mr. Butler.

"Really?"

"School's almost out. You've got the summer to relax. Be a teenager. But when you get back in the fall, we should start seriously discussing your college essays."

"My essays?"

"Yeah. You're gonna need them. Part of the application process. Every school requires them. I'm thinking you could craft something on your *Romeo and Juliet* riff from class. Flesh it out a little. Hope in the face of hopelessness—the power of empathy in fiction. Something like that. It could be great."

"Mr. Butler," Luke said, "why were you with—"

There was a knock, and Luke stopped talking, because Scarlett Powers was standing at Mr. Butler's door. "Hey, guys," she said. "What's up?"

"Scarlett," said Mr. Butler.

She stepped in and stood over Luke.

"Um, I'll be with you in a minute. There's a chair down the hall, across from Mrs. Miller's office, if you wanna sit and wait."

"Oh, yeah. Okay." She didn't move, though; she just stood there, looking at them.

"No, it's cool," said Luke. "We can talk later—like, tomorrow or whatever."

"Luke, no. Scarlett, seriously. Come on."

But it was too late. Luke sidestepped Scarlett and took off.

47

"Well, that was pretty rude," said Mitch.

She was already sitting in Luke's vacated seat. "I knocked."

"Luke and I were talking. You could clearly see that."

"Not my fault he just jetted like that," said Scarlett.

"Actually, I'm pretty sure it was."

"You ever notice how scared they all are of me?" she said. "I mean, am I really *that* terrifying?"

Something was up. He could tell. Like Luke, she was acting differently, too. She usually projected total confidence, but she was flustered and upset now, sitting across from him with her arms crossed.

"It's typical, though, right?" she said. "Guys are scared of women who don't give a fuck. We're a lot harder to control."

Mitch suspected that Scarlett was right, and that this, minus the f-word, would also make a pretty great college essay. On the wall behind her, next to the clock, hung a poster of Kurt Vonnegut's Eight Rules of Writing. His eyes fell on the second one, his favorite: GIVE THE READER AT LEAST ONE CHARACTER HE OR SHE CAN ROOT FOR.

"How can I help you today, Scarlett?" he said.

She looked at his open door. For a moment, it seemed like she might close it. Thankfully, she didn't. "So with, like, office hours," she said.

"We can just talk, right? It's not like it has to be about *just* class? That's sanctioned, right?"

Mitch was now officially scared—embarrassingly so, in light of the girl's new working theory on men. He was an English teacher, so he was used to his students unburdening themselves to him with personal things. But this was Scarlett Powers. "What's on your mind?" he said.

She held her iPhone, clutching it in her lap with both hands. "Has Mrs. Butler said anything about me?" she asked.

"Mrs. Butler?"

"Yeah. Your wife. She's my therapist. *Was* my therapist. I don't know."

"No," he said. "I'm aware that you and she work together. But we never talk about . . ."

Her eyes were watering, tears threatening to spill over. Mitch was no longer afraid of her, and he felt like a shitty teacher for having been, if even just for a moment.

"I've had a really bad week," she said. "And I'm feeling very sad."

"Oh," he said. "Well, okay. I'm sure she's at her office. Do you have her number there? Maybe I could give her a—"

"She dumped me," said Scarlett.

"She . . . dumped you? Why would she—" He stopped himself. His wife saw a few of the students at school—four, in fact, including Scarlett. Jessica thought he should know who they were, just in case, but he knew nothing else, and he wasn't supposed to.

"Our relationship's been . . . *compromised*. That's what she said. I know too much." She held his gaze.

"Okay."

"Listen," she said. "Mr. Butler, I'm almost outta here. There's only a few weeks left, right? And, I'm actually graduating this time."

"I know. Congratulations."

"So I'm as good as gone."

"Well, we still have some books to get through after *1984*, but, yeah."

She looked down at her phone. "So maybe we can speak, you know, freely?"

That fear from earlier was beginning to return. She was upset, clearly, but the intensity radiating off her caused him to roll his chair back a few inches. "Well," he said, "I think that all depends."

"Mr. Butler, I know."

"You know?" he said.

"I *know*."

"You know what?"

She flushed at the neck. Blotches of crimson disappeared into the collar of her white uniform shirt. "Like, are you gonna make me actually say it?"

"Scarlett, I'm afraid you'll have to."

"I know about you and Mrs. Butler. About your thing. Your arrangement or whatever you guys're calling it."

The assorted arteries and veins in his neck that carried blood up to his brain tightened. "How would you . . . Did she te—"

"I saw her. With a dude. Her, like, other guy. And now she doesn't want to be my therapist anymore. But I really need to talk to her. I need her to help me."

"A guy?"

"It was an accident. Like, total Smalltimore bullshit. Wrong place, wrong time. At this house." She stopped to look at her phone again— a long text message. And then her eyes filled. A tear crested one cheekbone. "Mr. Butler. Do you think I'm a psycho?"

"What?"

"Like, do you think I'm too crazy to be with? Like, not worth the trouble?"

"Scarlett, where did . . ." There was no use in asking her this, or anything else. She was crying.

"Can you do me a favor?" she asked.

The metal box was opening again. His face was getting hot. "What, Scarlett?"

"Can you maybe ask her to take me back?"

48

Luke would've gone home immediately, but first he took a detour to the restroom to berate himself for running out of Mr. Butler's office like a complete spaz when Scarlett showed up.

Is there some magical age you reach in life, he wondered—like twenty-five or forty—when you find that you're able to make it through an entire day without totally embarrassing yourself?

"You are a complete tool," he told his reflection in the mirror. And then he hoisted his backpack onto his shoulders and headed for the parking lot, which was where he found Scarlett.

He stopped when he saw her. She was sitting on a bench by the bike racks in the junior/senior lot, staring off into space.

"Oh shit," he said.

He could try talking to her, of course. He could take a shot at redemption. But, being a complete tool and all, the odds of him saying something nonspastic were slim, so he made another break for it. He was nearly to his Jeep when he heard his name.

"Hey you," she said. "Luke."

He turned and acted surprised to see her. "Oh. Hi again."

"Do you think I'm a complete fucking bitch or something?"

"What?"

The lot was half-empty. Students who didn't have extracurriculars were gone.

"Why'd you bust outta there like that?"

"I don't know. You looked like you had something important to talk about."

She looked over toward the baseball field. There was a metallic ping of a bat hitting a ball. "Is that your car?" she asked.

He'd spent half an hour before school that morning figuring out how to take the ragtop down, and now he was glad he had. Parked there in the lot next to a couple of Hondas, the Jeep looked like something out of a commercial. "Yeah," he said. "Just got it."

"It's dope," she said.

Luke absorbed her compliment, willing himself not to say anything stupid in response. No one had ever told him anything that he had or did was dope.

And then she said, "You're gonna give me a ride home, okay?"

He closed his eyes when he let off the clutch to pull out of his parking space, because if he stalled he'd have to immediately kill himself.

His life was spared, though, and the Jeep rolled forward smoothly, as planned, and then he drove as slowly as he reasonably could toward the exit, in the hope that someone—anyone—would see him leaving school with Scarlett Powers beside him.

She fiddled with the stereo until she found what she wanted: a classic-rock station. "So, like, can I smoke in this thing or what?" she asked.

Luke told her yes, not because he wanted her to smoke in his new car but because he would've said yes to anything she asked him, without exception. Glancing over, he noticed that her eyes were red, like she'd been crying. She lit her cigarette with a little purple drugstore lighter and blew smoke out into the world.

"Are you okay?" he asked.

She wiped at her eyes quickly, like she was pissed at them. "Yeah. I'm fine."

"So, where're we going?"

"What?"

"Where do you live?"

"Oh. Head up Falls Road. Just keep driving. It's a ways. I'll tell you when to turn."

They rode in silence for a while, listening to power ballads. Every stoplight, of which there were many, was an emotional roller coaster for Luke. Waiting for green lights gave him a chance to look around and see people seeing him: a dude in a cool Jeep with a hot girl. But then, when the lights turned green, he had to deal with the clutch and first gear and the prospect of stalling.

He turned off Charles Street and headed toward Falls Road.

"So you, like, live by them, right?" she said. "Mr. and Mrs. Butler? They're your neighbors?"

"Yeah," he said. "Right next door." He slowed and steered around two cyclists. "How'd you know?"

Scarlett shrugged. "I don't know," she said. "Heard someone say it once, I guess. People know stuff. Left on Falls here. Get in the right lane and get around all these morons turning at the arrow, or we'll be stuck here all day."

In the city, Falls Road is as congested and annoying as any other street in Baltimore. In the suburbs, though, it opens up into a scenic highway through horse farms, like you're time traveling. Luke shifted into fourth gear, and then fifth, and the Jeep hummed. He'd never driven it this fast before.

"So, yeah," she said. "They're weirdos, by the way."

"Who? The Butlers?"

Scarlett flicked her cigarette butt out into the passing foliage and grabbed her hair to hold it against the wind. "I know they seem pretty chill. Like, the hottie shrink and the English nerd extraordinaire? Perfect little couple. It's all an act, though. Trust me. They're as fucked up as anybody."

He thought of his mother walking slowly up their sidewalk in the dark. "What do you mean?"

She looked at him gravely. "Sex stuff."

"Sex stuff?"

"Yeah. She's fucking some bartender. Young guy in the city. Hot—

like, *hot* hot. Like, half her age. And Mr. Butler? I don't know. Who knows what that guy's into?"

Two brown colts lifted their heads and watched them as they sped by.

"You never know what's going on behind closed doors, dude," she said. "Nothing's good. Everything's fucked. Turn left up here, at the sign."

Luke downshifted into third, then second, which was a rougher transition than he wanted it to be. He turned in to a neighborhood he'd never seen before. They drove by an ornate sign on a brick façade that read THE WOODS OF EAGLE RUN and then by a long expanse of perfectly mowed grass. Sprinklers misted the lawn and pavement. Beyond that, a series of enormous houses sprang up, each surrounded by towering trees.

"On the right," she said. "The gray one. With the Maryland flag."

He pulled into her driveway and rolled slowly up toward a mansion—easily one of the biggest houses he'd ever seen. "Wow," he said.

"Yeah," she said. "A couple of the Ravens live on this street. See that one with all the plants? That's the kicker's house, I think."

Luke said the kicker's name, and Scarlett nodded. "Yeah, I guess."

She let her hair go, and it fell over her shoulders. She'd slid her Sperrys off during the drive, and now she put them back on. Other than that, she was perfectly still. "I wish everyone didn't hate me so much," she said.

There were no lights on in the house, and no cars in the driveway. No flat-screens flickering or dogs jumping at the window. Nothing. "People don't hate you," he said.

She looked at him, and then out the windshield. "Yeah they do."

The radio was playing too loudly. A commercial for reasonably priced gutter cleaning. He turned it down and shifted into neutral.

"They think I'm crazy and that I'm a bitch."

He wanted to tell her that they didn't, but they kinda did. "Well, I don't," he said.

"My boyfriend dumped me last night," she said.

"You had a boyfriend?"

Scarlett nodded. "Yeah. For like a week. He was my first one."

"You've never had a boyfriend before? You?"

"I'm not a girlfriend kinda girl, I guess," she said.

"Did he go to our school?"

She laughed. "Fuck no."

"Oh. Right. Why did he dump you?"

Scarlett took her phone out of her backpack. She opened her text messages and started reading out loud. " 'You're a lunatic. And you're not nearly hot enough to be as big a psycho as you are, by the way. Nowhere near worth it. I'm fucking done with you. For fucking real. If you ever come near me again I'll mace your ass and call the police.' "

"Jeez," said Luke.

"He misspelled psycho," she said.

"Well," he said, "it's tricky. The silent *p* and all."

"Since he was my boyfriend, and since he told me how fucking crazy he was about me, I asked him if I could move in with him after graduation. I'm totally over my parents. He said that might be a little too fast, and then he laughed at me, like I was an idiot. So I got pissed at him and kinda trashed his room. And while I was trashing his room, I found a pair of underwear that wasn't my underwear. Really slutty. Like, a thong. And so I broke his window with a hockey stick."

Luke nodded.

"Reasonable, right?" she said. "Like, they have guys who can fix windows. What's the big deal?"

"Well, psycho or not," said Luke, "you're, like, basically the hottest girl I know in real life."

Scarlett looked over at him again. She didn't smile, exactly, but for a moment her face looked less sad. "Thanks for the ride," she said. "Your Jeep really is dope."

He watched her climb out with her backpack, which was as big and oppressive and weighed down as his. She walked up a cobblestone path to the front door. He put the clutch in and shifted into reverse and prepared himself emotionally for having to back out of her long, sloping driveway.

"Hey, Luke," she called.

She stood before a big red front door, next to a flowerpot. She set her backpack down and lifted her shirt, flashing two glorious breasts. They were gone before he even realized that he'd seen them.

When she went inside, Luke stared at the door. Then he stalled the Jeep.

49

They were out of Golden Oreos.

When Mitch opened the cupboard and discovered this, it hit him like a genuine tragedy, and his knees nearly buckled. "Are you fucking kidding me?" he said.

"I know," said Jessica. "We gotta put them on the list."

They didn't have an actual list of the things they needed, like something committed to paper. It was just a mental list, and it was full of holes and countless missing things.

They were in the kitchen again, in their respective spots. They could've mixed things up—maybe gone to a restaurant or a bar for such an important conversation—but having kids is sometimes like being held in a minimum-security prison, so there they stood. The kids were in bed, the house was mostly dark, and he'd just finished summarizing his conversation from earlier that afternoon with Scarlett.

"It's funny," he said. "I was fully content to never talk about this again. To just close the book, you know."

"Same," she said. "Which isn't great. If we were my patients, I'd say we needed to talk about all of it. Dig into the details. Explore how each of us feels. A full emotional inventory."

"Jesus," he said. "Are there any schools of thought that encourage patients to bottle everything up until they die?"

She told him that there wasn't, and then they played a quick round of Let's Move to Fenwick. There was no income tax there, which was nice to talk about because it had nothing to do with what they were talking about.

"Looks like we've got some pretzels in here," he said. "And some of the kids' Goldfish crackers. It says they're 'flavor blasted.'"

"I'm good," she said.

This is a funny expression, Mitch thought, *because she, he—everything, in fact—seems far from good.* He walked away from the cupboard and back to his spot: leaning against the kitchen counter across from her. "So," he said. "What were you doing there? When Scarlett saw you?"

"I went there to break rule number two," she said.

"Which one's number two?"

"No repeats," she said.

His heart felt as if it had dropped to a lower spot in his chest—somewhere a heart shouldn't be, jammed against a minor organ, a spleen or appendix or something. The word *affair* came into his mind, its letters all jagged and sharp like barbed wire. "I guess that's what the dress was for, then."

She was in a baggy sleeping T-shirt now, and a pair of shorts. "But then I didn't," she said. "I left."

"You left?"

"Yeah," she said. "I was about to walk out the door. The whole thing was about to be over. And then there she was. Scarlett, standing there in her underwear."

"She was in her underwear?" asked Mitch.

"Yeah."

"She didn't mention that at office hours," he said. "That'll make it worse. The story. When she tells everyone she knows on the planet."

"Maybe she won't talk," said Jessica.

Mitch made a face, because she was being naïve.

"Okay, maybe she will. But think of what it'll do for our street cred."

The dishwasher hummed and swooshed between them, one of the many sounds of marriage.

"Why'd you leave?" he asked.

"I don't know," she said. "Maybe I decided I didn't want to do it."

He kept looking at her, though. Finally, she nodded and ran her palm over their smooth countertop. "Luke texted me about the kids. Jude was freaking out. And then Emily was freaking out. They needed me, and I was nearly naked in a row house downtown."

He groaned at this—the bluntness of such a simple sentence. He filled a glass with water from the sink but didn't drink it.

"The E.T. nightmares are getting worse," she said. "He's a giant spider now, but with an E.T. head. Sounds awful."

"God, it's so easy to scar them," he said.

"It all suddenly felt so wrong," she said. "It always felt wrong, I guess, on some level. But when I saw Luke's texts, and when I thought about them, Emily and Jude, I couldn't rationalize it anymore."

Mitch rubbed his forehead. "Me neither."

He wished he hadn't pitched that joint down the garbage disposal a few weeks earlier. Pot, even more than Golden Oreos, would've made this whole scene easier. He told her about SVÄRTA night at Terry's apartment, about Kristen, and about how affected he'd been when he saw Terry's sons' depressing little bedroom.

"This Kristen girl," said Jessica.

"Yeah?"

"She licked you?"

"She did."

"Where?"

He touched his neck. "Body shots. It's what the youth do, I guess."

"Was she cute?"

There are so many words that describe female beauty—thesauruses full of them. *Cute* wasn't quite right, Mitch knew, but it was close enough, so he nodded.

"It was the kids, then," she said. "They're what stopped us from . . . what we were going to do."

"Yeah."

It'd been drizzling earlier, and now rain drummed on the roof and deck.

"Do you want to see him again?" he asked.

"Do you want to see her again?" she asked.

Neither of them answered the other's question. He suspected that, if they had, their answers would've been complicated.

Jessica touched a stack of catalogs on the counter. "He liked my lisp," she said.

"Your lisp?"

"Remember how much you used to love it?" she said. "It'd slip out, and you'd go crazy."

"I still do," he said, and he did, although he couldn't remember the last time he'd noticed it—the last time it had even crossed his mind.

"We're not gonna be one of those couples who stays together for the kids, are we?" she asked.

"I hope not," he said. It was a weak answer—passive and defeatist—but before he could correct himself and tell her that, no, they absolutely were not, sounds came from the stairs. A cough, and then a whisper, and then the kids hustling back up to their rooms. Emily and Jude had been spying on them.

"Shit," said Jessica.

They looked at each other. "What do you think they heard?" asked Mitch.

They didn't know. But they were parents, so they assumed the worst.

50

There's that first few seconds, right when you wake up in the morning, when your head is absolutely clear. It's like a computer booting up—its screen perfectly clean and white—before the train wreck of your desktop clogs everything up with its disorganized jumble of crap.

When Mitch woke the next day, he reveled in those few seconds.

There were no problems. No anxieties or regrets. Just the warmth of his floor bed and the dull hum of the house. The sun lit up the room while birds carried on outside, screaming like the world was ending, the way they always did in the morning.

Then the realities arrived, one after the other. All of their friends were divorced. Jessica had slept with someone. Scarlett knew about it. God only knew who she'd tell; who she'd already told. Jessica was under the impression that he, too, had slept with someone. His brain, that freshly booted hard drive, was about to obsess over all of those things in a downward-spiraling rainbow wheel of death when he rolled over and found his daughter lying beside him, wide awake.

"Boo," she said.

"Morning, babe."

"Did I scare you?"

"Yes. You're terrifying."

"The Oreos are all gone," she said. The golden ones."

"They are. But how do you know that?"

"I used a kitchen chair to climb up onto the counter," she said. "Jude showed me how the other day."

"Okay, maybe let's not do that anymore."

She nodded, which seemed like a lie.

"Is that why you're here?" he asked. "Keeping track of the Oreos?"

"No. I'm just laying down."

"Were you scared?"

"Not really. We just wanted to be with you guys."

"We?"

"Jude and me."

"Jude?" The boy was there, too, Mitch discovered. Jude and Emily had squished themselves between him and Jessica. Mitch thought of how cats and dogs sometimes climb into their owners' luggage, demanding to be taken along. "Well, look at that," he said.

"We're the only ones awake, though," she whispered. "You and me."

He looked past the kids. Jessica was huddled on her side, clinging to the small sliver of real estate she'd been left with.

"Are you and mommy fighting?" Emily asked.

Mitch did his best to replay in his head what she and Jude might have heard the night before. The specifics would be tough for them to grasp, but they'd apparently understood enough to know that whatever they were talking about was serious. "Not at all," he said.

"Are you gonna get divorced like Aunt Amber and Uncle Alan? And Aunt Megan and Uncle Terry? And Aunt—?"

He pulled her into a sideways hug, squeezing her bony rib cage. "Honey, no," he said. "We're not. I promise." He thought, for the thousandth time, of Emily and Jude staring, horrified, at a dying E.T. on the giant screen, and he understood just how much they needed him and Jessica.

"Can I tell you something?" she asked.

"You can just talk," he said. "You don't need permission."

"Okay. Well, I want pancakes," she said. "It's been about a hundred years since we had them, and I want some."

"I think we're out of pancake mix," he said. He was softening the blow here. The fact was, he *knew* they were.

"Well, that's okay. You can just go to Graul's and get some."

"Oh yeah? Just like that, huh?"

"Mm-hmm. Oreos, too. You should get like ten bags of them so we don't run out so fast."

He looked over at the alarm clock. 7:50 A.M. It was a good idea, actually. Breakfast. Families on the brink of ruin don't make pancakes on Saturday mornings and eat them together at the kitchen table, right?

"You hang here, okay?" he said. "I'll be back."

He flipped the wipers on to get rid of the morning dew, and rolled down the windows. He opted against NPR in the hopes that he could go the whole morning without interviewing himself. When he hit the Bluetooth feature on his dashboard, the car synced with his iPhone. It was set to random, which usually called up some deep track he didn't care about and hadn't heard in years. But on that morning, "Free Fallin'" by Tom Petty came on, so he turned it up, because everything's simpler when Tom Petty's on the radio. We're all just good girls who love our mamas, horses, and America, too, goddammit.

Mitch pulled out of the driveway and turned right. As he passed Ellen and James's house, he drove slowly so he could look at Luke's Jeep. It was out there, parked in the driveway with the top off, which was a total rookie mistake in the world of convertible ownership. By now the poor kid's interior would be soaking wet with dew, and it'd take hours to dry out. He made a note to himself to pass along the tip next time he saw him.

Graul's was a small grocery store on the edge of their neighborhood, one of those places that doesn't have much but still somehow manages to have everything you need.

It was just opening when Mitch walked through the automatic doors. One of the employees smiled at him from the registers as she counted change and hummed a song to herself.

The mission was simple: Get pancake mix, eggs, milk, and Golden Oreos, then hustle home and start making breakfast. As he made his way through the aisles, though, he realized that they needed more than that. In fact, they needed pretty much everything.

He started with the staples, then went from there—adding things like granola, dishwasher detergent, and a few little cans of espresso with Starbucks logos on them. His phone buzzed in his back pocket when he was in the cereal aisle. He expected to see a request from home—strawberries or Swedish Fish or something—but it was from Alan. No emojis, just words.

She broke up with me. DUMPED!

Mitch pulled his basket over to the side. He pictured Alan alone in his sparse new apartment, *SportsCenter* blaring on the flat-screen.

"Dude, you and your actual phone conversations," Alan said when he answered.

"Seemed worthy of an actual call," Mitch said. "What happened?"

"She did it over text. Can you believe that shit? Fucking millennials."

Mitch could hear the pain in Alan's voice. "What'd she say?"

"She said I'm old."

"Jesus, really?"

"Well, no. She said it nicer than that. But that's what she meant. Different life stages. Going different places. Blah, blah."

The fact that the girl was right was beside the point. Mitch's job here was to stand next to his packed cart of groceries and say nice things to his friend. "There'll be others, though, right?" he said. "Other fish in the apps? You met Jenny pretty quick. You'll meet someone else."

Alan groaned. He sounded hungover. "Fuck the apps, dude. I was just talking shit before. The apps are a nightmare. It's scary out there. Everyone's desperate, myself included."

"Oh," said Mitch. He found himself suddenly out of things to say.

"Me, Terry, Doug . . . fuck, we're all miserable. Terry's OCD-ing over his records. Doug's flipping tractor tires or whatever the hell he does in the gym all day. I'm wearing fucking cologne. Dude. Mitch.

You're lucky, man. Seriously. I'd give anything to have what you've got."

The cartoon captain from the Cap'n Crunch box was staring at him. He thought of Jessica back home in bed, the kids curled around her. They were the same age, Jessica and Mitch. They were in the same life stage. The middle part. Evolutionarily speaking, they should both be nearly dead by now. They were in it together. "Yeah," he said. "It's a good situation."

"Hold on to it, man, okay? Tight. On your side of the fence, the grass is green as fuck. On this side, there is no grass. There's just booze and sadness and fucking designer jeans."

They promised to get together soon—a drink or an Orioles game or something.

He pulled his cart up to the first register, where his favorite cashier was working.

"Hey there, Mr. Butler."

"Morning, Lester," Mitch said.

Lester had worked at Graul's for as long as Mitch had been going there. He wore a maroon cardigan over his work shirt. "You're up bright and early," he said.

"Feeling ambitious today," said Mitch.

Lester rang up his items slowly and precisely, like always. "Oh, don't you just love these Golden Oreos?" he said. "They're such a guilty pleasure."

"They are indeed."

Lester fixed his glasses. "Haven't seen you in a while. How are things? How's the family?"

Mitch smiled. "Hanging in."

Back outside, the parking lot was filling up. People were pulling in— like Mitch, loading up for the weekend. A dad hustled two kids in soccer uniforms into the store. Cars stopped for a lady pushing a walker.

He opened the rear hatch of his car and set his grocery bags between the pieces of bed frame. He made a commitment to himself to finally get rid of their broken bed. In fact, he'd do it that day. No more procrastinating. He'd google where to take discarded furniture. He and Jude could go together, a legitimate father-son outing. He returned his shopping cart to the cart train up front. Then, on the way back to his car, he stopped mid-jog.

A pickup was parked in a corner spot nearby, a row over from Mitch's car, and inside, there was a young, unidentifiable mutt; a shepherd mix, maybe. Two women walked by and smiled when they saw it, because it was such a cute, funny-looking dog. And, just like that old Lab from so, so long ago, outside the quirky pizza place near Hopkins, it sat in the driver's seat with its paws up on the wheel—all ready, it seemed, to speed away.

"No way," Mitch whispered.

He snapped a few pictures with his phone and looked them over. Then he dropped the best one of the bunch into a text to Jessica. The dog was smiling in that dopey way that dogs smile. He typed a short message and hit Send.

think you were right about Mr. Butler.

who dis?

Luke

how'd you get my number luke?

School directory

well played, stalker mcstalkington

Sorry

just taking advantage of the resources at your disposal. I applaud you

Thanks

not showing you my tits again though

OK

do tell. what did butler do?

Luke was lying in his bed. He'd been awake for an hour doing two things: building up the courage to text Scarlett, and piecing things together. There was the look on his mom's face when she'd stumbled into the house the week before. The look on Scarlett's face when Luke drove her home. The "sex stuff" comment. Mr. Butler had done something to his mom and to Scarlett. It was obvious. He was apparently some kind of creep. He didn't want to tell Scarlett anything specific

about his mom, though; not over text. Luke just wanted Scarlett to
know that he believed her.

You were right. Maybe we just leave it at that?

leaving a girl in suspense. nice move

He sent her a smiley-face emoji, hated himself for it, and then
watched her text-bubble.

how fucked up is 1984 btw?

I know, right?

mr butler can fuck off but that book is dope

what're you doing today?

He waited, endured some more self-loathing. Why had he asked
her that? He was just setting himself up for some savage reply, like
Nothing with you that's for damn sure. But thankfully, she wasn't mean.

I got some big plans actually.

Really?

yup. i'm gonna win my therapist back. If you're lucky maybe
you'll see me. later nerd

What?

No text-bubble this time. Nothing followed. She was gone, and his
mom was calling for him.

When he found her in the kitchen, she was heating up some Eggo waf-
fles in the toaster.

The flicker of optimism that had scared Luke so much—the one
that made him actually afraid she might off herself—was gone. It had
been gone all week, replaced with all-day pajamas and vacant eyes.
Her spiky new haircut wasn't spiky anymore. She'd pushed it down
flat against her head.

"Luke, honey," she said.

"Yeah, Mom?"

He waited for something important. A sign. A statement. Something to be worried about. Something to be hopeful for.

"We're out of coffee. Can you run to Starbucks for me?"

52

"Hey, Em." It was Jude, whispering. "Em."

"What?"

"I think Dad's back."

"How do you know?"

"I hear his car. Can't you?"

"That's not his car. It's way rumblier. It sounds like Luke's Jeep."

Jessica was awake. She had been for a few minutes now; she just hadn't told them yet. It was funny listening to them talk sometimes when they didn't know she could hear them. The things they said. "I think Emily's right," she said. "That doesn't sound like the CR-V."

"Oh, hi, Mommy," said Emily. "You're awake."

"I am. Where'd Daddy go?"

"Graul's. He left while you were sleeping. He's getting stuff for pancakes. And more Oreos, too."

"That's nice."

"Whatever," said Jude. "I'm checking anyway."

"Me too!"

"Put on shoes, you guys," said Jessica.

"Okay!"

"Okay!"

As they thundered down the stairs, Jessica did what she did every morning: She reached for her phone. She had a text message. When she tapped the green icon on her screen, she found a picture of a smiling dog in a pickup truck.

Sure, he's a bad driver. But he's a very, very good boy.

It was the same thing he'd said on their first date. She laughed then, and she laughed now. Mitch was telling dad jokes a full decade before he was even a dad, God bless him. She felt her eyes turn hot with tears.

She sat up and looked at the lived-in clutter of their bedroom—of their lives. Unfolded laundry wrinkled in a basket. Her running shoes next to his running shoes. Teetering piles of books that they'd get to eventually. They'd survive this. They had to.

She got up and put on a sweatshirt and looked at herself in the mirror. *Day one,* she thought. As backassed as it sounded, maybe their experiment *had* saved them. She slept with someone. He slept with someone. Now they were starting over. This was day one.

Her phone shook on the dresser, vibrating loud against the wood. She didn't need to pick it up to read it. It was from the phone number with no name.

I'm outside. Please come talk to me.

As far as Luke could tell, it hadn't rained overnight at all, but the interior was wet anyway.

"What the fuck?" he said.

He blotted the seats with some towels from the garage as the Jeep idled in the driveway. It helped a little, but eventually he accepted that by the time he made it to Starbucks for his mom's latte, he'd look like he'd wet himself. As he buckled his seatbelt, he realized what had happened. "Oh, right," he said. "Dew."

The seats and dashboard weren't the only things that were all wet. The pedals—the gas, brake, and clutch—had a slippery glaze of moisture on them beneath his sneakers, which caused a precarious start in first gear. But he managed to get it rolling without stalling.

Mr. Butler told him that someday the clutch would feel like an extension of his own foot, and he wouldn't even have to think about it anymore. "That's life, man," he'd said. "Stuff's hard at first. Then you get used to it."

It was good advice, but he was mad at Mr. Butler now, so he disregarded it entirely. It's a particular kind of grief when you realize that adults can sometimes be real assholes.

As he rolled down toward the end of the driveway, he looked over at the Butlers' house, like he always did. He saw Emily and Jude in the driveway wearing pajamas and sneakers, waving at him. He waved back, relieved that Mr. Butler wasn't with them.

There was someone else there, though. Luke noticed him at the same time the kids did. A young guy in jeans and a T-shirt stood by the mailbox next to a piece of furniture—an end table–looking thing. He thought of what Scarlett had said. "Some bartender. Hot—like, *hot* hot." This had to be him. He looked like a model.

The Jeep's front tire ran into the grass, so Luke pulled the steering wheel over, righting the course, and tried to focus on driving. He put the clutch in and came to a stop at his mailbox. He looked left, and then right. That was when he saw Mr. Butler's car coming up the street.

The windows were down. The music blared.

Mitch had flipped ahead in the album to one of his all-time Tom Petty favorites, "Runnin' Down a Dream." He drummed his fingers on the steering wheel and remembered a long-forgotten road trip back in college with the Husbands, before they were husbands.

He was young then, ridiculously so—his whole life ahead of him— and that was how he felt now. Seeing that silly dog had revitalized him. And, as much as he hated to admit it, so had talking to Alan. He felt bad for his friend, but for the first time in a long, long time—since The Divorces started—he felt absolutely certain that he didn't want what his friends had. The Husbands and the Wives, the rest of the Core Four. He loved them, but they could all go straight to hell, because Mitch wanted nothing more in the world than to stay married.

He was technically speeding. But who could blame him? He was speeding in the way everyone speeds when you're driving along a deserted street on a Saturday morning with a kick-ass song on the stereo and a boot lifted off your chest.

First, Mitch saw Luke, sitting in his Jeep at the end of his driveway—and he could see that Luke saw him, too, so he slowed down to wave. Luke didn't wave back, though. Instead, he glared. The look Mitch saw through their respective windshields was pure disdain.

Next he saw Emily and Jude, and after that, Jessica. The three of them stood motionless in the driveway. And then he saw the guy.

It was him.

Young. Handsome. *Really* handsome. Mitch recognized him instantly, but he wasn't sure how. As the CR-V rolled closer, though, he remembered date night. Bar Vasquez. Their waiter. White shirtsleeves rolled halfway up his forearms. This was the guy Jessica slept with. The guy who'd nearly ruined it all.

It's funny all the things that can go through your mind in just a few seconds. All these complex thoughts and feelings, and then the sound of a Jeep engine roaring suddenly to life.

From where she stood, Jessica had a perfect view of the crash.

The Jeep sprang forward from the driveway. Mitch swerved as best he could, and because his windows were rolled down, she heard him shout, just before impact, "Luke! Shit!"

The airbags all deployed in one big pop, and the four long wooden boards that used to be their bed flew out of the CR-V, like missiles fired from a destroyer, and fell clattering onto the street. One stopped at the kids' feet. One slid past Ryan and flipped his handmade end table over. The other two landed between the heap of crashed vehicles, like part of the wreckage.

Mitch turned off the radio and stepped out of his car. He blinked.

Luke stepped out of his Jeep, an equally stunned expression on his face. His Orioles cap was knocked sideways on his head. "My foot slipped," he said. Mitch still didn't say anything. They all just looked at one another. Both cars hissed and clicked. A neighbor's dog barked.

"Daddy!" yelled Emily. "You guys crashed!"

53

"*What* are you doing here?" said Mitch.

The guy looked over at the jacked-up cars, which at that point were one conjoined thing, and then he looked at Mitch. "Dude, are you okay?"

"I'm fine."

"Actually, you're bleeding."

Mitch looked down at himself.

"No. Right there."

Mitch touched his own neck. There was the slightest sting, and some red on his fingertips. One of the boards had grazed him on its way out the window, apparently. Later, he'd think seriously about how it easily could've killed him if not for a lucky inch or so, but right then he didn't give a shit. "I'm fine," he said. "Why are you here?"

The guy took a breath, steadying himself. They'd all been spread out: Mitch and Luke in the street, Jessica and the kids in the driveway, him—the guy—at the mailbox. Now, though, they came together at the bottom of Jessica and Mitch's driveway, close enough to touch one another.

"Who're you?" asked Jude.

"Yeah," said Emily. "Who *are* you?"

Jessica cleared her throat. "Mitch, kids, this is Ryan. Mommy's . . . friend."

"How do you know each other?" asked Emily.

Mitch looked at Ryan. So did Emily and Jude. Ryan looked at Mitch.

"Okay," said Ryan. "No one's acknowledging this, so I guess I will. You guys just got into a car accident. Should we, like, call the police or something?"

Luke gazed back at his Jeep and sighed. Mitch, though, looked only at Ryan.

"So, no?" Ryan said. "Fine. Listen, um, sir. Mitch. I've come to talk to Jessica."

"Oh, you have, huh?" said Mitch.

"Do you know each other from work?" asked Jude.

"How're you friends?" asked Emily.

"Give us a sec, kids," said Mitch.

"You should get a Band-Aid, Daddy," said Emily.

"I will, babe, in just a minute." Mitch was still staring down Ryan.

"Jessica, can we talk?" asked Ryan. "Like, maybe over there? I have something I need to say."

"Ryan," she said, "I think this is not a great ti—"

"Is this what you want?" said Mitch. "Jessica? Him? *This* guy?"

She tossed her hands up, barefoot there on the pavement. "Are we gonna do this now? In front of the—"

"Yeah," said Mitch. "We are. We're all in this together."

"Jessica," said Ryan, "I'm in love with you."

"Oh Jesus, Ryan," she said. "Stop it."

Maybe it was the adrenaline—low-level shock from the accident— or maybe it was the light trail of blood that was starting to pool at the collar of his sweatshirt, but that particular word coming out of Ryan's mouth made Mitch feel suddenly ill. And then it made him mad.

"I'm serious," Ryan said. "And I think you have feelings for me, too. In fact, I know you do. Maybe those feelings aren't love. Not yet. But I think they can be, if you give me a chance. I mean, we had fun, right?"

"Who the hell do you think you are?" said Mitch. "This is our home."

"Kids," said Jessica, "maybe you should go in—"

Next door at Ellen and James's house, Ellen stepped out onto her front porch in her pajamas and robe. Everyone turned and looked at her. She was holding a half-eaten waffle. "Luke?" she said. "Holy shit. What happened? Are you okay?"

"Mom, I'm fine," said Luke.

"They crashed," said Emily, pointing. "See? It was loud."

Ellen assessed the damage in the street and joined the huddle, holding her robe closed against the morning chill. "Hi, Jessica," she said. "Hello, Mitch. Is everyone okay? Who's fault was it?"

"Just hear me out," said Ryan. "Don't you think there's a reason you kept coming back to me?"

"Ryan, stop."

"It means something," said Ryan. "We've got a real connection. You can't deny it. I don't care that you have kids. Or that you're older than me."

Luke stepped up and stood next to Ellen. "Are you even gonna say hi to her, Mr. Butler? I mean, are you really that big of a dick?"

"What?" said Mitch.

Luke glared at him—the same glare from before the crash.

"Say hi to who? I'm kinda in the middle of—"

It was probably meant to be a punch, but the result was more like a slap. It certainly sounded like it. Either way, it hurt, and Mitch stumbled backward, holding the side of his face. "Luke? What the hell, man?"

And then Jude jumped into the fray, wrapping Luke around the waist like a would-be tackler. "Don't hit my dad!" he shouted. Jessica and Ellen went to their respective sons, pulling them away from each other.

"You had sex with my mom, you asshole!" yelled Luke.

"What?" said Mitch.

"Wait, what?" said Jessica.

"Luke," said Ellen. "Oh God. Honey, no."

"I don't know what you're thinking here, Luke," said Mitch. His cheek stung. "But, yeah. No. Your mom and I didn't—"

"We didn't, Luke," Ellen said. "We just—"

"You just what?" asked Jessica. "When? What the hell's going on?"

"What's sex?" asked Emily.

A car was coming now, and the group collectively stopped and watched it approach. It was a Mercedes-Benz, one of the super-expensive ones. As the big car rounded the curve, it slowed and then stopped in the middle of the street. The driver's-side door opened, and Scarlett Powers stepped out.

"Scarlett?" Jessica, Mitch, Luke, and Ryan all said this at the same time.

"Yo, what the fuck?" she said.

Emily gasped.

"Oh, I mean shit," Scarlett said. "No, not shit. Sorry. Luke, your Jeep."

"What are you doing here, Scarlett?" asked Jessica.

"I need to talk to you."

Everyone looked at one another.

"Me?" said Jessica.

"Yeah, you."

"How did you even find me?"

"School directory," she said. She looked at Luke and smiled. "I looked up this guy's address, because he's your neighbor. What's up, creeper?"

Jessica looked at Ryan. "Actually, how did *you* find me?"

"The Internet," he said.

"What?"

Ryan shrugged. "You told me your last name. The other night. I love you, Jessica."

"Stop saying that. Please."

"Yes," said Mitch. "I'm warning you. Do not say that again."

"I have to have you be my therapist again, Dr. Butler," said Scarlett. "You were right . . . about everything. You're *always* right about everything. I'm a mess without you. Just look at me. I'm having setbacks all over the place. See? I totally just stole this from a convenience store." She took a tube of cherry Chapstick out of her pocket and showed it to the group. "My lips aren't even that dry. I'm probably gonna get arrested again by, like, the end of the week. I'm crying out for help here."

"Scarlett, that's sweet. Really. But I explained why that's not possible. There are rules."

"Rules?" She laughed and waved her hand at them, the whole group, the entire scene. "You two are married. You're her side piece. I don't know you, but you're wearing your pajamas. There are two children here, which there probably shouldn't be. And you. You saw my boobs yesterday."

"*What* did she say?" asked Ellen. "Luke?"

"Those two cars are, like, destroyed," said Scarlett. "We're in the middle of the suburbs, and there're wood planks all over the street. Mr. Butler's bleeding. Does any of this look like following the rules to you? I mean, come on, who cares? We're good. Take me back."

"All right, listen, everyone," said Jessica. "Clearly, there's a lot going on right now. A lot of confusion. There's been an accident. Mitch and Luke may have concussions. People are punching people."

"What?" said Scarlett. "Who got punched?"

"I punched Mr. Butler," said Luke. "In the face."

"Really?" said Scarlett. "That's baller."

"It was a slap," said Mitch. "Luke, you slapped me."

"My dad had sex with Luke's mom," said Emily.

"What?"

"No."

"Honey!"

"Jesus."

"Emily," said Mitch. "Baby, Ms. Ellen and I did *not* . . . have sex."

"We almost did," said Ellen. "I mean, we were about to."

"Mom!"

"I'm just saying."

"Mom? Oh my God."

Scarlett had left the Mercedes's door open, and now the car started to ping. That was the only sound. And now Jessica was looking at Mitch.

"El," he said.

"What?" Jessica asked.

"El. El was . . . *is* Ellen."

"Oh. Ooooh. Really?"

"Who's El?" asked Jude.

"It was a misunderstanding," said Mitch. "Ellen and I found ourselves . . . in a moment." He turned to his neighbor. She was looking at the ground, still holding her robe. "Ellen, you're lovely, okay? I mean that."

Ellen looked up at him, shuffling a step in her slippers.

"I'm serious. Your dress was great. I can only imagine that the red one you told me about is even better. And any guy would be lucky to have *that* with you. But I couldn't do it. I'm in love with my wife."

"Mitch," Jessica said.

"We didn't do it."

"But you said—"

"I lied. I didn't have sex with her or anyone. I just thought that's what you wanted to hear."

"It wasn't. I just thought it was."

"You two really need to work on communication," said Ellen.

"I love you, Jessica," said Mitch. And then he said it again, looking at Ryan this time. "*I* love you. And no, it's not just because of the kids. We love them. Kids, we love you. But I don't want to stay with you because of them. No, we're *not* one of those couples. I want to be with you because of you. I have since the day I met you. The kids are like a bonus prize. This last month has sucked. It's been terrible. I don't want to be with anyone else. Ever. I don't even like anyone else. Just you."

"Aw," said Scarlett. "Mr. B., that's adorable."

"I want that, too," said Jessica.

"You do?"

"I don't want Ryan. Ryan's just hot."

"Hey," said Ryan. "That's not fair."

Ellen nodded. "Mm-hmm."

"Mom!"

"I'm sorry, Luke. But . . . look at him."

"You should see his roommate," said Scarlett. "Who's a complete douchebag, by the way. Ryan, you can tell him that for me."

"Jessica," said Ryan, "I made you a table." He picked his work up off the ground and set it back upright next to the mailbox.

"It's a nice, table, Ryan," she said. "Really. But this is my life. Mitch is my life."

"Okay," he said. "I get it. But can I just say something else?"

"Dude," said Mitch. "Are you serious?"

"*This* guy's your life?" said Ryan. "Really? The fact that you're even in this situation tells me that he didn't appreciate you in the first place. You *love* her, Mitch? Come on. If you love her—if you *really* love her—and if she really loves you, I wouldn't even be here in your driveway. And she never would've been in my bed."

Mitch had no more experience punching people than Luke did, so his swing missed entirely. He grabbed Ryan by the shoulders, gripping his T-shirt as hard as he could. Ryan did the same to Mitch, and for a few stupid seconds, the two men clung to and shook each other from side to side. Mitch called Ryan a son of a bitch, and Ryan told Mitch to "chill the fuck out, for fuck's sake."

Ryan quickly gained the upper hand, and Mitch felt himself being turned. Ryan was trying to put him in a headlock.

"I don't want to have to hurt you, Mitch."

"Screw you," Mitch croaked.

"You guys!" said Jessica. "Please stop it. Ryan, let him go."

Mitch slapped and punched at Ryan's sides, but his hands seemed to just bounce off, and Ryan was too lean to grab hold of. All the while, Mitch was vaguely aware that, below him and to the right, Emily had started counting. He didn't understand why. Caught up as he was in this completely unwinnable physical altercation, his daughter's swelling bravery simply didn't register.

"Emily, what are you doing?" asked Jessica.

". . . seven, eight, nine. *Ten!*"

"Sweetie!"

"Uh-oh."

And then Emily kicked Ryan right in the balls.

PART FIVE

DATE NIGHT

54

Midsummer in Baltimore can be pretty miserable.

The humidity becomes this omnipresent thing, as constant and relentless as impending death, and you can't so much as go outside to get the mail without sweating through whatever you're wearing. The complaints are constant, NPR puts out warnings to check on your elderly neighbors, crime decreases because it's too hot to break the law, attendance drops sharply at Orioles games, and everyone pretty much avoids human contact.

Thankfully, they weren't there yet.

It was June, and at just before 7:00 P.M., the air was pleasantly free of oppression, and Fells Point was bustling with people. Mitch walked along in no particular hurry, because as usual, he was right on time, and he was fairly certain Jessica would be late.

He passed a tattoo shop. Two inked-up guys stood on the sidewalk smoking cigarettes. He stopped outside the Sound Garden record shop and looked inside the open front doors, enjoying the dusty, hempy, vinyl-y smell wafting out into the street. Aretha Franklin was coming from the speakers inside. There was some protest art on a mural nearby, and the ground shook from a passing tricked-out Humvee with purple ground effects. An enormous cargo ship, like a tipped-over skyscraper, was docked at the port, spoiling his view of the harbor.

Luke was home with Emily and Jude, babysitting.

Things had been understandably awkward between Mitch and Luke for a few weeks, but, as teacher and student, they'd powered through it. As far as Mitch could tell, Luke also had a metal box for storing unpleasant imagery. It helped, of course, that Luke was a much happier kid now. Having a girlfriend will do that to a guy. Scarlett and Luke were dating now, because, according to Scarlett, she was "done with super-hot assholes." Mitch had chaperoned prom the previous month and taken special pleasure in separating them during the evening's final slow dance. "Dial it down, you two," he told them, slapping Luke on the shoulder. The kid had a look on his face like, *Can you believe this?*

Jessica relaxed her patient-therapist standards—standards that seemed more symbolic than hard-and-fast at that point—and took Scarlett back. "I kinda had to," she said. "In good conscience, how could I unleash that girl on another therapist?" Jessica couldn't tell Mitch anything specific, of course, but apparently Scarlett was doing quite well. She was even going to one of the local colleges in the fall. Her father had made a generous donation, so she was enthusiastically accepted, despite her checkered academic record.

As with Luke and Scarlett, things were going well for Ellen, too. The dresses that the Wives had helped her pick out at Nordstrom that spring were the beginning of a full-fledged makeover, it seemed— another postdivorce reinvention. Just that morning, Mitch had waved to her as she jogged up their street in a pair of neon-orange running shoes.

Mitch passed a few sports bars. More music and baseball. He passed an Indian restaurant, an Italian place, and an ice cream shop with about a hundred figurines bobbing and swaying on the windowsill. Two women walked out onto the street, both licking ice cream cones. They looked around and then tentatively held hands. As they walked toward him, Mitch discovered that one of them was Tara, his spin instructor. Her red hair was pulled back, and she was smiling. There was ice cream on the other woman's nose, and they laughed. Tara didn't notice Mitch as she and her smitten girlfriend walked away in the direction of the water.

"Good for you, Tara," Mitch said as he stepped around some pigeons who were eating french fries from a Styrofoam carton.

Things were understandably awkward between Jessica and Mitch, too, for a while, if he was being honest.

The speech about loving her that he'd given in the driveway, amid the mess of that morning, had been like the last scene of a thousand movies. The thing about movies, though, is that they always seem to end right when the real work is about to begin. So you never see the couple having breakfast the next morning or lying in bed a week later, quietly struggling to earn the romance that was woven into all those sentimental things that were said in desperation.

Bar Vasquez was a few blocks over. He couldn't see it from where he walked now, but he knew it was there, and he knew Ryan was probably working. Mitch was surprised how civil he felt toward the guy. A couple of months on, he harbored very little ill will. After all, how could he be mad, really? Ryan was a single guy in his twenties—too young still to understand what he had been tampering with. Ultimately, the only thing he was guilty of was the same thing Mitch had been guilty of for nearly two decades now: being in love with Jessica.

That said, seeing him get racked into oblivion by Emily had been nice. It was a direct shot, and the poor guy fell to the ground like a wounded animal. When he finally gathered himself, after Emily had brought Mitch a Band-Aid for his neck, Ryan offered to take the pieces of their bed frame. "The wood's pretty decent, actually," he said. "I can maybe do something with it." He took that goddamn end table with him, too, thankfully.

The restaurant Jessica had picked was new, next to a rebuilt luxury hotel along the water. It had an open-air plaza outside with tons of seating. In a few weeks it'd be too hot to eat anywhere that wasn't air-conditioned to the hilt, so she'd told him she wanted to take advantage.

There was a sign near the entrance directing outdoor patrons to go in through the main restaurant. Mitch did as it said, passing an empty hostess stand and an elaborate bar full of fellow Baltimoreans. Like so many places in the city, the décor was old-school, with paintings of crabs and boats and racehorses. A pretty girl with a nose ring smiled as she buzzed past him carrying a tray of drinks, and he wondered why there had to be so many beautiful waiters and waitresses in the world. Beautiful people in general. How much easier would life be if, the moment you get married, you take a pill, and everyone else turns plain and boring?

Mitch stopped at the entrance to the restaurant's outdoor section, which was partitioned off by some flowerpots and railroad ties. All the people and tables briefly overwhelmed him, and he wasn't sure if he had to backtrack to find a hostess, or if things were first come, first served, so he just stood there trying to get his bearings. His phone buzzed in his back pocket. It was a text from Jessica.

You're not going to believe this. I beat you.

He looked around. And there she was.

She was at a two-top table right in the middle of it all. She set her phone down and looked at the menu, and Mitch just watched her for a while. Her hair was up, because she'd come from work, and she almost always wore it up at work. She reached for it, and it fell down across her neck and shoulders. He scanned the crowd around her, registering the effect she caused. A guy walked by her table and glanced at her. Another guy, who was by himself a few tables over, glanced at her, too, thinking whatever he was thinking. An older guy—silver hair, a red tie—looked at her out of the corner of his eye while polishing his silverware with his napkin. The woman across from him didn't seem to notice. Jessica was oblivious to all of it. Or maybe she was just ignoring it. Mitch wasn't sure which, and, as he often did, he wondered how women can get through the day without flipping something over and screaming, "Will all of you please stop looking at me?"

"You need a table, hon?" It was the waitress with the nose ring. She was even prettier up close. "You look a little lost."

Mitch smiled. "Nope, I'm good," he said. "I'm meeting my wife."

ACKNOWLEDGMENTS

It takes a village, right? Well, this one took a bigger village than usual.

Ryan Effgen and Catherine McKenzie read this book when it was a mess. Their thoughtful feedback helped save it from the brink.

Jessica Anya Blau gave me the title. I ran into her at a coffee shop in Baltimore last year and told her the title I'd settled on. She said, "No, I don't like that. It should be *Last Couple Standing*."

My agent, Jesseca Salky, was everything that I needed her to be—like smart, kind, and absolutely relentless—as always. I'm so lucky to have her on my side.

The team at Ballantine was a writer's dream. Special thanks to Jennifer Hershey, Kara Welsh, and Kim Hovey for so much support. And to Mimi Lipson and Janet Wygal for their copyediting expertise. They saved me on nearly every page. And to Anne Speyer, my wonderful editor, who guided me and this book to a place I wouldn't have found on my own.

Finally, thanks to my wife, Kate, and our daughters, Caroline and Hazel. And to my Baltimore friends, to whom this book is dedicated. As far as big, sprawling, man-made modern American families go, we could do a lot worse.

ABOUT THE AUTHOR

MATTHEW NORMAN lives in Baltimore, Maryland, with his wife and two children, and holds an MFA from George Mason University. His previous novels include *We're All Damaged* and *Domestic Violets,* which was nominated for a Goodreads Choice Award for Humor.

thenormannation.com
Twitter: @thenormannation
Instagram: @thenormannation

This book was set in Fournier, a typeface named for Pierre-Simon Fournier (1712–68), the youngest son of a French printing family. He started out engraving woodblocks and large capitals, then moved on to fonts of type. In 1736 he began his own foundry and made several important contributions in the field of type design; he is said to have cut 147 alphabets of his own creation. Fournier is probably best remembered as the designer of St. Augustine Ordinaire, a face that served as the model for the Monotype Corporation's Fournier, which was released in 1925.